ONE MONTH IN MY MIND

ANNA KEENAN HILL

AKH

For

Robin, Oliver, Felix & my Mum

Cover illustrated by Lesley Danson
Cover layout by Rachel Britton

PROLOGUE

What a complete and utter shit.

There's no other way to describe such a despicable example of a human being. Well, I say human, but as far as I'm concerned Luke is a regenerated Neanderthal male, but with less charisma. In fact, that is quite possibly a *huge* insult to Neanderthals.

I mean who else would pack up all their worldly possessions and inform you they were leaving by scribbling a note on a post-it? *And* the pen was running out, and he couldn't even be bothered to find another one, so the end of the message is barely legible.

I'd only gone to Tesco. Admittedly it was to do a big shop. Big as in buying toilet roll and washing up liquid along with the groceries, not big as in there's time to wrap up my life with Gemma and drive off before she gets home, sort of big.

I KNOW I haven't been the easiest person to live with for the last couple of months, but isn't that what relationships are all about?

Aren't you meant to work through problems and help each other over the difficult times?

It's not as if we'd only just met, we've been together, sorry, stupid me, HAD been together for three years and living in the same house for at least two of those years.

It all started when Jeffrey died. Well, that and losing my job. OK, it wasn't the best job in the world but it paid the bills or at least some of them. But apparently, you can't have someone dealing with the public when they are unable to smile. I do get that, but surely they could have been a little more understanding.

After all, Jeffrey was my whole life before Luke came along. We shared everything, often my supper, which I had laboriously made after a long day at work and *always* my bed.

He had to move over when Luke came on the scene, which didn't go down well with either of the males in my life, but they both gradually got used to this unlikely trio.

But Jeffrey was thirteen, which is a good age for a Spaniel, and finally the inevitable happened.

Jeffrey died, peacefully in his sleep, wedged between Luke and I one Sunday morning.

Actually, when I really think about it, the problems with Luke had been apparent for months before this and, I don't know whether it was because of the loss of Jeffrey or the realisation that things were far from well with Luke, that I started feeling more and more miserable.

Finally, after months of lying here on my settee, watching daytime TV and dissecting every conversation we ever had, I had reached the point that I needed to see the doctor.

I couldn't sleep, was barely eating and cried at the drop of a hat.

My doctor and I talked at length, over several appointments, and finally, it was decided that antidepressants might be required.

I really wasn't keen on this. Although I felt miserable I didn't think I was *that* far down the line, just yet.

Eventually, Dr Wright agreed to give it a bit longer and suggested taking a long walk every day for the next month. We would then reassess the situation.

As I lie here, wrapped in a blanket, flicking between channels, I think it's an excellent idea and I will certainly give it a try.

Tomorrow.

DAY ONE. WALK ONE.

Look at it. All trimmed, neat and tidy. How do these people find the time to keep everything so orderly?

Actually, it looks *too* precise. I don't like the sharp, stubbly edges with a symmetry so exact it leaves nothing to the imagination.

So what would it be, Brazilian or au naturel?

If you can be so formal with your garden hedge then I'm betting it's Brazilian.

Then again, looks like the house belongs to an older person.

How does that work? Do older people still have Brazilians? I don't really want to think about that.

Now I can't get the thought out of my head.

Good job this is the part with the hill. I can focus on pushing on up the incline rather than considering the nether regions of the baby boomers.

At least I'm out here, in the big wide world, attempting to tackle this 'persistent, low and negative mood', as Dr Wright called it, without having to resort to taking any medication. He seemed pretty sure that a daily walk would help.

I'm a bit fed up really that I've been unable to drag my reluctant brain out of the depths of despair without the help of a doctor, but he was right, something had to be done.

How the hell did I get to this point?

Oh, yes, well there's Luke, of course, he's long gone and it's such a strain putting on a, 'I'm happy and coping face' for Mum and Dad when I'm clearly not.

I didn't do much last night after getting home from the doctor's, apart from crying myself to sleep, but, I feel much more inclined to give it a go this morning.

After all, what have I got to lose?

So I reluctantly crawled out of bed and forced myself to get dressed. Usually, I would have stayed where I was until mid-afternoon and, more than likely, not got dressed at all.

I even forced myself to have a mug of reasonably hot coffee and dunked a ginger biscuit in to count as breakfast. I mean, a girl needs something for energy if she's to go for a damned walk.

At least my disturbed sleep allowed me to plan a route.

In theory, this should take about 45 minutes if I walk quickly.

It starts with a long but fairly gradual incline, levels out for a while and then for the final stages there's a more gentle, downhill stroll until I get home.

So here I am, currently on the hill, slightly out of breath and ruminating about what is an appropriate age to stop having a Brazilian.

What did my foggy brain call this in the middle of the night? Oh yes, a fairly gradual incline. Who am I kidding? It feels like I'm climbing a mountain, well, maybe not a mountain, there are houses either side of me, but still...

What's that smell? It's rather nice, like freshly cut logs, but that noise, Jeez, it's unbearably loud and getting louder.

No!!!!

How can they? Murderers.

Oh, the poor tree. It has probably been there for years and years and suddenly its limbs are being sawn off and rammed through a mincing machine.

I can't stand the thought of it.

There it was, happily biding its time.

One minute casually providing us humans with the air we can breathe then stripped down and mushed to a pulp in a matter of minutes. Can't these people see what they are doing?

Oh and the smell.

It's a strangely comforting smell really, that makes you think of small country cottages with open fires and flowers around the window frames. But the grinding sound brings me back to the reality that this man is murdering this tree.

God, I'm *so* furious.

I could grab him and shove him bit by bit into his own mincing machine and watch as the owner of the house comes running out to see what is happening, only to be splattered all over by the remains of the tree surgeon.

Which reminds me, 'Fargo'. I must watch that again, it's such a great film.

Umm, the sound of the machine is distant now.

Maybe I better not mention the tree surgeon episode to Dr Wright.

Somehow I don't think he would see it quite like I did.

Of course, I'm not actually going to do it. It's only a thought.

Doesn't everyone have random thoughts like this?

What's that man doing?

Looks like he has come from the van and he's wearing a high vis jacket to make himself look official.

The woman just opened the door. She looks really old. God, I hope she's OK?

What if he's just trying to get into her house to steal her life savings?

It could be anything in that carrier bag.

A hammer maybe, to viciously attack the poor, unsuspecting woman and render her unconscious?

He might pull it out of the bag as soon as he gets inside.

Maybe I should go over and intervene. Just let him know I'm here and have clocked him?

'Well thank you so much. I'll see you again tomorrow.'

Oh.

Looks like he was just delivering her lunch or something. Oh well, at least she's safe.

Downhill now. That's a relief; I'm shattered. I didn't realise how unfit I had become.

WHO THE HELL PARKS LIKE THAT???

Huge bloody people carrier parked completely on the pavement. I can't even get past without walking into the road.

What if I was blind? I'd walk straight into that stupid car. What makes them think it's OK to block a pavement? Lazy sods. Bet they couldn't be bothered to walk the extra few inches, so parked on the pavement.

They want to get out for a daily walk like me.

Maybe then they wouldn't be such idiots.

Jeez.

Wish I had some paper with me; I'd leave a very rude note.

Oh well.

Here I am. Back home.

Thank goodness.

50 minutes. Not bad but I'm sure I can improve on that.

DAY TWO. WALK TWO.

It's cold. All I want to do is to crawl back upstairs, climb into my warm, inviting bed, pull the duvet up around my ears and GO TO SLEEP.

But what makes me think I would anyway? I was awake half the night so there's no reason to think I'd nod off now.

I suppose I'll just finish this coffee and go for my walk. I did promise myself, and Dr Wright, that I'd give it a good go.

Shit, now I've spilt lukewarm coffee down my front. Oh, I really can't be bothered to go *all* the way back upstairs just to change my shirt.

This scarf will do. It's bright and cheerful and, more importantly, will cover up the coffee stain beautifully.

Ta Da. Somehow I have managed it, I'm all set. Walking boots on, gloves at the ready and off I go.

At least I've managed to get outside. That's better than last week when I stayed indoors for several days on the run, as I couldn't be bothered to move.

But now I'm outside the door, I've shut it, locked it and checked that I have locked it several times.

I'm off.

Not sure my legs are up to this hill today, they're still aching from yesterday.

But you can do it, Gemma.

Well, a little self-motivation won't do any harm.

Oh, look at that cat in the window. What a dear little thing. It's a tortoiseshell one with lovely colouring. Tortoise. That has always struck me as rather an odd word but the worst thing is the way some people say tort-*toise*. I much prefer it when it sounds like tortus. In fact, catch me at the wrong moment and if you say tort-*toise* I may just go for your jugular. Maybe that's a slight overreaction but that's what I'm good at just now.

Oh, hang on, those two workmen look like they are coming my way.

They definitely are and it looks like they want to talk to me.

Don't panic Gemma. You are quite capable of holding a short conversation, now just smile.

Keep smiling – but not like you are a lunatic, jeez, listen to the men and take that fixed grin off your face.

So, they only wanted a sandwich shop. Oh hang on, I sent them to the supermarket but, actually, I remember now, there's a little shop just around the corner. Should I run after them and tell them?

Or would that just make me look like the grinning idiot they met earlier was now chasing after them and appears slightly more deranged than they had at first thought?

I'll leave it. Surely they'll see the little shop and, if they don't, it isn't exactly the end of the world, is it? Or will they think I did it on purpose?

For God's sake stop this.

IT DOESN'T MATTER.

I'm still cold but at least I'm making some progress up this damn hill. Those birds are chirpy. What are they so happy about? Actually, they're not happy, that's the clack, clack, clacking of a decidedly unhappy mother bird. There's probably some cat after its babies. Doesn't it realise its dog eat dog in this world? Whether you are a human, cat, bird or, well, a dog. She's going to have to fight to rear those fledgelings. That's how it is for us all. David Attenborough should do a film covering a few feral children and their mum yelling to get them in at night. Only his calm, soothing voice could make that sound OK.

I think this is about halfway up the hill, thank goodness. I'm starting to actually warm up now which is quite a relief.

Look at that old man coming out of his house. Oh, bless him. He's all wrapped up with his hat and glasses on. Can he make it to the gate? He looks a bit unsteady and his stick is wobbling. Please don't fall over. I'm not sure what I would do. Oh God, he's going to reach the gate when I do and it's too late to alter my course.

How sweet! He said hello and smiled at me and I managed to say hello back. That's progress! Well, it is for me anyway. He's still leaning on the gate and looks rather out of breath.

What right do I have to be so pathetic at the moment? I have my health, I can walk, I'm young; I've got it all compared to that poor old man.

Well, OK, my boyfriend did leave me but he was a shit anyway. He must be. If he couldn't cope with someone being a bit depressed for a while without running off, well, he's not worth it.

I'm too good for him and that's the end of the story.

He's still a shit though.

It's getting a bit quieter now and the houses are much bigger and posher. Or it would be quieter if half of them weren't having extensions.

This one seems interesting though. It looks like they are doing it themselves.

There's Dad and two sons and the other guy is possibly an *actual* builder. I suppose they have to have *someone* who knows what he is doing.

Surely there are laws about building things. I suppose that's why this other man is there.

Oh look, it seems someone has smashed that little pane of glass! Dad will not be pleased with that. I can just imagine him giving them a hard time over their supper tonight. I'll have to keep an eye on this.

Oh, hey up, here comes a jogger and I'm pretty sure it's the same guy I saw yesterday. Just keep walking and smile if he does.

Ooh. We're on nodding terms. That's good! Maybe I'm not as ugly and unattractive as I thought. Or, maybe he's just being polite. But whatever, if I can manage to return a smile when I'm on a brisk walk, red in the face *and* out of breath then that's some sort of progress. I think.

THANK YOU VERY MUCH...

Great, pressure washer guy has managed to cover me in mucky, muddy, sludge. It looks like someone has thrown a bucket of filthy water over my bottom half.

Is he even bothered? He looks like he's just said something but I can't hear a thing over the noise.

I'll just smile back and pretend I'm not bothered. I AM BOTHERED but I shall be grown up and pretend.

There, that wasn't too bad, was it?

Even if I do feel uncomfortable now and my feet are squelching in my trainers.

What a relief. It has flattened out just before the downhill bit and it feels so much easier.

I'm also drying out and my trainers have stopped squelching which is good.

But that's one hell of an eerie looking house on a pretty normal looking street.

There just seems something funny about it.

I guess it looks reasonable enough but it's so cold and uninviting. It feels like it is just a front of respectability when inside there's some massive trauma going on.

You know, kidnapped children being held hostage in the cellar or maybe, mass murder and slaughter and it's the home of a serial killer.

But everybody just walks past like nothing is going on.

The postman delivers the mail every day without giving it a thought. Or does he? Does he also suspect there is more to number 16 than meets the eye?

I'll have to watch it around here.

If it is the home of a mass murdering serial killer then I don't want him realising I have a routine that brings me past his lair at roughly the same time every day.

Now I'm getting paranoid. It's probably a normal man, minding his own business and getting on with his life.

Still looks *really* weird though.

Here we are, back around the circuit at pressure washer guy. At least he has moved down the road a bit so I should be safe from a drenching this time.

I think he's trying to smile at me. It's probably an apology really.

Or maybe he's laughing at me. I don't know and quite frankly I don't actually care.

It's true! I don't care; surely this is a good thing? I have managed to stop my brain from sabotaging my thoughts for the next half an hour to mull over my soaking by a workman.

That's great, I feel *so* much happier now.

Small steps I know but lots of small steps make up a whopping marathon in the end.

At last, home again. How come it still took me 50 minutes? I thought I'd been faster this time.

Maybe tomorrow.

DAY THREE. WALK THREE.

Here I am again, out in the big wide world and wrapped in a huge scarf to keep warm...and to hide away.

I'll set off at a really brisk pace and see if I can improve on my time. It's quite exciting to set myself little challenges.

Although, I still haven't got used to this hill. It feels so much steeper than if you go up it in a car.

Obviously. What did I expect? Sometimes my thoughts can be so stupid.

Oh look, this house has a monkey-puzzle tree in the garden. I really like them; they are so different from all the others.

Mind you, looking closely, they are a bit odd. They are actually rather scary with sharp edges and a bit prickly.

Maybe, I wouldn't have one in my own garden, there's something slightly sinister and spooky about them and I don't think I would find it at all relaxing looking out onto something like that.

Look at that poor woman; she is so fat! Oh hang on, now she

has turned around it isn't fat she is obviously pregnant, very pregnant.

How can a body stretch to that size? Surely it's not possible?

Obviously, it is. She's still walking around and unloading things from her car.

Maybe I should ask her if she wants some help?

I don't want to freak her out. She doesn't know me and could think I'm some sort of nut.

I'll leave it and just walk on by.

Nearly at the top of the hill now thank goodness. It did actually feel a little easier today. Maybe it's my imagination, I wouldn't have thought only a couple of long walks could make a difference. But it certainly feels like they have done the job. Just imagine what I'll be like after a few months of this!

There are a couple of women up ahead. They look an unlikely duo. One of them seems a bit embarrassed as she picks up the small, steaming pile her little dog has just left on the pavement. Well, you would wouldn't you?

They're getting nearer now, one woman carrying a small bag of faeces and with a rather cute dog on a lead and the other woman earnestly talking on regardless.

"My daughter has just been tested, her reading age was 5 years and 0 months."

No! I'm out of earshot and will never know the answer!

Is this a good thing or a bad thing?

Is she 10 years old but has the reading age of a child of 5 years and 0 months or, is she 3 and a child prodigy?

How frustrating! Maybe I should go after them and ask. No, I can't do that; I'm not *that* crazy.

Relief! Finally, we have levelled out and my poor calf muscles can have a bit of a rest. Temporarily I felt quite elated but then two people managed to squash that feeling almost as soon as it started.

The first one was walking along with an adorable little puppy and I told her how nice it was.

SHE JUST STARED AT ME. No response whatsoever. How rude can you get? As if that wasn't enough, a matter of only seconds later, I put a brave face back on and smiled at this chap walking in the opposite direction. As we met I said hello and he, VERY BEGRUDGINGLY, responded.

That's it. I give up on people, they are such hard work and have the ability to cripple my feelings in a nanosecond and it then takes me days to get over it. What's the point?

Hang on, there's a woman with a pram coming towards me.

What should I do? Ignore her like those two idiots just did to me or try and make an effort?

I'll have to look at her. I simply can't walk past and completely ignore her it just isn't in my nature.

Here goes, she's getting near now.

Trying to lock eyes, engage her and make her speak.

But no, she's having none of it. She's just staring down at the ground and avoiding me completely.

It must be me; do I look really grumpy and terrifying?

Or maybe she's just protecting her cub. I could be anyone. An axe-wielding maniac woman for all she knows.

But I don't *think* people generally assume you are a terrible person and about to attack them.

I know I have phases of that but it isn't a normal thought pattern, surely?

It must be my expression that is putting people off.

I think I better stand in front of a mirror later and study my face a bit.

There I go again simply assuming it's me who has the problem.

It might be her. She could have been up all night nursing a fractious baby and is now feeling stressed and exhausted.

Come to think of it, how do people manage that?

I can barely look after myself. I'm certainly not eating properly, and getting dressed is a bit of a hit and miss affair as far as colour coordination is concerned.

Maybe in this particular incident, it's 50/50. Partly me being half-crazed and thinking way too much about it and partly her being too involved in her own situation.

That feels like a bit of progress may be creeping slowly in.

Better watch that or I may just start feeling a bit human again.

That was hilarious! I have just nodded to a postman who is walking up a side street and ahead of me on the main road is his van.

Nothing unusual in that, but there's a woman sitting on the bonnet (well nearly sitting on it or maybe you could call it heavily leaning.)

By this time the postman has turned the corner and is now behind me. He can also see the woman, especially as she is now waving her arms about to attract his attention. Then she started shouting, 'Have you got my parcel? I'm not waiting 24 hours to get it redelivered.'

So basically she is stalking the postman.

I turned and he looked a little bemused but sort of smiled.

Annoyingly, I then walked past the van and couldn't really stop just to listen in. It would appear very rude. I suppose I could have pretended to fall over or something but that would have really disrupted the flow of the interaction.

Whatever, it has had me chuckling for the last 5 minutes and actually, I'm home!

Wow, I didn't even notice the last bit of the journey today.

What's the time?

That was just under 50 minutes. Getting better, slowly.

DAY FOUR. WALK FOUR.

Here we go again, puffing up the hill and seeing what the world has to offer today. At least I am out, for a while this morning I thought I was going to slip back into my more typical sloth-like behaviour.

I like sloths. It must be so nice to just sit about, halfway up a tree, and barely move all day long. Nobody expects them to actually *do* anything. That would suit me perfectly at the moment.

But I do remember being on holiday when I was little and some tourist running up shouting, "Quick, quick, there's a sloth!"

That's always amused me.

Maybe in another life, I can come back as a sloth, sit in a tree and laugh at all the people rushing around down below.

What a racket! Who on earth has a cockerel when they live on a housing estate? Bet they're popular with the neighbours. It's 10 am now, I wonder if it has been making that noise since sunrise or if it has adapted to estate life and generously waits until mid-morning before singing its little heart out?

I certainly wasn't expecting that. Maybe it's here on holiday, just a visiting cockerel, confused by the change in environment and numerous streetlights. There's a thought, maybe the lights have him shouting all night long. Now that would certainly cause a few problems. I should take a stroll one evening and see what is happening, or maybe not. If it is making a racket half the households around here will be up in arms with plenty of banter over the Bantams as they lean over the garden fence.

Actually, probably more than banter and more like outright turf war. I think I'll stay away.

Oh look, a couple of schoolgirls coming towards me. The one on the left is pretty and chattering away whilst the one on the right looks most awkward and uncomfortable. Poor girl is large and lumbering and looks desperate to gain some approval from her attractive counterpart. What a start in life, it just makes you realise that how we perceive the world is largely related to our genes. Had she not been so eager to please the other one then she'd be in school now getting an education and paving the way for a bright and interesting future. Instead, she's following Miss Pretty Face like an enthusiastic puppy. I wish I had the guts to confront them and send them packing. But I don't, she'll have to fight her own battles. Of course there is always the possibility that I may be misreading the situation and actually, Lumbering Lady is fully in control and Miss Pretty Face is tagging along to try and gain some rebel kudos.

Why is life so complicated?

I need to focus on my own issues before I start solving imaginary ones for other people.

Oh, a ladder.

I can't go under it; that would be bad luck for the next million years. I have to go round, which means stepping out into the road and risking getting mowed down by a speeding motorist.

I'll take the road option.

What's he doing up there anyway? Looks like he's fitting one of those massive dishes. One that looks like a carbuncle on the face of, well a rather ugly house actually.

But the point is that the carbuncle will be contributing to the cultural black hole that currently exists. The inhabitants will have so many reality shows to watch they could literally just sit there all day, vicariously living the most 'unreal' of lives.

Mind you, I have to admit to being drawn into a few myself, sometimes it's easier than juggling your own life. But I can't help wondering if everyone is trying to strive for these perfect, fame-fuelled lives and consequently they'll never be happy. It's not real, any of it.

God, why can't I just enjoy these things for what they are, entertainment? Why do I have to question everything instead of just having a laugh at someone else's expense?

Here we are, back at the DIY building site and Dad doesn't look happy. In fact, both the boys look pretty miserable too. Maybe he really did have a go at them about the broken window?

They should be excited, the cement man is here, pouring his cargo into a wheelbarrow and then one by one they are distributing it all over the place. They're all wearing wellies and are wading around in the sticky sludge as they try to even it out before it dries. I better not distract them or there will be a young man forever encased in the foundations of their extension.

At the very least they need to make sure it's flat or they'll be walking uphill every time they want to go to the next room, or glasses of water will constantly roll off the table and smash into a thousand pieces on the new carpet.

Oh, I did get a slight smile from the youngest son. That's good; I don't like seeing other people miserable.

Maybe that's how Luke felt watching my sad face day after day.

NO! I WILL NOT BE THE BADDIE HERE. I COULDN'T HELP IT.

It's Luke; he's the shit. Probably always was.

That's funny; the lady at number 80 is usually sitting at the table in the window. It all looks very formal, there's a very white tablecloth, a rather nice teapot with matching cup and saucer and a small plate of biscuits. The last few days she has been sitting there, under the comforting light of a standard lamp and I like to think she's doing a crossword.

But she's not today. It's all set up but no lady.

I hope she's OK. Perhaps she has gone to the toilet and she'll be back in a few seconds. Or maybe she slipped in the kitchen; on the milk she spilt as she transferred it from the carton to the jug. Or maybe she tripped and fell over the cat – or – STOP IT.

Why, why, why do I have to turn everything into a drama?Surely there isn't really a catastrophe waiting around every corner?

When I think about it I have walked this route a few times now and nothing terrifying has happened. I've thought of a few weird scenarios but they haven't *actually* happened. Well, I don't think they have. I suppose it could be that I have some sixth sense or something, but generally, I think I'm pretty normal and just having a bad few months.

Aren't I?

COURSE I AM.

Stop being such a lily-livered, iceberg, wet lettuce and get a bloody grip.

Of course, I'm normal, I'm just readjusting after a difficult period of my life but the fact is that I'm going to be bigger and better, well, not bigger, especially after all this walking, but smaller and better than I ever was before.

I will be in full control of my life and making decisions because *I* want to and not just to please everyone else.

Thank goodness I'm on the downhill part now, it's difficult enough trying to motivate myself without my calf muscles burning and my face glowing like a belisha beacon.

It's still so cold out that I'm wearing several layers plus a scarf, hat and gloves but look at that man sitting waiting for a bus in just a blue-checked, short-sleeved cotton shirt. Is he mad?

What is it with some men, and I include Luke in this, obviously, that they have a need to appear macho and the big tough guy by wearing completely inappropriate clothing?

You know, shorts and t-shirts when it's snowing, that sort of thing. Do they think it impresses us females?

Should we tell them that actually what we are thinking is, 'Look at that complete idiot,' and not 'Jeez, he must be a good catch? Look how his metabolism can deal with extreme temperatures without the need to wear more sensible clothing. Yes, I definitely what to have *his* babies.'

Actually, I don't think we should tell them, I guess it's natural selection at its best really.

At last, the final few minutes walking before I get home and can put my feet up and have a nice, strong cup of coffee.

I *might* even have some toast. Umm, I can smell it now. I think I will.

But what do I put on it, marmite or marmalade?

Seriously Gemma, LISTEN TO YOURSELF!

We are talking toppings for toast here not some major life decision that will have repercussions for years to come.

OK, marmite it is.

48 minutes. Not bad.

DAY FIVE. 1/2 WALK FIVE.

What an idiot I am.

I got up with every intention of going for my usual walk but no, I get dragged onto the settee and forced to lie there staring at the ceiling and thinking.

It's not as if I've been pondering about anything constructive like planning my future or internally debating my work options. No, I've been lying here trying to justify why I'm not halfway up the hill by now and seeing what is going on in the big, wide world.

It's not too late. I could get up, right now, get dressed and set off, all within the next five minutes.

But I can't. My body simply doesn't want to move. It is as if it has been welded to the base of the settee and I'll be here forever. Maybe one day, in a month or two, when someone, somewhere finally realises I haven't been seen for ages, the police will knock the door down with one of those big ramming things.

They'll fly through the door as the wooden frame splinters and then stop in their tracks.

I'll be lying inert on the damn settee, pale and wan with

one arm dangling gently down towards the floor. They'll be overcome with grief at the loss of such a beautiful young lady and worry that more could have been done to save her.

Or, they'll find a slowly decomposing body and a room full of flies. The smell will overcome them and one by one they will exit the room to vomit on the driveway.

No, I don't like that idea. Not one bit. I think it's the smelly part that really puts me off. I don't want some strangers coming into my home and thinking it stinks, only to realise it's actually me, or rather the remnants of me.

Perhaps they'll just find a skeleton.

I'll be perfectly positioned with my bony arms folded serenely over my bony chest. There will be hundreds of cats in the house, roaming around looking distraught. There are always hundreds of cats when a body is found.

But what about mum and dad?

Surely they would notice if I didn't call on a Monday evening? Just imagine how they would feel to find their only daughter had gone, and all that was left were her sad remains, and a house to clear out.

I can't do that to them, it isn't fair. It's not like it would be an accident or the result of a horrific illness. It would be down to me and me alone, unable to get my act together and get on with my life.

Jonny would be sad too.

Admittedly he'd go straight for my vinyl collection and guitar and hotfoot it back to his place with my treasured possessions. But at least they would be loved and used.

Brotherly love is more than that though, he'd miss me too; especially our arguments over the best music currently being churned out.

STOP IT GEMMA! JUST STOP IT.

What is wrong with you? You have everything to live for and you're behaving like a deranged woman.

It's not as if you haven't been dumped before, is it? There's been plenty over the years when you think about it, and the same was happening to all your friends.

It's a part of growing up.

You meet someone, spend a few weeks with them thinking they are the love of your life, then cry solidly for two hours when you split up before going out and meeting someone else. And so the cycle continues.

Eventually, though you find someone and it's different.

It feels right and they make you laugh. You miss them when they go out just to the shops.

No, not the shops, I'll never be able to think of Tesco shopping again in the same way. It will always be blighted by the terror of returning to an empty house and a post-it note.

But that's the thing, all my friends are now living with people, and seem happy enough, and that's what makes this hard.

Maybe I should get another dog? Losing Jeffrey was just the worst thing.

Actually, it was harder than losing Luke now I think about it.

Jeffrey loved me and didn't choose to go. Time just caught up with him and off he drifted, peacefully in my arms.

Luke, on the other hand, planned to leave when I was out! Unbelievable, and it looks like he had another woman all along. Well, maybe not all the time but she was certainly on the scene long enough to get pregnant.

That's the good thing about friends, when the chips are down they turn up with a bottle of wine and tell you your boyfriend had been playing around for months, and they didn't want to interfere.

That went down well. But would I have behaved differently if the roles had been reversed?

Would I have had the courage to tell *them*?

Probably not.

If this hadn't happened to me I don't think I would have said anything.

Now I would. Any hint of a misbehaving boyfriend and I'd be straight on the phone.

But would I? Would I really want to be the one who caused all the heartache to follow?

Oh, I don't know.

Why don't you stop churning yourself up inside Gemma and think of something a bit nicer?

That's easier said than done, that's why.

But I will force myself to get off this settee and get dressed.

I will make myself put my shoes on and then frogmarch myself out for a walk.

I don't think I'll do the usual walk though. I've managed to spend the entire day pontificating about life and the universe and it's getting a bit late.

I think I'll just go for a short, brisk walk in the park instead.

Unfortunately, the park is still full of idiots. I used to come here all the time with Jeffrey and practically every tree holds a memory for me. There has always been an odd assortment of people hanging about but it didn't bother me, I was there for a reason.

But now, what is that woman shouting about?

Her son, I assume it's her son; he's about three and

running ahead of her. Then there's her *possible* boyfriend, but definitely not the father of the child.

I'm not sure why I think that. Maybe it's because she's screaming at the child to stop running ahead and he hasn't said a word.

'We're not going that way,' she has just yelled at the poor child to make him stop. He dutifully did stop, and then guess what, they *did* go that way.

What sort of a message is that? Next time the boy won't listen to her and she'll wonder why. Be consistent you stupid woman.

And another thing, whilst I'm on the subject, why can't he run, he's three, in a park and letting off steam. Surely now is exactly the time he should be running.

Here we are again, people.

They are so engrossed in their lives that they can't see what is going on right in front of them.

Now she's telling her boyfriend that the nursery teacher has told her the boy will be in the top sets of everything when he starts school....

But will he? Doubt it looking at you, love.

God, I'm such a bitch when I'm in this sort of mood.

Thankfully they have gone now. They will just about be reaching town by now on the other side of the park. Maybe they are going there to find a nice restaurant and enjoy a lovely family meal.

Or maybe they're not.

However, here I am, nearly back home.

It wasn't as eventful as my usual walk, and I do feel I have cheated myself by only getting out for 20 minutes, but it's better than nothing and that was the alternative.

So actually, Gemma, you should pat yourself on the back for turning things around, even if it was only in a small way.

The good thing is that I also feel a little peckish!

Excellent news, I can make some coffee and maybe some toast and sink back into my settee.

But I did it. I made myself go and I do feel better for it. Excellent.

DAY SIX. WALK SIX.

What a glorious day!

The sun is shining, the sky is the most beautiful shade of blue and there's barely a cloud in sight.

I should take great big lungs full of crisp, clean air and clear out my system a bit.

Umm, maybe I'll try that when I get to the posh area where there are fewer cars churning out carbon monoxide at a ridiculous rate.

I suppose I could get a bus somewhere remote and take a walk there, but I just know I wouldn't keep doing it. I need to set myself achievable goals, so, for now, this is it, carbon monoxide and all.

Oh look, there's the postman up ahead getting into his van. He'll be moving onto his next section so I'll probably see him again soon if I get a move on. Wonder if he has noticed me?

If he has he must be thinking I'm a bit odd, out walking on my own day after day.

But do I care what he thinks? Yes, I do really, but why?

He's nothing to me, other than another human being who crosses my path from time to time. I should just treat it as that, a chance, occasional meeting. But it's not, is it? It isn't a chance meeting, he's out doing a job and I happen to walk near his route every day. I could alter it by setting off at a different time or walking in the opposite direction but I don't. I choose to go this way at this time so he'll just have to put up with it.

Hang on, Gemma; don't be so bloody stupid.

He has only ever smiled at you and never given you any reason to think he's fed up with seeing you.

It's me, once again putting my own mad thoughts into someone else's head. He actually seems a reasonable sort just getting on with his life, delivering the mail and looking forward to payday.

Jeez, it's actually much colder than I thought it was going to be, I wish I'd brought my hat with me. My ears are nearly dropping off.

Huh. Imagine if they did. Drop off that is, my ears. I'd look like I had been mountaineering up Everest rather than strolling around a few blocks. I don't think mountaineering would be my thing really. Trudging about with a huge rucksack on my back and wondering if there was going to be an avalanche at any moment. Not to mention trying to sleep in a tent halfway up a mountain with only a few Sherpas for company.

No, I don't think I'll bother, even though the views must be spectacular and certainly more dramatic than these rows of houses and a church.

But look, there's a lady coming out of the church carrying a small baby. It looks like she has been to some mother and baby event, in fact, there's the notice, 'Fun Music Classes'.

Oh God, can you imagine. A room full of yelling babies, all completely baffled as to why they are being forced to shake a maraca whilst their parents beam with pride. Maybe it's one of those things that are impossible to understand until you have your very own squirming, item of humanity sitting on your knee.

I get the feeling I'm not very maternal yet.

But even so, why has this poor woman come out of the session to sit in her car feeding the baby?

It's quite sad really. After all, it's only natural, isn't it? Feeding and growing are what babies are meant to do. It's all they do really, apart from filling nappies I suppose. That's another reason I don't think I'm ready for having children. I really can't see myself clearing up after a really dirty nappy.

Plus, there's the fact that I don't have a boyfriend. Even my limited knowledge gleaned from GCSE Biology, (and a highly embarrassed biology teacher), alerts me to the fact that it definitely takes two to make a baby.

Granted, the male can then bugger off if he likes, job done, but he is required to at least be there at the conception.

Having said that, look over there. That chap is still around for his child and it appears that the child is giving him the runaround.

It's hilarious, he has got out of his car and gone to get the child but she has locked all the doors and is laughing at him trying to get in.

He's quite calmly, or rather, outwardly calmly, asking the child to let him in.

He could be there for hours. I don't think I can walk any slower just to see the outcome. I assume at some point he'll either get the child to unlock the door or, he'll have to break in.

That's his problem though; I can simply walk away and enjoy the fact that no small person is running rings around me.

Here I am, I've reached the DIY building site already. Amazing what a few incidents en route can do to pass the time.

It looks like the bricks have been delivered and they are making excellent progress. Actually, they all seem happier today and the youngest son even said hello to me. That was nice.

See, a little greeting is all it takes to make someone's day. I even had the courage to tell him how much it's coming on now.

Yin and bloody yang.

I'm all happy about the building boys when I nearly get run over by a learner driver.

There are so many of them around here but I guess it's a pretty good place to learn. The roads are fairly quiet and there are plenty of junctions to practice stopping and, hopefully, starting again.

It's fun to try and judge what stage of learning each driver has reached. This one, for example, is completely incompetent and shouldn't be allowed behind the wheel of a car. She is crawling along, but, actually, she isn't kangarooing, so maybe she is slightly further up the list than I first thought. But she certainly isn't ready for the bigger roads yet.

But what's that bumper sticker all about?

'Beware – Sudden Braking'.

If you need a sticker saying that then it should be in great big letters, clear for all to see, not so small that you only manage to read it as you smash into the back of them.

Good news is I've reached the posh bit so there are more trees, and birds and it all looks very serene. But look at this place, it's rather grand and very orderly except for one of the upstairs rooms which has tarpaulin draped all over it.

What's that all about?

Is it the home of a serial killer and that is his kill room? Unsuspecting walkers get dragged from the street and are never seen again. Or perhaps the family are decorating. Who knows?

But you don't see many walkers around here and most people don't completely shroud a room in tarpaulin just to decorate. Just saying, it seems a little OTT if you ask me.

Maybe I'll put a bit more effort in and get past this bit, just in case.

Here's the other building site and boy do they look fed up. What's the matter with them?

They've also had their bricks delivered and should be happy to be moving onto the next stage but they certainly don't look happy. They're all working in silence apart from the noise from that huge flame-thrower thing.

What on earth is that used for? Do bricks need heating up before cementing into place? I don't know and, by the looks on their faces, I don't think I'll bother asking either.

At least they should be able to spot it if someone is dragged off into that house over there. It could be their good deed for the day. Use the flame-thrower to get the murderer to release the poor victim before it is too late.

I'm getting a bit worried now. Why am I so preoccupied with serial killers? I was thinking about them the other day, it was a different house though. But surely, the law of averages says that there aren't going to be two serial killers living within walking distance of my house.

Or maybe there are and they are just very good at not getting caught.

Why do I keep suspecting people of something as horrendous as that?

It's rather a dark, deep, nasty thought to have. It would be much nicer to imagine they are decorating to refresh the room rather than about to kill their seventh victim and then dispose of the body in some unknown fashion.

I suppose it shows my current state of mind more than anything else.

Or maybe *I'm* one, a potential serial killer in waiting. It only needs one small thing to happen that will trigger off a chain of events beyond my control.

Perhaps I should hand myself in now.

Don't be stupid Gemma, you can't even swot a fly without feeling guilty for the next 12 hours as you imagine all the baby flies waiting for their mother to come home.

Pretty pathetic really, I'm certainly no murderer.

Who'd have thought that so much thinking about death and destruction could get me all the way back home! I barely noticed the last part of the walk.

I really do think I need to work on controlling my thoughts a little more. It's surely not healthy to lose half an hour of time to such nasty thoughts. But the good news is I really fancy a bowl of muesli.

DAY SEVEN. WALK SEVEN.

Oh, it's much nicer today, still, clear-blue skies but not absolutely freezing like it was yesterday. Consequently, I am completely overdressed with my face bright red and sweating and I've only been going for 10 minutes.

In fact, I'll take my hat off and stick it in my pocket, that's marginally better but I bet I look a complete fright. My hair will be plastered to my face, which will complement the red glow wonderfully.

Not that I care. I really don't. People can think what the hell they like about my appearance.

If they want to come over and discuss it with me then fine.

I'm likely to kill them but if they choose to insult me then it's their own fault.

Who am I kidding? Of course I care. Well, at least enough to find matching socks today which is a vast improvement over the last few months.

What is it with socks?

Why is it so difficult to put them in the wash and actually retrieve the same number an hour and a bit later?

Where do they go? Is there some sort of sock heaven where they go to rest after a lifetime of sitting on some smelly feet?

I only wash for one; surely it can't be too difficult to find several socks that are meant to go together. At least when Luke was here I had the excuse that he may have left some at the gym, well, I told myself it was the gym but the reality was he probably left them under the bed of his mistress as he rushed to get away before her husband came home.

Mistress.

Do I like the word mistress? No, not really, mistress sounds controlling and authoritative which isn't really the impression I have of the trollop who lives a mere three miles from my own home.

They are welcome to each other and the tangled web of lives and lies that they are wading their way through.

Funnily enough, this is the first time I've thought about them without crying!

Yeah! Go me!

That's put a spring in my step, I really don't want Luke in my life anymore and I actually mean it. I'm not just saying it to try and convince myself.

Excellent. This is a red-letter day.

In fact, right on cue, there's the postman. It's as if he's delivering my freedom as he goes on his rounds.

Oh stop it, you stupid cow, don't be so dramatic. The postman has nothing to do with it but at least he smiled and nodded at you.

And I smiled and nodded back which is certainly an improvement on yesterday when the poor chap was unwittingly the recipient of one of my internal, and quite mental, rants.

Look, there's a woman coming out of the monkey-puzzle house.

I'm a bit disappointed really. I thought she'd be a rather spooky, witchy, wrinkled, wart-ridden lady with her eerie tree and her eerie house but she's not.

She looks perfectly normal. In fact, she looks like Mrs Suburbia going off shopping in the supermarket to stock up on food for the week ahead.

Tedium. Tedium. Tedium.

I much preferred it when I thought of her as evil and mysterious.

But isn't it amazing what you see if you actually open your eyes and take a good look around, like that husky dog in the window over there?

It's a huge beast and it's only a small bungalow but there it is, sitting in the window, casually watching the world go by. I wonder what it makes of it all and whether it is concerned about the lack of snow? After all, snow is in its genes. Well, not literally, obviously, but generation after generation of huskies were used to living in the freezing cold, sleeping curled up in the snow and thinking nothing of it. But this one is happily sitting in a warm, centrally-heated lounge and doesn't appear to be concerned that global warming may have caused so much damage that all his snow has gone.

Hold on, that would mean the dog would have to be aware that different countries lie on different latitudes. Can they do that?

I'm sure all animals are much more aware than us humans give them credit for but I'm not sure I'd go *that* far.

Whatever, husky house is way back there and I have other things to think about and observe on my daily hike.

It all seems very pooch orientated today, I have just walked past the most gorgeous dog, with its owner. It had such beautiful eyes which seemed to be saying, 'Morning', as it sauntered by and such a wonderful, long, woolly coat. A most unusual dog and after a cursory look at the owner they were actually very similar. Her eyes also seemed to smile at me and her hair well, not that I'm one to question someone's hair, I haven't been to a hairdresser in months, but hers was pretty much long and woolly like the dogs.

But there you have it, nice dog; nice owner.

Funny that, why is it that owners look like their dogs?

I mean I'd love a bloodhound. Not now but when I'm older and more settled. I'd have to be at home all the time to look after it properly so maybe when I have a young family would be a good time. I can see it now, me striding out with a pram, a toddler and a bloodhound as we go for long, rambling walks to tire the children, the dog and hopefully for me to recover my shape after the strain of carrying two children.

But does that mean I'm going to turn out to be all saggy and dribbling like a bloodhound?

It's not a look I'm really going for and I must admit it's certainly not a look that will encourage my husband to stay around and care for his family.

Surely it doesn't mean that owners *always* look like their dogs.

Then again, if I had one now, right now, I bet people would be thinking, droopy sad-faced dog, droopy sad-faced owner.

That would be quite appropriate.

Here we go, Lycra alert. As I'm going down the hill there's a man on a bike puffing his way up. It's not just that he's wearing Lycra that's causing me some concern but that it's a multi-coloured affair.

What *does* he look like? Especially, well, he's a man of a certain age, with a body which doesn't exactly lend itself to wearing tight-fitting clothing.

But all credit to him, at least he's out here trying to do something about it.

I'll smile some encouragement at him to help reach the pinnacle, as in peak, top. Not the pinnacle of Lycra wearing.

That would take *much* longer.

I don't believe it!

He looked away.

He actually looked away rather than smiling back or making eye contact and saying hello. He simply didn't want to.

Maybe he couldn't. Maybe the tight fitting outfit and the extra exertion of the hill rendered him completely speechless.

Or maybe he's from the, 'Look the other way', branch of society. Oh, there are plenty of them. Holier than thou, all outwardly concerned but when it boils down to it they simply can't be bothered.

Oh hang on, he's turned around and is coming past again.

Fairly flying past but then it is downhill for him now and he's getting quite a speed up.

Nope. Still not speaking.

I hope his brakes fail at the end of the road and he careers into a tree.

I'll walk past and look the other way.

Arse.

Just when you've given up on the human race someone goes and spoils it all.

This time it was the jogger. He was coming towards me at quite a rate and it was plain to see that the path wasn't big enough for the two of us, thanks to an overgrown bush.

Luckily for him, even after the Lycra man incident, I still feel humane enough to step out of the way, into the road actually, to allow him to pass without having to break his stride.

It was rather nice of me I think, especially as he's a man and I'm not particularly keen on them right now.

But, hallelujah, he not only smiled at me but he also raised an arm in a silent thank you.

He was rather nice actually, pity he wasn't the one wearing Lycra.

Good heavens, Gemma, is this the stirring of some long lost emotion?

No, I don't think so but at least I have looked at a man without wanting to rip his Adam's apple right out from his throat in one, swift but deadly move.

And here we are, home again.

I think I'll have a bath and I may possibly shave my legs.

DAY EIGHT. WALK EIGHT.

Blimey, it's blustery out here today. Good job I decided to wear my hat or I'd look a real fright as the wind whips my hair into an Einstein-esque style.

Still, it didn't do him much harm did it? His uncombed hair and distracted ways are now synonymous with genius.

I love the story of him being on a train and, when the conductor arrives, he frantically starts searching his pockets for his ticket.

'Oh don't worry Mr Einstein,' the conductor said, 'I recognise you and you can travel for free.'

'Thank you', replied Einstein, 'but if I can't find my ticket then I won't know where to get off the train.'

Snort.

I just love that. It's *so* like me; without the being recognised or the genius bit, of course.

Or maybe I am? Maybe I'm a genius in waiting. Waiting to find out what I can actually do that will amaze the world.

Frankly, in my case, I think the sight of my fuzzy, windswept hair is more of an outward and visible sign of an inner disturbance than anything else, but we shall see.

Here comes another learner driver, let's see how this one fares. Well, she appears to be a little more in control than the one the other day but boy is she gritting her teeth as she crawls along.

Not as much as the instructor is though.

They are both going to need teeth guards if she doesn't pass her test soon.

Perhaps there could be some sort of deal between dentists and driving instructors.

I can see it now, a huge poster by the side of the road, 'Book Five Lessons and get a free Tooth Guard – one each.'

Maybe that isn't exactly the image an instructor would like to portray but it amused me for a good few hundred paces.

I do enjoy reading body language and that incident over the road just now was a perfect example of one body screaming, 'Go away,' whilst the other one is yelling, 'Let me in.'

Hilarious.

The woman, who obviously lives in the house, as she was standing in the doorway, was all smiles and pleasantries. However, to the trained eye, she was leaning on one side of the door with her arm casually, but quite purposefully, stretched out across the entrance, barring the way.

Whilst her face was saying, 'Hi, so nice to see you,' her body was screaming, 'you've done what you needed to do now go away, I'm busy.'

The other woman, oblivious to this, or maybe she just didn't care, had one foot on the step as she tried to gain entrance and the battle of wills continued until the visitor seemed to get the message and said her goodbyes.

This all happened in the few seconds it took me to go by.

How come I can pick up on the body language of

complete strangers and yet I didn't notice anything unusual in Luke's behaviour in the months he was SLEEPING WITH ANOTHER WOMAN RIGHT UNDER MY NOSE?

Ugh, I still feel sick when I think about it. What a waste of time, energy and my emotions.

I'd sooner he had just come clean and told me he had found someone else rather than give it a few months to see which one of us he preferred; especially as he obviously preferred HER.

For God's sake Gemma, let it go. You've been doing so well these last couple of days, don't let the scheming, pathetic little shit creep back under your skin again.

You're free of him. FREE! Remember that life is better since he left. Really, it is.

Maybe if I just keep telling myself this I will eventually believe it. What is it they call it? Oh yes, 'self-fulfilling prophecy'. That's it. All I have to do is keep telling myself I don't need him, don't want him and I'm better off without him. Simple really.

I sort of believe it too, most of the time. Now it just seems that every so often I let my guard down and he deals an almighty blow to my subconscious.

At least that's better than him constantly undermining me.

So, pat yourself on the back, Gemma, go on do it.

No, not really, you idiot, now I just look bizarre.

Like a mad, windswept woman patting herself on the back as she strides forth along the road.

I do wonder about my sanity sometimes but people often talk to themselves like this don't they? Surely they must do, it's just an inner argument as you weigh up the right thing to do, whatever the scenario.

I mean I've done it for as long as I can remember. It isn't

simply a reaction to Luke but a known and tested strategy that has helped me get to where I am today.

Umm, OK, maybe not so good then.

Where exactly am I?

No job. No boyfriend. Wavering on the brink of needing antidepressants. STOP IT.

I've had a job, had a boyfriend, still have a house and will drag myself back from the brink if it's the last thing I do.

That's better, you tell them, girl.

Which reminds me, last night I realised I had done a whole week of this walking lark and I worked out how many steps I had taken. I couldn't believe it. I used the app on my phone and the distance varied from between 4,789 steps to 5,085 steps each walk.

I guess it depended on how many times I fell off the kerb or detoured around a screaming lady sitting on the postman's van.

Anyway, if we say, for ease of calculation, and because it's a nice, round, figure, that on average, whilst walking this route, I take 5,000 steps. Apparently, that's about 4.51 Km, which is an astounding 2.8 miles a day!

That's not bad and is certainly 2.8 miles further than I would have walked the entire of the previous week.

But then I started feeling really proud, 5,000 steps every day for a week is a grand total of 35,000 steps, which is 31.57 Km or a whopping 19.6 miles.

19.6 miles over the week! Who'd have thought?

AMAZING!

I had no idea that just by putting aside less than an hour a day I could manage to walk those sorts of distances.

In fact, I was so pleased with myself after working this

out that I walked straight to the kitchen and ate some chocolate to celebrate.

This wasn't really part of my game plan but all the excitement made me lose my senses temporarily. Well, for long enough for me to eat chocolate instead of a proper meal. This is obviously something else I need to address.

But HANG ON, I was just praising myself and celebrating what is, in fact, a huge leap forward for me, and somehow I have managed to turn it around and talk myself down to a much more familiar mood.

Fed up and angry.

STOP IT GEMMA.

Go on, treat yourself and wallow in the unfamiliar feeling of satisfaction, just for a change. You never know, you might even grow to like it.

Jeez. I have just passed the really spooky house, where something terrible must be going on for the place to look *that* eerie, and guess what, there's tarpaulin up in one of the rooms.

I haven't noticed it before which means there must have been someone in there recently. Well, within the last 24 hours actually.

Shit, that other house also had tarpaulin up in one of the rooms. There seems to be a theme developing here and it's not a good one.

I'm afraid we are back to the serial killer's theory.

Which is why I am almost jogging now as I get as far away as possible from this place.

Ugh, it gives me the creeps.

Oh God, now *the* jogger is coming over the horizon and I must look a right state.

He's all toned and coordinated, with a black sports

top, matching black shorts, which allow me a very good look at his tanned and rather nice legs, and expensive looking trainers, plus he's barely out of breath. Whilst I, on the other hand, am wobbling along, as my legs really aren't used to being used at speed, red in the face after a few hundred yards of jogging and wearing the most unattractive, old, scruffy coat that I used to use for walking Jeffrey. Some faded black leggings, which are definitely saggy around the bottom (although luckily he won't see that thanks to the oversized coat) and a pair of old walking boots finish off my shambolic attire.

Question is, do I continue jogging and make it look like I meant to be running all along or do I slow to an acceptable fast walking pace and try to save some face?

Has he even noticed me?

Oh no, he's nearly level with me. He must have been going at a sprint rather than a jog.

It's too late now, I'll have to keep running and try to act normal.

Snort. Normal. Me.

'Hi!'

'Oh, Hi,' I spluttered with the last ounce of air left in my lungs.

Shit. Did I seem nonchalant?

Doubt it, he happened to pass me just as I snorted at my own incompetence, which more than likely sealed my fate as the completely mad and dishevelled woman he comes across whilst out running.

It's OK, Gemma, you don't care, remember?

Plus he's probably about three miles away by now the pace he was going.

But I do care.

I don't want to be seen as disorganised and, well, quite frankly, ugly. That's it. I'm ugly and always will be.

Why am I still running?

God, I have such a stitch, I'll have to bend over here until it goes.

Take some nice, even breaths, Gemma.

'You OK?'

Sigh.

Please, not him, jogger man returning from his half marathon before lunch.

'Oh, hello,' thank you, God, it's not.

'Oh,' again. It's only Lycra man from the other day, dismounting from his bike to check on me.

'Thank you, but I'm fine, just taking a breather.'

'That's alright then, you just seemed to be struggling a bit so I thought I'd check.'

'That's very kind of you, you know, to check, and not look the other way.'

'What?'

'Oh, nothing, I mean, just thanks. That's all.'

Stop talking Gemma you're just making it worse.

'OK, well, bye then. Enjoy the rest of your ru-walk.'

'Will do, bye.'

He's gone. He has mounted his bike and is disappearing into the distance. What a relief.

Come on, Gemma, stand up and get moving before anyone else has to pick you up off the bloody floor.

Actually, now I'm at a safe distance; that was quite amusing.

When I get home I'm going to look at some more appropriate clothing. I'm not really ugly I just need to take control of my appearance and put a bit of effort in.

Here we are, 46 minutes.

46 MINUTES, all that running and I only knocked two miserly minutes off my time?

Mind you, how long was I prostrate before Lycra man arrived.

Whatever.

DAY NINE. WALK NINE.

It's still blowing a bloody gale out here, when is this dreadful weather going to pass over and give us all a break?

It's almost impossible to try and work more on my appearance when every time I step outside I'm almost blown off my feet.

Why exactly did I bother to straighten my hair this morning?

Oh yes, because after yesterday's shame I decided to take myself in hand and make more of an effort.

Consequently, I am now sporting a new pair of joggers, black with neon orange trim. I'm hoping that the trim will have the same effect as go-faster stripes on a car.

I really splashed out and also purchased some very expensive, well *expensive* to me, running shoes. I know I'm not actually running, it's more of a fast walk but I did break into a jog yesterday, which justifies the outlay in my mind. Also, the sales girl did a very good job of selling the extra support to my arches.

I've let myself down with the coat though. Once I have

recovered from the shock of the trainers I may go out and invest in a more ladylike coat.

But for now, I shall just have to appear only half decent.

Oh good, Lord!

What is that man doing running out into the road wearing only his dressing gown?

I know he's only wearing his dressing gown because the unfortunate timing of a blustery squall allowed me a full view of his genitals, and a pair of wiry, knobbly legs minus any footwear.

It was not a pretty sight and I may well be traumatised for weeks to come.

He is totally oblivious to my presence as he is staring down a side street.

There's nothing for it, I shall have to break into another jog just to nosey down the street before whatever he is so distressed about disappears.

Blimey, it was a man, probably about 60 and pulling a little travelling case behind him that looked stuffed to the gunnels.

I wonder what their story is?

Are they secret lovers who have been arguing all night and, as one man leaves, the other can't help running out to take a final look at his only true love?

Or maybe the man with the case has just robbed the other guy and the contents of the case are all dressing gown man's most treasured possessions.

Either way, I shall have to stop jogging now as I can barely breathe and both men are now out of view anyway.

Whatever has happened there the whole scenario appeared to be one of sadness.

I hope he's OK?

Maybe I should go back to his driveway and check on him.

I don't want to come past in half an hour and find him swinging from a tree having tied his dressing gown cord around his neck. Apart from the trauma that would present, the thought of the lack of cord holding his dressing gown in place is not a nice one. I've seen more than enough of that gentleman already thank you very much.

He probably wants to be alone anyway. He certainly doesn't want to explain it all to a complete stranger, or not one who is having enough trouble sorting out her own emotions without trying to find a long lost sense of empathy with the males of the species.

No, I'll leave him to lick his wounds in private.

Besides, I'm not actually sure which driveway he came from and I can hardly go knocking at doors and inspecting people's dressing gowns until I find him. I'm not even sure I'd recognise his face and I certainly can't ask to see everyone's nether regions until I find someone with a perfect match.

But it is a timely reminder that I'm not the only person out here in the big wide world with problems. The trouble is that when you shut yourself away, as I have done for some time, it's easy to become so insular that you lose your way a bit.

I guess this is me acknowledging that coming out for these walks has actually been a good thing if only to force me into some sort of routine and out of the house for a while every day.

And that, my dear Gemma; is another teeny, tiny glimmer of an improvement.

Here we are, another learner driver, it's the gritting teeth one, not the absolutely horrific one. It looks to me like she has speeded up a bit from the other day. She's definitely a bit more confident but her teeth are still clenched as if she's developing lockjaw and the instructor's knuckles are white as he grips the dashboard.

Can you imagine spending your entire working day feeling like you were on the scariest ride at an amusement park?

Surely it can't be good for you. I wonder what the rate of premature deaths amongst driving instructors is? Heart disease, alcoholism and divorce must be rife amongst those who spend their days permanently tense.

Thank God I don't have any burning desire to take *that* up as a job. It may well tip me right over the precipice if I did, free-falling into oblivion.

OK, so there is some improvement in my mental state but it is obviously rather tentative and should, therefore, be treated with caution at this stage.

Is there no respite on this bloody walk?

Now I've reached the eerie house. I will make myself slow down a bit and try and get a better look at the place.

Ugh, surely I can't be the only one who senses there is something not quite right here?

Looking at it now, it just seems cold and empty. Not empty of belongings as I can see the top of a settee, which must be just underneath the window, and there are a few ornaments on the fireplace, but there doesn't seem to be any *life* there.

It's as if the whole human part of a home being a home has been sucked out into a black hole and disappeared. The basic structure is there but there's a complete lack of warmth.

Shit. Shit. Shit.

I'm sure I saw a person, or at the very least a shadowy figure, lurking beside the curtain.

Quick, Gemma, get a move on and try and look nonchalant.

OK, so suddenly darting off and breaking into a run isn't particularly nonchalant but what else could I do?

Whoever was in there didn't want me to see them. I wonder how long they had been there?

Did they see me peering in as I slowed down to go past, trying to get a better look?

I really hope not.

Am I being stupid or is there a child held hostage in the cellar or the next victim of a serial killer lined up waiting for the right moment for events to unfold?

I have no evidence whatsoever that anything untoward is going on inside other than a gut feeling, and quite frankly can my gut feelings be trusted?

If I were to try and explain all this to the police they'd laugh me right out of the station and right into the local psychiatric hospital for assessment.

No, I'm going to have to find something a bit more concrete to go off, preferably not some with a person encased inside.

I'll come back tonight, when it's dark, and try to get a bit closer.

What's going on down there? It looks like that lady might need a bit of help. Oh God, I wanted to dash home and make a plan for tonight's reconnaissance trip but the poor woman does appear to be in some distress.

'Hello, are you alright?'

'No, I'm hanging on to this scaffolding for dear life. This

wind has brought it down but if I let go it will blow straight into that car and house over there.'

'Oh, yes, I see, let me grab a bit for you. Is there anyone around to help us?'

'My daughter has called my husband and he should be here anytime now, with one of his work colleagues'

'Well, that's a relief as I'm not sure how long I can hold this, my hands are freezing already!'

'It's very kind of you to help, my arms are about to drop off but you've managed to take some of the strain.'

'Err, exactly how long will your husband be?'

You better say he's just pulling up now or I'm going to let go before this thing pulls my arms out of their sockets.

'Well, he said he was nearly here a couple of minutes ago.'

Oh hello, who's this I can see as I peer under my right arm, just below my armpit?

'Are you going to be long it's just I think that scaffolding might just blow onto my garage roof or even the car if you don't move it soon?'

Seriously?

Does the old bat that obviously lives next door think we are doing this for fun?

'It's OK Mrs Davis, Brian should be here in just a minute, why don't you go back inside where it's nice and warm?'

Well, I'm certainly not imagining that being said between gritted teeth.

I'd better add my thoughts or the old dear might get harpooned by one of these metal rods.

'Yes Mrs Davis, if I were you I'd just step inside out of the way.'

I'm going to have to shift my weight a bit here before I let go of the bloody thing.

'I'm just going to turn around so I can hold on with my other hand for a bit longer.'

Good, looks like Mrs Davis has taken our advice and buggered off but where is this husband?

Does he even exist or am I being sucked into some dreadful plot?

Somehow I don't think this very likely, the poor woman looks ready to cry and I can't say I blame her. I feel like that and I've only been here five minutes.

'It's OK, here he is, just pulling up.'

Thank Christ for that, my arms are burning now.

'Very good,' I reply with a false smile.

'It's OK, love, I've got it now, me and Jim can sort it out, but thanks for your help.'

'Right, excellent, I'll, err, leave you to it then.'

Jeez, my arms are sore, I'll have to shake them about a bit to get the blood moving.

Well, they all seem a bit preoccupied so I think I'll just skulk off, I've done my good deed for the day.

That certainly warmed me up a bit apart from my hands, which feel like they are burning they are so cold; the rest of me feels nice and toasty.

I'll do a semi-jog home, it's not far off, and set about a plan for tonight.

DAY NINE AND 3/4.

Right, I think that's everything.

I have my torch, changed my off-white dog walking coat for a dark mac and found a black beanie hat, so I really do look like I'm about to go undercover.

I've been waiting for ages for nightfall when most normal people have shut their curtains and are now huddled around the T.V. sets.

Unfortunately, it appears to be very nearly a full moon, which is providing a bit more light than I had bargained for but I'll manage.

This is actually quite exciting!

For the first time in ages, I feel like I have a real purpose. Even if my suspicions are a bit vague and quite possibly a figment of my imagination. I have to find out what is so odd about that house.

Right, time to go, one last check.

Shit, I knew there was something. I didn't charge my phone.

Not to worry there's about 40%, which should be fine, providing I don't get kidnapped.

If I do I'll be furious with myself for forgetting to check such a basic piece of equipment but that's not going to happen is it?

Oh stop it, Gemma, just get going and stop being such an idiot.

These walks are certainly doing my stamina good as I've semi jogged all the way here and I'm still standing!

But now I need to take care, as this is the street of the eerie house.

I'll just keep to the path, as near to the garden wall as I can until I reach the house.

All the other houses are shut up for the night by the looks of things, which is exactly what I wanted.

Should I crawl along under cover of the wall?

No, because if I do happen to come across another nocturnal rambler I don't want them to think me suspicious.

Anyway, there's nobody here so it's irrelevant.

This is it, it's the next house along and it looks pretty much in darkness.

Here goes, I'm up the driveway and right next to the lounge window.

I'll just take a little peek inside to see what is going on in there.

Precisely nothing. How disappointing, but, I'm not done yet.

I mean if I'd kidnapped someone I wouldn't have them bound and gagged and just prostrate on the floor in the lounge.

I'd have to be much more discreet than that.

I think I'll open this side gate and have a little look around the back.

Umm, mental note to self, next time I decide to go

undercover I really must bring some oil with me. That gate made enough noise to wake the dead.

I daren't move for a minute or two in case someone is inside and I have just alerted them to my presence.

I don't hear anything apart from my own heart beating rather rapidly, so I shall continue.

I'm semi-crawling, semi-standing, maybe I should call it scrawling. Oh no, that's the thing children do on scraps of paper with multicoloured crayons. How about stawling? Not sure if that's a word or not, I'll have to look it up when I get home and if it isn't a known word I shall make it my purpose in life to introduce it into everyday vocabulary.

I've always been interested in etymology. Take the word 'quiz' for example. Apparently, a theatre proprietor in Dublin had a bet to see if he could introduce a new word into the city within 48 hours. He wrote the word quiz on lots of pieces of paper and after the performance that night asked all his staff to write the word on walls around the city. Sure enough, next morning everyone was talking about the strange word that had appeared, and soon it became part of the language.

The annoying thing is that the taxi driver who told me this, on what was supposed to be a romantic weekend in Dublin with Luke, didn't tell us what the prize was. Must look that up too.

Oh stop it, Gemma, now is not the time for your random ramblings, especially as you're now round the back of the house and this window above you must be the kitchen.

If I stand up very slowly and just take a little look...

Arghhhhh.

Ouch.

Dear Lord, who the fuck was that and why have I ended up sitting in a very prickly bush?

Oh God, they're coming out, I need to get out of here.

'Hey, who's there?'

Shit. He's put the light on and I can hear him unlocking the door but I seem to be frozen to the spot.

Well not so much frozen as tangled up in this damn bush. Ouch, there's another scratch to add to the collection.

'Umm, what exactly are you doing wedged in my rose bush?'

Double shit. It's only *the* jogger man, looking very pleasant in jeans and a jumper whilst I lay entangled in his bush with no explanation that I could possibly give to him that doesn't cement his view of me as a complete idiot.

'Hi!'

He's coming closer, it's only a matter of time before he realises it's me.

'Do you need some help?'

He's holding his hand out to pull me up and his voice sounds calm and concerned, but his face tells me he is very amused at my predicament.

'Yes please, that might help.'

If I can just pull my hand out from underneath me then I can offer it up for some assistance.

'Ouch, shit that hurt.'

'It will do, you're stuck in a rose bush remember.'

'How could I forget, there's one sticking right up my, oh, that's better, my hands free.'

Here it comes; hand to hand contact.

Um, nice and warm, firm and...

'Hey, that hurt!'

'I'm sure it did but at least you're standing up now.'

Oh God, now what do I say, he's bound to ask why I'm creeping around his house.

'So, why exactly are you in my back garden and scaring me half to death by peering in the kitchen window just as I went to fill the kettle?'

'Why didn't you turn the light on?'

'Hang on, I'm meant to be the one asking the questions.'

What do I say? I was just checking if there were any hostages inside, or do I let him think I was simply checking him out? I can't do that, it's more than checking someone out to break into his garden, it's stalking!

'I'm not sure you'll believe me when I tell you, it's a bit, well, umm, unusual.'

'Tell you what, why don't you come in and let me clean you up a bit and you can explain it all over a cup of coffee.'

Is he trying to lure me in and I'm the one that is going to be the hostage or is just being kind?

'That would be lovely, thanks.'

Obviously, my inner instinct is telling me that he must be OK.

'Come on then, milk and sugar?'

'Just milk please.'

This is surreal.

Nice kitchen though. It's much more modern looking than I thought it would be from seeing the front of the house.

'Here, take this flannel and wipe the mud, and not insubstantial amount of blood, from your hands.'

'Thanks, I must say you are taking this rather well. Weren't you concerned I was an intruder?'

'You are an intruder.'

'Oh.' Maybe he isn't as laid back about this as I first thought.

'But I would imagine you're the only intruder around that wears dark clothing but brilliant orange piping. I must admit you gave me a real fright when I saw a face at the window but as you flew backwards and your legs flashed by, I immediately knew I had seen that piping a few times before.'

'You're laughing at me.'

'I'm allowed to.... you squashed my rose bush.'

'True, and thanks for the coffee.'

'No problem, but are you going to tell me why you're here?'

Think, Gemma; quickly, come up with some brilliant excuse in the next nanosecond.

'I thought there was someone being held hostage here.'

That is far from a brilliant excuse.

He's looking at me very blankly.

'I said, I thought there...'

'I heard what you said but for heaven's sake, why?'

He does genuinely look bemused but that's hardly surprising, only a few minutes ago he was having a quiet evening in and then *I* happened.

'It's complicated.'

'I'm sure it is but I'm all ears.'

'Look, OK, I'll explain.'

I think I'll have to go for the truth; anything else would just sound stupid. Ha, as if this won't!

'I've been going for these walks recently,'

You don't need to give him your life story, Gemma, just keep to the main points.

'and I walk past this house every day.'

'You walk past me every day too when I'm out running.'

'Yes, that's right, isn't it funny!'

'I don't know yet, that very much depends on what you say in the next few sentences.'

He's still laughing at me; I can tell by the way he's looking at me, with one eyebrow raised. It's rather nice actually.

Focus, Gemma.

'Well, I kept thinking, whenever I went past, that this house looked a bit, you know, odd.'

'Odd. In what way?'

'Empty, like some terrible thing was going on inside.'

'It is.'

Shit. Why did I come in here? I was right, he's going to leap over the kitchen counter and throw me into the cellar any minute.

Can I find my phone in my pocket without him seeing?

It's not there! It must still be outside in the bush.

This is getting worse and worse.

'So, umm, what is happening that is so terrible?'

Keep him talking, Gemma, engage him in conversation and make him think of you as a real person with a real life to live.

'My Mum died two weeks ago. After the funeral, which was held down south, as she wanted to be buried next to Dad, I had to come here and empty the house. I've been at it for days. It's such a depressing job I make myself go out for a run every morning just so I can face the task ahead.'

He's good, very good.

Or maybe he's telling the truth.

Actually, as I look around it doesn't look that eerie from this side of the garden fence. Maybe it is true after all.

If that's the case I feel awful. The poor man has had enough to deal with without me barging into his life.

'So actually you are right. The house does have an eerie

feel about it as I'm breaking up a lifetime of memories as I sort through all her things.'

What have I done?

This poor man is grieving and now he has a slightly demented woman in his kitchen.

'Does that answer your question?'

'Yes. Yes, it does and I'm so sorry. God, I'm so stupid and not quite myself at the moment. I'm afraid I seem to have let my imagination take over and, well, got the situation entirely wrong. You know, two and two makes four, I mean five. I think I should stop talking and leave.'

'No, finish your coffee at least. I'm not mad at you; I'm actually quite pleased for the distraction. It's not every day a lovely lady breaks into your property and tells you she thinks you are a kidnapper.'

'See, you are mad.'

'No, no I'm not mad.'

Yes he is, he thinks I'm lovely. He is definitely lying about that, look at the state of me. Covered in scratches and mud, no makeup and the only good thing is that my beanie is hiding the fact that my hair has longer roots showing than the rose bush has in the soil. Oh, shit, the beanie seems to have come off in the bush attack so actually, he *can* see my roots.

This is not going well.

'No, I'm not mad but I must confess I am slightly amused. It does seem a rather strange theory to come up with after walking past a house a few times and seeing it empty.'

'I know, I know, but I was sort of right. Not the hostage bit but the eerie bit. Except it wasn't eerie I was picking up on but sadness. I guess you could say I'm just very in touch with my emotions.'

He's actually laughing out loud now; maybe that was a step too far.

'Oh, you're funny, but I must say it feels great to laugh. It has been such a horrible time here, I didn't realise it would hit me this hard.'

'I suppose some good has come of this then.'

'Tell the rose bush that, I don't think it will ever be the same again.'

'I doubt it, what with my hulking weight landing on top of it!'

'You're far from hulking, I'd say just about right if you were to really push me.'

'Really!'

'Yes, really. Is that what all this walking is about?'

Careful, Gemma, just as he's starting to think you may be normal after all you don't want to blow it now.

'No. No, of course not. It's well, complicated and I don't want to bore you with all that now. I think trespassing on your property and ruining your garden is enough for one day.'

He does make rather nice coffee, that's a bonus, it isn't often I find someone that likes their coffee as strong as I do.

'Sorry, I forgot to say, do you want more milk in that coffee? I tend to make it very strong and most people start getting jittery after just a few mouthfuls.'

Is he a mind reader?

'No, it's lovely thanks, just how I like it in fact. It's actually a relief to have a cup I can drink and enjoy rather than pretend it's perfect whilst thinking it tastes like dishwater.'

'Ha! You certainly have a way with words. Would you like another one?'

'No, no thanks. I think I should be getting on now and leave you in peace.'

'Honestly, it's fine, I was only watching some crime programme on TV which was then interrupted by my very own intruder.'

'I'm so sorry about that. I hope you don't think me too mad?'

'Of course I do! But in a nice way, look, if you don't want another coffee why don't I walk you home to make sure you don't get into any more trouble?'

'No, no, no, it's fine. Honestly. You get back to your programme, you may be in time to find out whodunnit. But thanks for being so understanding.'

'Well, if you're sure. Look here's your hat stuck in the bush. There are only a few spikes in it, it should be fine once you've shaken it out.'

'Thanks, I'll, um, clean it up when I get home. But I'm sure I'll see you out and about, you know, jogging.'

'I'm sure you will, I look forward to it.'

'Bye then, thanks for the coffee.'

'No problem, see you.'

Good grief, I'm out and managing to walk in a reasonably straight line despite the prickles that seem to be lodged in my knickers.

I could hardly sort *that* out in front of him.

Snort.

Even *I* wouldn't do that. Shit. Did I just snort out loud? That's the second time I've done that when he has been there. He's going to think I've some sort of breathing problem. But why is he still in the doorway?

Is he making sure I leave his property?

I wouldn't blame him really but I shall have to try and walk as normally as possible until I get around the corner.

Thank goodness. Freedom!

His house is in the distance and I can finally sort my knickers out.

What time is it? Shit, my phone. It must be in his garden somewhere.

I can't go back now, I'll have to make do and see if I have the courage to call in tomorrow and pick it up.

Let's quicken the pace and get home so I can take these damn clothes off and look at the damage the rose bush has done.

I think a nice long soak in a warm bath is in order.

DAY TEN. WALK TEN.

After last night's escapades, I feel like I have been steam-rollered. Who'd have thought flying through the air and landing in a bush could be so painful? It's as if I can feel every muscle in my body.

Maybe that's my penance for being such an idiot?

I really don't think I want to see him again. It's so embarrassing.

But why then, Gemma, are you out at exactly the same time as usual and walking exactly the same route?

Because it's part of my treatment, that's why.

I'm a creature of habit and this walk has become important to me. I certainly feel slightly fitter but, most importantly, my mood has altered.

I still feel confused and unsure of the direction my life should take but not in such a gloomy, death is the only escape, type of way.

It seems that watching the everyday events that happen just in this small part of town are somehow helping me to see that life goes on regardless of how you feel.

Look at the little tortoiseshell cat. She's always sitting in the window at this time and I like the fact that I smile at her and she looks back at me. Who knows if she sits there waiting to see me but I think about her when I get to this part of the road.

A week or so ago I wouldn't even have noticed her. But then I wouldn't have been out on a walk either.

And look how much the building has come on at the DIY builders' place. It's amazing! They were only digging out the foundations when I started this and now the bricks are up to the second floor.

It just shows what can be achieved with a bit of hard work. Well, that and the help of half the family in this instance, but whatever, it's amazing.

So amazing that I shall smile at them as a way to encourage them to continue.

It worked! The younger boys smiled back! OK, their Dad didn't but then he was grimacing from the strain of a very heavy-looking wheelbarrow rather than gurning at me, I think.

At least that has put an extra spring in my step. It makes such a difference when someone takes the time to be nice and it doesn't cost a thing. People should try it more often.

Oh, shit. I know that figure in the distance coming ever closer at an alarming rate.

It's him. The jogger.

Should I take evasive action?

Well unless I want to jump over the wall and land in the building site amongst all the bricks and cement then I shall have to continue on the path. There isn't anywhere else to go and I really don't want him seeing me 'intrude' into someone else's garden. He really will think I'm bonkers.

I shall have to put a smile on my face and pretend I am not at all ashamed of last night's little incident.

'How are the scratches this morning?'

So he's going for the direct approach.

'Much better thanks. I had a lovely bath when I got home and managed to extract a further 28 spikes. I hope your bush forgives me.'

'Well, I can't say it has fully recovered but it is still alive.'

'That's a relief!'

It's rather nice that he's the one out of breath from running whilst I feel cool and in control for a change.

'By the way, I found your phone in the garden this morning. Luckily it stayed dry last night and it looks to be OK. The screen saver, it's a nice picture.'

'Thanks, thanks for finding it, I'd be lost without my phone but mainly all the pictures on it. I can't bring myself to change that one yet. It's too soon. You know, too soon after he died.'

'I'm so sorry. I'd no idea. He looks so young. What a dreadful thing to have to deal with.'

'Well he wasn't *that* young really, but yes, it has been very tough.'

'Not that young? He can only be in his twenties, I'd say that was young.'

'No, he was thirteen.'

'Thirteen! But he had stubble, practically a beard!'

'Not really a beard, just soft, silky, wispy hair. God, I miss him.'

'Wispy hair? Hang on that cut is at least a number two.'

'Oh shit, no, not him. That's Luke, a complete bastard. I mean Jeffrey, my springer spaniel.'

'What?'

Why does this man seem to make me act like a complete

imbecile every time I see him? I can feel myself going red now; none of the initial composure is left at all. I better explain myself. Again.

'Luke was my boyfriend but we split up. I'm not upset about him. Not in the slightest, he was such a shit. No, it's Jeffrey who I can't bear to remove from the phone. That picture happens to be a really nice one of him.'

'Oh, I see.'

He's laughing at me again. I can sense it.

I really am his main source of amusement at the moment. Only source really if you account for him having to take apart the family home all on his own.

'Well, I'm glad it has allowed you a little mirth, especially given your current circumstances.'

'Sorry, I'm not laughing at you. But you must admit the misunderstanding was rather amusing.'

'Umm, I guess so. If the roles had been reversed I suppose I would have been laughing out loud by now. At least you are slightly more restrained.'

'There's another thing I thought of in the night, I couldn't sleep after you left. I suppose all the excitement got the better of me. But I don't even know your name. I'm Dan by the way.'

He's putting out his hand for me to shake.

Do I take it?

Of course you do you silly cow, he's only being polite. What harm can it do? After all, he has seen you upside down with your legs akimbo.

Umm, nice but strong, and a bit sweaty if I'm honest.

'And yours?'

'My what?'

'Your name! Goodness, it's like getting blood from a stone!'

'Sorry, sorry, once again bloody sorry. All I seem to do to you is apologise. It's Gemma. Yes, Gemma.'

'Are you sure? You sound a little uncertain.'

'No, it's definitely Gemma! Always has been!'

'Great, finally we have contact. Look, I'm sorry about your dog, Jeffrey. It's always hard to lose a pet but I must say I'm quite pleased that Luke is off the scene.'

'Yes, me too. It was a bit of a shock, coming home and finding he'd left, but good riddance to him I say!'

'Exactly, that's the spirit. Look, would you like to meet up later for a drink or something? You know, start again with slightly more normal introductions.'

Uh oh. Now what. I do like him but I really don't think I'm up to talking small talk in a pub with him just yet. But then why not, what else would I be doing tonight?

'OK, that would be nice. Maybe we can put the intruder thing behind us and start again.'

'Lovely, how about the 'Hare and Hound' at 8 o'clock?'

'Perfect! See you later then.'

Walk away Gemma, stop smirking at him and walk away.

'Umm, great. You can let go of my hand now and I'll see you later.'

Shit. Shit. Shit. Why do I do it? Now he thinks I'm clingy and basically lacking in social skills alongside everything else. At least he has jogged off and can't see my blushing face. Although it's so red he can probably feel the heat from it even at that distance.

What's all that clapping?

Oh my lord. All the DIY builders have been eavesdropping on the entire conversation. Surely they didn't hear it all?

'Have a nice time tonight, Gemma, it will help you get over Jeffrey!'

They heard. No doubt about it, they are all doubled up laughing now.

'Thank you. Happy building, chaps.'

Chaps? Who uses the word chaps these days?

Just go Gemma, and don't say another word.

Every time you open your mouth you put not just your foot in it, but your entire leg.

At least I've put some distance between us now. No doubt they will want to know all the nitty-gritty next time I pass. Well, I shan't tell them! It's my life and, whilst they are a part of it for a few seconds every day as I walk by, they don't need to know all the ins and outs.

What a turn up for the books!

I'm on the second stage of my walk and not only have I amused the local builders but I have secured myself a date for tonight.

Not bad, Gemma, especially when you think that you had no intention of meeting anyone ever again when you had your toast this morning.

It's all rather exciting.

But.

Why does there always have to be a lingering 'but' with you, Gemma?

What do I wear? What do we talk about? How long should I stay? It's more than three years since I went out like this; I've no idea how to behave anymore.

Anymore? What you talking about, Gemma? It's not like you haven't met up with Dan in rather more trying circumstances so far. Going to the pub should be a breeze compared with breaking into his garden and landing upside down in his foliage.

I just need to relax about it and try to enjoy myself. That

will be a novelty in itself. I don't recall enjoying myself for some considerable time.

No, it's a good thing and I mustn't talk my way out of it.

In fact, even though it's only mid-morning; I think I should speed up a bit and get home. I have lots of planning to do, mainly deciding on what I should wear.

DAY ELEVEN. WALK ELEVEN.

I don't seem to be able to stop grinning!

Even my friend, the little tortoiseshell cat, seemed to notice I was perkier than normal and appeared to twitch her whiskers with approval. Well, I'm telling myself it was approval, but she could have been trying to avoid the distinct smell of Guinness which is still lingering on my skin after I managed to spill Dan's entire pint over myself.

That was embarrassing, especially as I was wearing a cream skirt at the time. Whatever made me wear that? I rarely wear skirts as it is, but cream. Seriously?

I'm the clumsiest person around so it was asking for trouble really.

However, looking on the bright side, it did break the ice as we were both laughing so much. Him with actual amusement and me with forced, 'It's fine I really don't mind sitting here in a wet skirt with a black stain down the front, sort of smile.'

After that, the conversation just flowed completely naturally.

We chatted about all sorts of things and the good news is that Dan loves animals too.

There is no way I could continue a relationship with someone if they didn't like animals. Dogs in particular.

Get you! Continue a relationship. Are you serious, Gemma?

It was only a drink in a pub, hardly the hottest date that has ever occurred, especially when it came immediately after me breaking into his garden.

Which, thankfully he seems to have put behind him now.

Although I'm not sure I *can* forget it.

I don't think he has someone held hostage any more, which I guess is progress, but I did have those thoughts originally and I'm not sure I can live with the embarrassment.

Oh, for God's sake, Gemma, of course you can!

It's the sort of story that will be handed down the generations and at some point, in the distant future, my granddaughter will be sitting on my knee and asking if I really did fall into Grandad's rose bush when I was spying on him as a young girl.

Snort.

I think you're getting a little ahead of yourself, Gemma. Don't fall into that old trap again. Just take it for what it is, a bit of fun.

Fun has been distinctly lacking in my world for some time now and laughing with a friend, even if it is over my clumsiness, is an excellent tonic.

So stop reading too much into it and just enjoy the moment.

'Hi Gemma, how was the date?'

Oh shit, how have I got to the DIY builders without even realising it?

I would have detoured to avoid them if I hadn't been so wrapped up in my own thoughts.

I can't really ignore them, that would just be rude, so I'll keep it brief and turn up the speed a bit to get past as soon as I can.

'Oh, hi, we had a very nice evening, thanks.'

'So did Dan manage to take your mind off Jeffrey then?'

Jesus, can't he see his dad is not amused and is looking daggers at me? He obviously wants his son to get on with the job and stop gossiping.

For once I'm in agreement.

'Sorry, can't hear you. You're making such good progress with the build that you're up to the rafters. Catch you another time. Bye.'

Well, I managed to handle that OK.

He's just staring after me and looking a bit disgruntled.

Ha. He'll be even more disgruntled by the time his dad makes it up the ladder to give him an earful.

For once I'm delighted Dad has full control of his boys and can take the heat off me.

Hang on. This is where I usually bump into Dan when he's out on his run.

Where is he?

He said last night that he'd see me tomorrow, usual time and place. We both laughed and he then said we would have to go out again. I'd agreed, so there's no doubt in either of our minds that we wanted to meet up.

But where is he?

Maybe he's running late. I'll just carry on and enjoy my walk. Maybe I'll see him further on.

Good grief. Pregnant woman is literally going to explode if she doesn't have that baby soon.

She is actually waddling. I thought that was something people just said but she really is waddling. She's also struggling to pick up those bags from the back of the car. Maybe I should offer to help.

Yes, I will, woman to woman. OK, I've never been pregnant, so have no idea how she must be feeling, but I do know that I find it difficult bending over after one of Mum's Sunday lunches, never mind being massively pregnant.

'Excuse me, would you like me to get those bags for you and carry them in?'

'Oh, hello. That would be lovely, thank you so much. I'm really tired today and this little bump doesn't seem to want to keep still.'

Little. It's massive. Even bigger than I thought it was now I'm up close. Surely she is going to pop and fly round and round in circles until all the air has gone out of her and she floats gently to the ground.

'If you could just stick them in the hall, that would be wonderful.'

'Of course, no problem. Are you sure you don't want me to carry them through to the kitchen?'

'No, honestly, love, they're fine there. I'm going to put the kettle on and my feet up for a bit before I unpack. My ankles are like puddings.'

Jesus. You're not kidding. They are the size of a couple of footballs. Just how much does the female body have to distort in order to have a child?

I think I'll stick to dogs, I really can't see me going through all that.

'If you're sure, it's no trouble. You looked like you needed a hand.'

'Your very sweet and thanks but I'm fine now I'm in. You get off and enjoy your walk. I see you come past sometimes and think how lucky you are to be slim. I haven't seen my feet for weeks.'

'It's OK, I'm glad I helped. If you need anything and see me passing then please just ask.'

'Thanks, dear, see you soon.'

'Don't forget, it will all be worth it and you'll see your feet again pretty soon.'

'Hope you're right, I can't stand this much longer! Bye then.'

'Bye.'

Poor woman. She looks worn out and it's not like she will get any rest when the baby arrives. From what I can tell they seem to want to feed constantly, fall asleep on you and you daren't move or they need their nappy changing. That pretty much sums up babies.

Yes, I'll stick with dogs. They are so much easier. And they don't ruin your figure.

I seem to have reached the grand house with the tarpaulin at the upstairs window. Let's see what's happening there. Surely they have moved the unusual drape by now.

Oh, no. They haven't. In fact, it looks even odder than it did last time. Not only is there a tarpaulin up at the window but the window has also been blanked out with newspaper.

Someone really doesn't want me, or anyone else, to see in there.

What on earth is going on?

STOP IT GEMMA.

You can't assume something terrible is happening just because you think it all looks a bit unusual.

Don't you ever learn? Didn't the embarrassment of the Dan situation teach you anything at all?

Walk on by.

That's it. Keep walking and don't look back. You really don't need to. It's all perfectly fine.

There.

That wasn't too bad, was it?

I've managed to force myself onwards and from now on I will not let my stupid mind run riot without taking a reality check first.

How many times do I need to reassure myself that not all houses hold dark secrets?

Mine doesn't.

Apart from the secret stash of chocolates I have hidden in a cupboard. Obviously, I have hidden them from myself which sort of defeats the object but at least I'm trying.

Wow! Just wow!

That was amazing. There I was minding my own business, and walking at quite a pace, I might add, when I came across an amazing sight.

This man was collecting up council roadwork signs and slinging them in the back of his truck when he suddenly stopped.

I could see him in the distance, kneeling down and wondered what he was doing.

As I got nearer he waved me over and there, right next to him, on the grass beside the road, was a beautiful little robin.

It wasn't at all bothered that our two faces were peering down at it and the workman said it had been there for ages, watching him move the signs.

We stayed there quite a while enjoying our close brush with nature, and then told each other how lucky we were, before smiling and getting on with our days. He returned to his sign moving and I continued my walk. Just before turning the corner I did have a look back and the dear little robin was still standing on the grass watching the man throw the signs very noisily into his van.

Maybe they have struck up an unlikely friendship.

Speaking of friends, where on earth is Dan? I still haven't seen him and I'm nearly at his house.

Have I got it all wrong and he is really laughing at me behind my back and it has all been a sick joke?

No, I really don't think so. He seemed so keen to meet up again.

Mind you, am I the best judge of such things at the moment?

Probably not, I feel like I am making progress but I do seem a bit scatty still, even for me.

Well, here we are, Dan's house and it looks pretty much as it did the last time I was here.

No lights on, no car, no movement at all.

Should I go and ring the bell?

No, I won't. I shall keep on walking right past and look as if I really don't care. Just in case he is in there, watching me from behind the bloody curtains.

That's it; I've had it with men. Again.

I can't believe I let one of the creeps get under my skin, even a little bit. Why do I let this happen?

I need to concentrate on myself and avoid all contact with any male, ever.

Well maybe not ever, but at least for the foreseeable future and certainly until I have seen Dr Wright again.

I'm sad now.

I thought Dan seemed nice and now I feel deflated and let down.

I'll semi-jog all the way home. That should make me feel better and burn off some of the anxiety, or kill me?

That wouldn't, necessarily, be such a bad thing as I'm such a dreadful judge of character.

Actually, I think it *might* just kill me; I'd better slow down a bit. Maybe that was more of a sprint than a jog.

But it has done the trick; I'm nearly home. When I get there I will lock the doors, shut the curtains and lay low for a while until I feel better.

Maybe channel surfing on the TV is all I'm good for after all.

DAY TWELVE. WALK TWELVE.

It has taken a superhuman effort to get out here today. I did spend the evening in a comatose state, lying on the settee and rarely moving. In fact, I think I only got up to find my secret stash of chocolate, and then lay down again eating chunk after chunk, barely registering the milky delight. Things must have been bad.

I couldn't even be bothered with the television. Every channel was annoying me and after flicking through the endless tripe for about half an hour I switched it off altogether and simply replayed the events in the pub over and over again in my mind.

It didn't matter which way I looked at it I still felt sure that Dan had meant what he said. I really am crap at reading people and consequently, I now feel unsettled and stressed.

But now I am making a valiant attempt at putting it out of my mind and focusing on a fast pace walk up this hill.

Obviously, I am failing miserably at this, as so far, for the entire walk my thoughts have been about Dan and my mood.

Not even my tortoiseshell cat friend has managed to raise a smile, although she did look at me expectantly. I hope I haven't ruined her day too. It does show just how much our actions can affect those around us and even those we don't think will notice.

Just imagine if that cat is so put out by my lack of acknowledgement that she gets off her windowsill and grumpily stalks around the house hoping for some reassurance. Only to find the house empty of humans, which fuels her angst even more, so by the time they get home she is in a right old strop and they don't understand why she is being so belligerent.

After that, her humans pick up on her bad mood and before you know it the entire house is full of fed up and grumpy individuals, falling out over what to eat, what to watch and what to talk about.

All of this stems from my lack of a smile for a poor little cat who had done nothing wrong.

Alternatively, the cat didn't care one iota about me and has turned over and fallen asleep.

Stop torturing yourself, Gemma, and just walk, as fast as you can, to get this bloody walk over so that you can return to your cocoon in the lounge and while away the day in blissful nothingness.

I think I might be very slightly later than usual today. It's probably only by a couple of minutes, three at the most, but there are very subtle differences. For instance, I would normally pass one of the postmen at this point. Every single time I have walked along this road I have seen him. But today he is way up the road still. I can see him in the distance but he would normally be here and refilling his bag from the van.

That's strange, I don't make a conscious effort to always be at the same time but my routine seems to dictate it. What has caused me to be out of kilter today?

I haven't knowingly done anything different, other than talking myself into going for a walk, but I tend to have to do that most days. I haven't yet made it to the dizzy heights of actually looking forward to it. Although maybe I'm doing myself an injustice, there have been the odd occasions when I have actually wanted to get out here.

But does the teeny, tiny difference in time really make that much difference?

It shouldn't, but now I'm thinking about it maybe it does. Everything seems very slightly different. The postman is 20 or 30 paces further away than usual and look, now I've arrived at the house with the teapot and guess what, she is there, in the window, with her newspaper.

Bless her, she looks a dear thing and just as a granny should look, even down to a grey bun at the back of her head!

So she's a creature of habit too. It's not that she has fallen over in the kitchen and is lying there with a fractured hip or died in her sleep with no one to look after her. This would be my normal assumption. But no, she probably sets the little table up ready and then nips to the toilet or something before settling down with her tea and her paper.

She has even sensed me looking and is smiling at me. I hope I haven't scared her; I've not been standing there staring in her window have I?

I don't think so; she doesn't look scared and is, in fact, giving me a little wave.

There, I've waved back and smiled. It's as if I have been able to right a wrong that was done to the poor cat. It just goes to show that a few seconds can make all the difference to a scenario.

It sounds like the plot of a film. Actually, it is the plot of a film; I've seen it. Two different versions of how a girls life panned out depending on whether she caught the train or not.

Hang on Gemma; I know what you are up to. You are trying to justify why Dan wasn't there. Go on; admit it.

Well, I hadn't thought of it until now but yes, I guess if he had been delayed for some reason we could feasibly have missed each other. He might be just as fed up as I am and wishing he could get in touch. But he doesn't actually know where I live yet or have my telephone number so he is totally reliant on bumping into me; or me calling around to his mum's place.

See, this is what you do, Gemma, you put the onus back on yourself. Just STOP IT.

If he had wanted to see you he would have done something about it. Stop picking at it as if it is an old scab and just forget about Dan.

And, another thing, why do you assume everyone is watching your every move and analysing your actions?

They probably don't give two hoots about you and may not even have noticed you.

That's not true though is it? The pregnant woman said she had seen me a few times; the DIY builders *definitely* see me and make judgements. Well, they do now, since the Dan/Jeffrey incident.

But I'm pretty sure most people are just getting on with their lives. They may clock me and give me a moment's notice but it will probably barely register on their consciousness. Just because *I'm* constantly analysing doesn't mean everyone else is!

Anyway, here we are at Mrs Terribly Pregnant woman's house and all seems quiet and tranquil. I do hope she is sitting in the lounge with her feet up or, even better, having a sneaky sleep, in preparation for the work ahead that will surely follow. It's funny how I have never seen Mr Pregnant. But actually, it isn't really, is it? He's probably at work. Someone has to pay for all that shopping and it is a rather nice house which presumably has a rather large mortgage attached to it. God, he has his hands full then, work, pregnant wife, juggling it all.

Here you go again Gemma, making assumptions and worrying on behalf of people you don't know. Could it possibly be Gemma that they are sublimely happy and extremely excited about pending parenthood?

Of course, they are! She seemed pretty together the other day and just responded to an open and honest request to help her.

Why am I such an idiot that I have to create trauma all around me and if it isn't there then I'll happily make it up?

Speaking of which, here is the weird house.

The tarpaulin and newspaper are still at the window but look, there's an extremely expensive car in the driveway. I know it's a posh house but that car is in another league.

What's that all about? I do wish I'd seen the car arrive and then I could have had a glimpse of the owner. Jesus, I'm so nosey. That is all it is. I am simply the nosiest person on the planet.

I'm not even going to look up at the window now, just to prove to myself that I can do it.

It's just a house with a nice car, Gemma; leave it at that.

Oh, hang on; I'm pretty sure I saw the corner of the paper move then. Dare I stop and look properly?

NO. YOU MUSTN'T. JUST MOVE ON.

OK, it's OK, the house is behind me and I will not give another second's thought to the rather extraordinary goings on in that place. It is all my imagination. It is just a house for Christ's sake.

But at least this weirdo thinking has got me to Dan's road. What should I do?

Alter my route to avoid it? Hang around outside in case I see him?

No, I'll stride past without giving it a second thought. Why should I alter *my* plans for him?

See, I can do it, I'm almost level and I haven't slowed down or stopped to tie my shoelace, which doesn't need tying.

I have walked purposefully past and not even given the house a glance. Well, that's a tiny lie; I did peep into the lounge, very briefly, and saw absolutely nothing of note.

So that's it. I continue on my way, with no hesitation, repetition or deviation of any sort. Nicholas Parsons would be proud of me.

Although I haven't managed to keep it up for more than thirty seconds never mind a minute as I'm already imagining Dan running across the lawn, calling my name and pleading for forgiveness.

As it happens, simply nothing has happened, a big, fat nothing. And my thoughts are particularly repetitious, deviant and, certainly, hesitant. I would actually go as far as to say my thoughts are completely random and wholesale destructive.

Get your act together Gemma, you're meant to be clearing your mind on these walks not muddying the waters even further.

The good news is that I'm on my way home and thankfully

walking briskly in a downward direction towards safety and obscurity.

I'm even back at the teapot house and look; she's waving at me again.

Oh, actually I don't think she is waving. She's trying to attract my attention.

'You OK?'

She's pointing a finger at me and I think the way she is wagging it means she wants me to wait.

I can't be sure of that but she does seem to be getting up from her chair. What do I do?

Go down the path towards the house or have I misread the situation. I don't want to frighten her.

Actually, she's surprisingly nimble and is already opening her front door. From the sound of the number of bolts she is pulling back, security is very much on her mind.

'Hello dear, you couldn't help me could you?'

'Of course, are you OK?'

'OK, of course, I'm OK, just because I'm old doesn't mean I'm stupid you know.'

'No, no, of course not. What can I do to help?'

Jeez, she's touchy, I had her down as gentle and quietly spoken but she's fairly shouting at me. Maybe she's deaf, my Gran was like that, she bellowed at you when you were sitting right next to her but strangely she could hear you open the biscuit tin from the other room.

'I'm stuck, dear.'

She doesn't seem stuck; she's almost jogging up the garden path towards me.

'Right, what exactly are you stuck with?'

'Glancing rebound?'

'What?'

Is she mad?

'Glancing rebound? I can't get it and it's driving me insane.'

She's definitely mad.

'Can't you hear me, Glancing rebound? 12 Across.'

'Oh, I'm with you,' splutter, 'How many letters?'

'Eight.'

'Easy, ricochet, got to be.'

'Excellent! Of course; thank you.'

'It's O....'

Oh, she's gone.

The bolts are being put firmly back in place.

Glad to be of service.

That's me. Rebound. How prophetic. I'm on a glancing rebound between Luke and Dan.

Except the only ricochet I can think of relating to Luke would involve a bullet and a .44 Magnum, and I don't mean ice cream.

I think I need to clear my thoughts and get back on track tomorrow.

Couch, here I come.

DAY THIRTEEN. WALK THIRTEEN.

Tra la, la de da.

This is little old me being happy, yes, happy!

I have put the last few days behind me and think that it is high time I took control and stopped behaving like a lovesick teenager.

In the wee small hours of this morning, I managed to convince myself that it was only one drink in a pub and therefore nothing to get so worked up about.

But I'm my own worst enemy. I always have been a worrier but the events of the past few months seem to have pushed me to the limits. Now I need to take control and sort myself out. I must say that Dr Wright was right; these walks do seem to help, even if I'm only in the early stages.

Somehow they give me time and space to think and I feel fitter than I did before. That seems amazing as it's only walk thirteen but it really does seem easier than it did when I started.

'Hi Tortie,' yes, I am even talking to a cat through a window today. My little tortoiseshell friend seems remarkably unmoved by my positive mood but I will not be deterred. At least she raised one quizzical eyebrow at me, which I like to think was a small greeting in some way.

I do believe it is also slightly warmer today and that infernal wind has certainly died down. That's a relief as I was getting so fed up with detangling my hair after a windswept walk.

There also seem to be a few more people about than usual. Maybe the break in the weather is encouraging some of the more reluctant walkers outside for a change. Either that or they are all patients of Dr Wright and he has had some busy clinics as he persuades half his list of patients to get off their backsides and do something.

Here come the DIY builders, let's see what they are up to today. Blimey, they really have reached quite a height, I'm not sure I would like walking about up there on the rickety looking scaffolding.

'Hi, Gemma, how you doing?'

'Oh Hi, I'm fine thanks, how are you?'

'Great thanks, Dad is out for the day and we are really enjoying some peace! I swear he is watching us every second to make sure we don't waste any time.'

'Ha, he does seem rather keen I must admit, but no slouching whilst he's away or he'll never leave you alone again.'

'Good point, I think we'll have to make sure there are some visible signs of progress when he gets back or he'll have us working by torchlight tonight.'

'He wouldn't, would he?'

'No, I'm only joking, he's a good man and just wants this extension finishing so we can all get on with our lives again. We're about to have a tea break, do you fancy a cup?'

'That's very kind of you but I'm on a mission to break my own record today so I better push on. I'm aiming for 45 minutes but I think I may have already blown the chances of that!'

'No you haven't, just get cracking now, you can do it.'

'I'm glad you have such faith in me, see you later and don't go falling off there, it's a long way down.'

'Tell me about it, I can't stand heights so this is getting to be a real challenge.'

'One that I'm sure you are up to, especially if your dad is around. See you.'

'Bye, enjoy your walk.'

What a nice man, isn't it funny how a few weeks ago we wouldn't have talked to each other and now we are chatting away like long lost friends.

Here we are at the Teapot house and everything looks just as it should. Table laid, cup and saucer at the ready and teapot lady about to settle herself down with her paper by the look of things. Do I wave?

No, maybe just a little nod of acknowledgement if she looks up.

She hasn't so that saves me having to actually do anything. But I'm pretty sure she noticed me then, she's a wily old fox and quite a character.

I must say it all seems very quiet today; all the learner drivers seem to have gone. That's weird. They can't all be taking their tests today, maybe there's some sort of driving instructor rebellion going on? Although I must say it's rather nice to walk along the pavement without fear of death from an uncontrolled vehicle.

OK. A bit more positive motivation needed as I near the house of Dan. Tra la, la de DA.

I will continue on my way with not a hint of tension; as I am so over all that stress stuff.

WHO THE HELL IS THAT?

A woman. Standing calmly as you like in the middle of the lounge, talking on a phone.

She was very pretty too and about my age. I don't believe it. Not only has he disappeared without a word but also he has moved someone in! This is outrageous.

Oh God, she's looking at me but then that's hardly surprising as I'm standing stock still in front of the house and staring at her.

Move Gemma, you really don't need to be seen staring like a lunatic at some woman you have never met before just because she is ensconced in Dan's house.

She's staring back and looks quite quizzical actually. Time to go and hotfoot it home. I will not allow myself to be embarrassed by her and her shiny, bouncy hair.

Sod this; I shall even break into a run.

Um, maybe not, certain parts of my anatomy wobble when I run, and not in a good way.

I shall walk calmly and yet briskly away.

There, see, that wasn't so bad. I have managed to put some distance between us and I shall now put her, him and the damned house of kidnapping behind me forever.

Breathe, Gemma, nice, gentle, even breaths. You really need to stop hyperventilating before someone comes chasing after you and puts a paper bag over your head.

Actually, it may be better if they put a plastic one on and then left me to slowly suffocate and put all this shit behind me.

Don't be ridiculous, Gemma. You know you don't mean that so why are you even thinking it? Positive thoughts remember.

They are all that are allowed today and from this moment forward.

You get out of life what you put in it, so the more positive you can be the better the outcome.

There, that's better. I feel like I have managed to talk myself down.

Down as in to improve my mood, not down as in standing on the edge of a high building and about to throw myself off.

Oh God, teapot woman has seen me and is making her way to the door. I suppose I should wait and see what she wants this time.

'Encourage – breathe in. Seven?'

To the point, don't bother with any small talk, will you?

'Inspire.'

'Oh, of course! Thank you.'

'No problem.'

Oh, she's gone again.

Well, I think we can safely say she's a crossword, rather than a Sudoku, kind of woman. At least that's one of my questions answered.

I must admit I'm pretty impressed with my crossword skills so far.

'Gemma, you're never going to make it in 45 minutes unless you sprint the last bit.'

Who, oh, it's builder boy.

'I know; there have been a few distractions today but thanks for reminding me.'

'No problem, we just had a bet on to see if we could get you running. Looks like we can't.'

'Well I'm delighted to have given you something to chat about but you're right, I'm not running. See you tomorrow you cheeky bugger. I'll tell your dad about you if you're not careful.'

'You wouldn't do that, would you?'

'Course not, now get back to work you slacker.'

'See you.'

'Yes, bye.'

Jeez, these walks are getting weirder by the day!

Mad, old women and their crosswords, young builders full of banter when their dad's out of the way and then there's the freaky house but I haven't even acknowledged that one today. I was too busy wondering where all the learner drivers were at that point.

Maybe that's where they all went. They've been herded into the house and locked up in the tarpaulin room.

Here you go again, Gemma, with your mad ideas.

At least I'm home; let's see how long I took.

55 minutes. That's ridiculous. Mind you, I did waste quite a bit of time chatting with the builders and staring at some random woman.

Never mind. There's always tomorrow.

DAY FOURTEEN. WALK FOURTEEN.

I slept well!

What a huge achievement and one I was rather surprised about if I'm honest. When I went to bed there were a million thoughts floating around my brain but I lay there quietly for a while and, before I knew it, the birds were singing, the sun was shining and the new day was ready for the taking.

So I have scaled my clothing down a bit today, as it does seem to be getting warmer. Obviously, I still have the old coat, which reminds me I really do need to go and buy a new one, maybe later today. But I have ditched the scarf and hat and even left my gloves at home.

Spring must really be trying to break through the stubborn cold weather.

Take some nice deep breaths as I march up this hill.

That's it, Gemma, fill those lungs with clean, fresh air.

Well, maybe not that fresh and clean but you know what I mean. It's just good to be out and moving around.

In a way, seeing that woman at Dan's house seems to have been a catalyst for change.

I have moved on from anxious thoughts about him and now I am focusing on getting myself feeling good again.

I really want to have positive and encouraging things to say to Dr Wright when I see him next. He's such a nice man and has taken the trouble to talk to me at length and try to help. It's the least I can do really. Apart from that I also *want* to feel good again. I've wasted too much time just lying on the settee and hoping everything will resolve. Action was required and action was taken, so here I am fairly brimming over with positive thoughts.

Where's Tortie today? I hope she's OK. No. Stop it. Positive thoughts remember. Just because the damned cat isn't in the window doesn't mean she has been run over as she took her morning stroll. Although I'll just have a quick look around, just in case. No, no sign of her. Hopefully, she is lying on a bed in one of the upstairs rooms, bathed in sunlight and so comfortable that she has forgotten it's windowsill time.

There, that's better, nice and positive.

Looks like Dad is back on building duty today as there's silence on the site. No radio blaring out like yesterday and the boys are way up high and concentrating on their work. Apart from the sly wave, the youngest boy has just surreptitiously directed at me, that is. I think a little nod of acknowledgement is all I dare to do with Dad's beady eye on me. But it doesn't matter as I am on a mission today and will not be distracted from my brisk and positive thinking walk.

Even the teapot house looks calm and quiet as Mrs Teapot peers down at the paper, deep in concentration. Hopefully, she'll manage to complete the crossword today before I make my descent back down the hill. Having said that, it is quite amusing that I have become part of her crossword ritual.

It really is quite warm out here, especially as I'm pushing along at a startling rate. I'm not going to be dictated to by my watch though, I am going to enjoy the walk and make a good time if I can.

What's going on up there?

I can hear shouting but can't see anyone or anything out of the ordinary. Actually, that's more than shouting it sounds like nothing else I've heard before, almost guttural screaming. There's something basic and very human about it.

What the hell is going on? There's no one about at all. I'm approaching, oh, Mrs Pregnant woman is coming out her door and staggering up the driveway.

'You OK?'

'Humphhhh, Can you, urghhhh, help me?'

Shit, what's going on?

'Of course, what's the matter?'

'I, arghhhhh, think, shit, help me!'

Right. Well, I'm no doctor but she looks pretty distressed to me and she usually appears very calm. The way she's clinging to her stomach makes me think that the baby is imminent.

SHIT. THE BABY. NO, I DON'T KNOW WHAT TO DO.

Oh my God, she's grasping onto me like I'm the last person she's ever going to see. What do I do?

Get her inside, Gemma, there's nobody to help out here, let's get her inside and call an ambulance.

'Come on, hold on to me and we'll get you sorted.'

'Thank God you appeared, I was mopping the floor in the kitchen when I thought I must have kicked the bucket.'

'No, you're definitely not dead, I can vouch for that.'

'Not that bucket, the bucket of water, it was everywhere; water all over the place. But I hadn't. The mop and bucket were just where I left them. My waters have broken.'

'OK, don't panic, we're nearly inside now, let's get you comfortable on the settee.'

'Arghhhhhhhhh. Nooooooooooo.'

'Ouch, could you take your nails out of my forearm a second. That's it, you sit there.'

'I can't sit, I definitely can't sit.'

'Why's that, surely you'll be more comfortable whilst we wait for the ambulance.'

'No, haven't called yet. Can't...find...the ...phone.'

Oh great.

'And I need to push.'

'No, no you don't. Honestly, you really don't need to push. Just sit down.'

OK, don't sit, squat on the floor on all fours then.

This is not looking good. Where's *my* phone? I need to call the ambulance and then Google, 'delivering a baby'.

'Why have you stopped yelling?'

'Because I'm pushing.'

The way she said that, through very gritted teeth, makes me think she *really* is pushing.

Fuck. Where's my phone? Thank God it's here in the bottom of my coat pocket where I left it last night.

Noooooooooo. The battery is flat. This cannot be happening.

'It's coming, the baby is coming, do something.'

'Right, you are fine, you're doing really well.'

'No, I'm not, I'm meant to be in the hospital, in a lovely warm birthing pool with my husband by my side and some lovely whale music playing. Arghhhhh.'

Whale music? What the fuck is that? Maybe now is not the time to ask.

'Look, just stay calm, we shall get through this together. Just breathe nice and slowly...in and out.'

'Can't. It's com.... arghhhh.'

OK, so pregnant woman doesn't have the gestation of an elephant after all as this baby is not for waiting.

'Where's your phone?'

'Upstairs...I...think...but don't leave me....grrrrr.'

I couldn't if I wanted to; you're gripping my arm so tightly I may never be able to move it again.

'It's OK, everything is fine, just try and hold on.'

'Hold on! No way, it's here, right now. Can't stop...'

Jesus, I can see something. It's horrific! Oh, my God, it's a head.

'Pant. That's what they said at antenatal classes.'

'Right, OK.'

'Not you, me!'

'Oh, of course, you pant and I'll just hold on tight to the coffee table as I feel a bit faint.'

'Here's another one coming.'

'Another baby? Not got this one out yet?'

'No, contraction.... arghhhh.'

Think Gemma. Cast your mind back to those lessons at school when they showed you a video of someone giving birth. You must have watched some of it in between the sniggering and utter shock. You are a woman and need to help this poor lady. Take control and put her at her ease.

Well, as at ease as she can be with a complete stranger looking at her genitals whilst a rather large-looking head gradually appears. This is like some sort of horror film.

Get a grip, Gemma.

'You're doing really well. I want you to breathe away, pant if you need to but listen to your body and tell me when the next contraction is coming. I need to brace myself for it.'

'You need to! It's here, right now....'

'That's it, nice, even pushing. I can see the head you know, not long now!'

Please God, get this baby out before I either throw up or faint.

'Oh, look, it's out! The head is out! This is absolutely amazing!'

'An...o...th...er one com..i..ng. Cat...ch the b..abyyyyy.'

She really is panting. I seem to have got that one right.

Jesus, it's coming out. Oh, my God, it's slithering all over the place. There's blood and gunk everywhere. I've got it. I'VE GOT IT!

'It's here! It's here! That was absolutely mind-blowing.'

'Is the baby OK? What is it?'

'It's perfect. Just perfect. It's a, ummm, well, it doesn't have a thing so it must be a girl!'

'A girl, I have a girl!'

I should get something to keep her warm. That's what they do isn't it, they wrap the babies up? This will do. There's a shirt here on a pile of clothes, probably an ironing pile. That really will have to wait now.

'Here, let's wrap her in this, it looks like it might be her Dad's shirt. As he couldn't be here at least his shirt will have helped out.'

Why am I crying? I don't seem to be able to stop. But *not* pregnant woman is crying as well. We're all crying now, baby has joined in!

'I need to push again.'

'No, surely not. There can't be another one in there. Can there?'

'Placenta. Cord. Need to cut. Don't panic, you're doing great. Go and find the phone upstairs.'

'You sure? You don't know me. You sure you don't mind me rummaging about upstairs?'

'Ha! You've been rummaging about in much more personal places than upstairs! It's fine, just call an ambulance.'

'Right. Yes, I guess so.'

This is so weird.

Nice carpet on the stairs though. Maybe they can get a matching one for the lounge as I doubt they'll be able to clean that one up.

This looks like it might be the master bedroom. The phone should be in here. Yeah, thank goodness, something is going right. Let's make that call and get the poor lady some proper medical attention.

'They're on their way, I explained the predicament and they should be here in just a few minutes.'

'Thank you. I don't know what I would have done without your help.'

'I think you would have done just fine, I didn't really do anything other than be amazed at what I was witnessing.'

'Isn't she adorable?'

'She's the prettiest baby I have ever seen. Do you want me to call your husband?'

'No, he's on a flight. I'll call from the hospital later. She wasn't due until next week. He'll be horrified he missed it but at least you were here.'

'I guess this little lady was in too much of a hurry to wait for her Dad to get back. The main thing is that she's OK.'

Where the fuck is the ambulance? I don't think I can keep up the charade that I'm coping for much longer.

I want someone to check them both over. I think I can hear the sirens. Please let it be coming here.

'It sounds like they are nearly here. Thank you again. They'll probably want to get me straight to the hospital.

When I'm out again, please call in so we can say thank you properly.'

'No problem, just try and keep me away! It's not every day you get to introduce a new human being to the world. Look, they're here.'

'Alright love, you look a bit peaky.'

'Very funny, I am a little shocked but these two are your patients.'

'We'll take it from here. You look like you've done a good job, well done!'

'Really?'

'Yes, look, for a first baby, she's done well not to need stitches. That's probably thanks to you.'

'Really?' Stop saying 'really', Gemma.

'Yup, well done. Now we need to get them both to hospital. Do you want to come too so they can check you are OK?'

'No, no. I'm fine. Thank you. I'll just take myself home I think.'

'Right, well, clean yourself up when you get there. We need to be off.'

'OK, good luck.'

'Let's get you on this trolley, love, you can hold your baby, don't worry.'

'Thank you so much. Before you go, what's your name?'

'Gemma. It's Gemma.'

'Thank you, Gemma. I'll never forget what you did for us.'

'Don't think I'll forget it in a hurry! You two take care.'

'Bye.'

Blimey. There they go. Mother and daughter off to hospital in the ambulance. Whilst here I am standing in the driveway grinning like an idiot.

I'll just pull the door to and go home. I can't continue my

walk after that and especially not looking at the state of me. I'm covered in blood!

I'm sure Dr Wright won't mind that I didn't do the whole session today.

'Gemma, you OK?'

Now what. Who the hell is after me now? I just want to go home.

'Jesus, Dan. What? How? Where have you been?'

'My God Gemma, what has happened? Are you alright, you look like you've been stabbed?'

'I'm fine. It was a baby. A BABY! I can't believe it.'

'Whose baby?'

'Pregnant lady of course. Although she isn't now, pregnant that is. She's a mum!'

'But where did you come into all this?'

'Long story and not one I wish to go over just yet.'

'At least let me take you home Gemma, you look a bit pale and well, quite frankly, horrific.'

'No. No, I can't deal with you at the moment. I just want to go home. You get back to the bouncy hair woman.'

'Bouncy hair woman, what are you talking about?'

'Look, Dan, I've had quite a morning and really don't want to hear your excuses right now.'

'I want to explain why I went. It's not what you think and she's not what you think either.'

'Well, maybe we'll bump into each other again, but not now. OK. See you soon.'

'You crack me up Gemma, first you think I'm harbouring kidnapped people in my deceased mother's house, then you appear in the street covered in blood. I've never known anyone quite like you.'

'Well, I'm glad I have been able to amuse you once again. Now, if you don't mind, I shall be on my way.'

There. That told him. He can stew for a while. I need to get cleaned up and sort my thoughts out.

He's still looking at me. I can sense he's still there. But I won't turn around. I shall walk with as much dignity as one can muster when covered in blood and with legs that feel like jelly.

Oh for God's sake. That's all I need. Teapot woman is coming out now.

'Massacre – 9 lette... Oh, doesn't matter dear, I've got it.'

'What was it?'

'Slaughter.'

Great. Glad my appearance solved the puzzle today, as I really don't think my mind would have been up to it.

Home sweet home. Never have I been as pleased to see you as I do right this moment.

I'll just hang this coat up and, Jesus, I caught a glimpse of myself in the hallway mirror.

I really do look horrific. There's blood all over me, including my face, which looks like it has been smeared on during some sort of tribal ceremony, and rounded off with a nice panda effect thanks to the sobbing fit I had just after delivery.

Note to self, *never* wear mascara if there is any chance you may end up delivering a baby.

DAY FIFTEEN. WALK FIFTEEN.

Well, don't I look smart? After the trauma of yesterday, I decided I would treat myself to a new coat. Partly because my old one was blood-stained and looked like I may have been working in an abattoir for the last few months, but also because I felt I deserved it. Yes, I really did think that little old Gemma had done remarkably well under extreme conditions, and the least I could do was get myself the new coat I had been planning.

I'm rather pleased with it. It's black, to match my joggers, but without the orange trim, and is quite fitted which I must say has rather a pleasant slimming effect. So now I really look the part of a serial walker, as opposed to a serial killer, who incidentally I still think may be lurking in the tarpaulin house.

It also seems to have made me turbocharged as I'm going up this hill with quite some pace today. I wonder if that's because I am getting fitter, or maybe it's the residual adrenaline from yesterday still coursing through my veins? I suppose there could also be a psychological effect of having a nice new, sporty coat. Perhaps the 'breathable fabric' is stimulating me to shift up a few gears. I suppose it doesn't really matter what the cause is the reality is that I feel good, a new baby arrived safely into the world and Dan appears to be on the scene again and keen to talk. Well, we shall just have to see what happens in that department. I'm not doing any chasing but I suppose there's no harm in seeing what he has to say if we 'happen' to bump into each other.

'Morning Tortie, glad you seem to be fit, well and back on your windowsill rather than flattened under a bus or something.'

No response of course but she did take a little look at me. One day her owner will be there and wonder who the hell it is, chatting away with her cat. But it's not as if I actually stop and hold a conversation with her through the window, it's only a brief acknowledgement as I go past.

And a wave from Teapot woman, things really are looking positive today. That's good; I had been concerned that I may have traumatised the poor woman forever with my grisly appearance yesterday. But it seems that she wasn't bothered in the slightest. I guess that from her point of view, she got the answer she needed for the crossword and it didn't really matter how or why.

When I think about it I suppose it was lucky I *hadn't* been stabbed, as she didn't bother asking if I was OK but accepted my appearance without a question. Actually, that's a bit worrying. Does she think I'm mad enough to walk around looking like that?

Probably, but who cares. The sun is shining and I'm revved up and raring to keep going.

'Hi, Gemma, nice coat! Much better than the old one.'

'Thanks, guys, I didn't realise you had noticed it, especially from way up there?'

'Course we did. Even Dad mentioned it. He asked us why you were wearing a coat that was several sizes too big.'

'Oh great, thanks for that. That makes me feel really good. Where is he anyway?'

'He's gone to the shops but will be back in a minute so we better get on.'

'You do that, you can't be far off completing this extension.'

'Umm, well, it will need a roof.'

'Oh, yes, of course. Obviously, building isn't my thing. See you later.'

'Yes, bye.'

Now, how am I going to play it when I see Dan? It might be today, it might not, but I want to be cool and seem nonchalant about the whole thing. He must already think I'm slightly unhinged, well, maybe not slightly, more totally fallen off the wall, but he did seem genuinely concerned yesterday. But then I suppose he did think I'd been stabbed. You'd have to be really callous not to show any concern for a person if you thought they were about to expire from a fatal wound.

One thing's for sure, we humans are really complex. There are so many factors we take into account either consciously or subconsciously. The slightest movement or gesture can tell a lot about us. That's pretty scary. I wonder how much I give away without realising it? Actually, I don't know myself very well so it would be a great help if someone picked up on a few signals and told me about them.

It would be chaos though. Imagine trying to walk down the street in a hurry and people kept stopping to say things like, 'Do you know that the way you keep looking around makes me think you have been up to no good.'

Although it could be positive I suppose, 'I like the way your hair bounces when you walk.'

Speaking of which, what do I do about bouncy hair woman?

Nothing is the obvious answer. Dan did say she wasn't who I thought she was.

How does he know who I thought she was?

I could have thought she was looking around the house with a view of buying it for all he knows.

Having said that, I think Dan has probably seen enough of me to know I'm more than likely to jump to *any* conclusion other than the correct one.

All may be revealed soon as I am approaching his house at a rapid rate. Maybe I should slow down slightly, not so slow that he thinks I'm deliberately hanging around outside, but slightly slower than this manic pace I have set today.

Apart from anything else I want to catch my breath a bit. It wouldn't do to arrive panting and red with exertion.

Here goes. House of Dan is looming. Is there movement inside? There was the merest hint that a person was in the lounge. Let me just take a peep.

Shit. Shit. Shit.

There was, bouncy hair woman. She stared straight back at me and then seemed to smirk. Yes, smirk.

She may have even been saying something but I didn't stay around long enough to find out.

How embarrassing.

Whoever she is she is going to think I'm very odd. Both times I have seen her I've been peering in the window. At the very least she'll have me down as a peeping tom and consequently no threat to her position with Dan. Unless of course, Dan has a thing about peeping toms, but I'm guessing he doesn't.

Quite frankly I'm probably lucky she hasn't called the police. I would if I saw the same stranger looking through my window on two occasions.

I tell you what though, Gemma, you really need to stop looking in people's houses. It's going to get you in some serious trouble one day.

'Gemma, stop. Wait.'

Who the hell is that now?

Oh, my word it's Dan and he isn't wearing his running things. So why is he sprinting towards me?

'Please, just wait.'

OK, umm, why are you running around outside with no shoes on?'

'I was in a hurry and forgot them.'

'That sounds more like my behaviour than yours, are you OK?'

'I'm fine, but can we stop walking as now you've bought my attention to my lack of shoes I realise how painful it is?'

'Of course. Are you sure you're OK you look a bit, well, flustered.'

'I am, as you so kindly put it, flustered. I was at home when my sister yells out that this strange woman is peering through the window again. I asked if she was wearing a huge, scruffy coat and she said no, a black running top.'

'Ah, yes, I can explain.'

'No, no, listen, at first I thought the only person likely to be staring into my house was you, but when she said they were wearing a black coat I thought it can't be, but ran in to have a look anyway. Unfortunately, you were just walking away and I couldn't see you very clearly, and I didn't recognise your coat so thought it must be someone else. Then when you crossed the road I saw your orange go faster stripes on your joggers. As you know I'm already familiar with your legs so I realised it must be you after all.'

'Ah, yes, I.'

'No, please, let me finish. So once I realised it was you I knew you would have jumped to *any* conclusion other than the right one, so thought I would catch you up and explain.'

As I thought, he knows me too well.

'Right, so, what exactly are you explaining, your sudden disappearance, your sister? Did you say sister?'

'Yes, my sister.'

Shit. Gemma does it again. Bouncy hair woman isn't some unknown lover but his sister. He'll be telling me he disappeared because of work next.

'Also, I'm so sorry I didn't get back in touch, I really wanted too, but I had to go back down south for work.'

Knew it. Work.

'One of my clients is rather needy and had a problem. As they are also one of my best payers at the moment I had to go down and sort it out.'

'Clients. What are you, some sort of counsellor by the sounds of it? Needy client reeks of a psychologist or something. That could be handy, you know, with me. Ha.'

Please stop talking, Gemma.

He's smiling again. Why does he find me so amusing?

'No, I'm not a psychologist, although, as you correctly pointed out, it may have been handy if I was, especially if we are going to meet up again.'

Oh, interesting, meet up again. This sounds promising!

'No, I'm an architect. I've been working on his house for months and it's in the final stages now. He was having a panic and I had to go and calm him down. The thing is, he has other properties and I'm hoping he'll keep me on. So, it's a case of running around at his beck and call at the moment.'

'Right. Work then.'

'Yes, work.'   ·

He's grinning now. I think he's actually enjoying my discomfort.

'I wanted to let you know I'd only be gone a few days but I didn't know how to get hold of you.'

'Right.'

'I do want to see you again you know. Maybe you could give me your number or tell me where you live so this doesn't happen again?'

'Right.'

'Are you OK, Gemma, it's just you keep saying right?'

'Oh, sorry, yes, I'm fine. Just fine. In fact, I'm more than fine!'

'Good, that's a relief. When I spoke to my sister whilst I was away, and she said someone had been looking in, I guessed it must have been you and I knew you'd be mad about me disappearing like that.'

'How? How did you know it would be me, it could have been anyone?'

'Umm, well, you do have a history of peering through my windows don't you?'

'I guess I do. Sorry about that.'

'Look, forget it. Can we meet up tonight and start afresh. Again?'

'Yes, that would be nice. How about the pub?'

'Sounds good to me. I'll be there at 8. Can you give me your number in case any problems should arise?'

'Here, I'll put it in your phone, then I know for sure you have it.'

'By the way, what was that all about with the blood-stained look and talk of babies?'

'Oh, you know, just a normal day. I was out walking when a pregnant woman asked me into her house to deliver her baby. Everyone's fine. The baby, the woman and me.'

'Gemma, I'm beginning to wish I was a psychologist rather than an architect. Maybe I should retrain just to cope with being with you!'

'Thank you, but that won't be necessary. Delivering a baby isn't something I've had to do often. In fact, until yesterday I hadn't done it at all.'

'That's a relief, I shall go home before my feet freeze and see you later at the pub.'

'Oh, I'd forgotten about your feet! Yes, please go and warm them and I'll see you later.'

Fantastic! I knew today was going to be a good one!

I'm meeting Dan for a drink and I only managed to make him think I was half mad rather than a complete sandwich short of a picnic.

Excellent.

'Hey Gemma, why are you grinning? Bet you've seen Dan again haven't you?'

'None of your business you cheeky sod but as it happens, yes, I have.'

'Looks like it went well. Are you meeting up again?'

'Not that it's any of your business but yes we are meeting up again. Tonight in fact.'

'Great, I look forward to hearing all about it tomorrow.'

'No chance, don't be so nosey!'

'You know you won't be able to resist telling me and anyway, your face usually says it all.'

'Really? Am I so transparent?'

'Put it this way, I bet I can guess where you live just from looking at you.'

'No way. I don't believe you. OK smart arse, tell me.'

Well, he's scrutinising me. Surely that just isn't possible.

'I'd say, about three roads down that way, the house in the middle.'

'What the f... um, hell, how did you know? That's pretty scary.'

'Oh, don't be scared, Gemma, it's amazing how far you can see from all the way up here!'

'Oh, you little bugger! Well, I suppose that's marginally better than finding out you are a stalker.'

'Your face was a picture, that's so funny.'

'I'm glad to have brought a little sunshine into your day. Now I suggest you get on with some work and let me get home. I've things to do.'

'Bye then.'

'Yes, bye, see you tomorrow.'

He makes me laugh. It'll be a shame when they finish building, I won't see him anymore.

Now here comes Teapot woman. I swear she has started lying in wait for me.

'Respectable – 6 letters?'

'Decent.'

'Yes, of course. Speaking of which, you look better than yesterday.'

'Thanks, I think.'

'Much cleaner coat.'

Wily old fox, she did notice.

Right, now to increase the pace again and get home. I need to prepare for tonight.

DAY SIXTEEN. WALK SIXTEEN.

What a fantastic evening! We never stopped talking and laughed until our sides hurt. In fact, we got a few strange looks from the other customers and eventually moved on to another pub where we got equally strange looks.

Is it so odd to be openly enjoying yourself? Maybe people need to loosen up a bit and realise it's OK to have fun. Get me! Miss, I was so miserable I could barely put one foot in front of the other, suddenly advising the world to be happy.

It's certainly weird how things turn out. I haven't thought about Luke for days now and that's not all down to Dan. I seem to have turned a very important corner as far as Luke is concerned. I really don't care about him any more and if I'm honest with myself it feels like a huge relief. The fact that things hadn't been great for a while just seemed to gnaw away at me. I think I was willing to keep on trying just because the situation was familiar and the idea of changing anything seemed frightening. But the reality is that now I have started getting out more I am seeing that there is a whole new world out there waiting to be discovered. I'm not stupid though, I know I'm only in the early stages of feeling better about myself but I do think it's possible to have a positive future.

I mean, the one fact that without my help that little baby girl may not have survived birth, is a pretty strong incentive to grab life and get on with it. I guess there's nothing like a huge amount of blood and gore to put things in perspective.

If it looks like there is anyone at home I may call in today and see how they are doing.

Dan was amazed by the whole story. In a way, it's lucky he did see me covered in blood and in a post delivery haze, as I doubt he would have believed me otherwise. I mean, had I just been telling him all about it as we sat in the pub, I'm pretty sure he would have thought I had made the whole thing up. Things like that just don't happen to people like me.

But actually they do, and there's one little girl more in the world to prove it. You do read about amazing births from time to time when the mother to be has been caught off guard and delivers on the bus or in a taxi or something, but it's not *that* common. So I'm grateful really that I was there to help, as it has helped me almost as much as the poor mum.

But we also laughed about me assuming the bouncy hair woman was a secret lover. Dan did point out that it would have been much simpler to think she was a relation rather than a lover, but I swear he never mentioned a sister before. Why is that? Surely clearing out your mum's home is the sort of job siblings would do together? I did mention this to Dan and he agreed with me but said his sister is a law unto herself, and he didn't really think about telling me about her at the time. She's a powerful lawyer in London and couldn't just leave the case she was dealing with until sentencing had taken place. She had been working on it for years and couldn't wait to see the man sent down. Apparently, he is now residing at her majesty's pleasure for a very long time, and Elizabeth, that's Dan's sister, is delighted with the outcome, and is now able to help sort the house out before she returns to London.

But on the whole, we mainly spent the evening laughing about almost anything, including the other customers, although thinking back that may have been the cause of the dirty looks. I've always enjoyed people watching and got Dan hooked on it as we scanned those around us. I must admit I do tend to elaborate a little, and it's probably highly unlikely that the couple at the next table were really under-cover FBI agents, but it made us laugh. It wouldn't have been half as amusing if I'd said he was a painter and deco-rator and she worked in a shoe shop. Where's the fun in that? It's much more fun to imagine a whole secret and exciting life surrounding the very normal, and actually quite boring looking people, sitting next to us. I hope they didn't hear what we were saying. That would be a bit embarrass-ing. But actually, they seemed too engrossed in their own conversation to be bothered about us.

'Hi boys, how's it going up there today?'

'Morning Gemma, fine thanks, how was your date?'

Date. I guess it was really but I hadn't actually thought of it like that. That sounds like quite an old-fashioned term but I like it.

'Oh we had fun thanks, it was a wonderful evening.'

'You certainly look like you enjoyed it, you're all glowing and happy looking.'

'Well thank you again but get back to your roofing before you get into trouble. I can see your dad in the kitchen and he looks like he's about to come out again with drinks for you all.'

'About time, he went in ages ago and I'm really ready for a brew.'

'Enjoy it then, see you later.'

'Yes, see you.'

He's such a nice boy, his older brother doesn't say much but at least he gives me a smile from time to time. It must be hard when your dad is as strict as theirs seems to be. I've been so lucky, my mum and dad are pretty laid back but have always been there for me when I needed them.

Now, here we are at the no longer fat/pregnant woman's house. There are lots of cards up in the window and several bouquets of flowers. Shit. That's a thought. I should have brought a gift with me. Something for the mum and at least a birth card.

Oh, she's there; the mum has seen me and is waving. It's too late now, I'll have to go in and say hello, minus a present.

'Hi, I'm so pleased I saw you, I've been looking out as I wanted to catch you and thank you again for the other day.'

'It's no problem, honestly, I'm just delighted it turned out as it did. I haven't delivered a baby before!'

'You did a fantastic job the midwife who checked me over once I got to the hospital was amazed. She said for a first baby it was so unusual for it all to happen so quickly and without the need for stitches.'

Ugh. Stitches, down there? How repulsive.

'Really, that's so nice to know! I guess mother-nature took over really as I hadn't a clue what I was doing.'

'Maybe not, but you remained calm which was exactly what I needed at that moment. I was terrified.'

'You didn't seem it, to me you looked like you were the

one that was calm and I was dithering about and shaking so much I could barely hold the phone to call the ambulance!'

'Come on, come in and meet your namesake.'

'My namesake, you mean you called her Gemma, after me?'

'We did, we were going to call her Sara but after you saved the day we thought it would be much more appropriate to call her after you.'

'Wow. I don't know what to say. That's such an honour. Are you sure?'

'Of course we are! We've already registered the birth, it's official; look, here's the certificate.'

'Oh, my word. There it is in black and white. Gemma Green. That's amazing! Can I see her?'

'Of course, she's asleep in the crib but you can take a peek. Here see.'

'Oh, my word. She's so beautiful and has masses of hair! I didn't see that before as she was so, well, gunky.'

'Ha! She was as you put it, gunky, but once they cleaned her up at the hospital all this black curly hair sprang up.'

'She's absolutely gorgeous. I'm not sure why I'm crying but oh my. Look at her little hands and fingers, she even has tiny, tiny nails! I'm so pleased for you both. Where is your husband, I'd like to congratulate him too?'

'He's out I'm afraid, once we settled little Gemma down for a nap he told me to go to bed for a bit whilst he went shopping.'

'Um, so why aren't you in bed then?'

'I couldn't settle; I wanted to see if I could catch you.'

'That's so sweet. How long will she sleep do you think?'

'She's a baby, who knows! But probably another hour or so.'

'In that case, I am going to go and you are going to grab some rest whilst you can.'

'Yes, miss. I think I will doze off now I've seen you.'

'I'm sorry I didn't bring a gift, I really should have done.'

'Please don't worry about that. You brought us the best gift of all, the safe arrival of our baby. We can never thank you enough.'

'Seriously, don't. I think the experience did me as much good as it did you and little Gemma. Now, go to bed!'

'I will but just one more thing, who was that man I saw you talking with as I went off in the ambulance? He looked rather nice.'

'Oh, that was Dan. He is rather nice actually and was pretty amazed by the whole story. I told him all the gory details last night in the pub.'

'Hopefully not *all* the details. Some things are best left to the imagination!'

'That's for sure! I think it should be compulsory for young girls to watch a birth for real, it would be the best form of contraception ever!'

'You're not wrong there. From where I was lying, or rather squatting, it wasn't the best of times but I must say it's completely worth it now I have her here.'

'Yes, she's adorable. Now you go off to bed and I'll let myself out. I'll call around again some time to see how you and little Gemma are doing.'

'That would be lovely, thanks, Gemma. See you soon.'

'Yes, bye and sleep well!'

Wow. Just wow! A new little human named after me. That is such an honour.

Oh, a text from Dan. I didn't hear that come in. I guess I was a little preoccupied.

He said he ran past and saw me in with the new mum and hopes to see me later. That's nice and there's even a kiss! A kiss, is that significant? I hope so. Now I have even more of a spring in my step than before. I'll reply saying yes, definitely meet up later. Do I put a kiss too? No. Or maybe yes. Or, oh, what do I do? Sod it, two kisses back seem about right. There. Sent.

Maybe two was too much? I don't want him thinking I'm over keen. Or do I?

Oh, stop it, Gemma. There's nothing you can do anyway; it's gone already. Two is fine. Honestly Gemma, relax about the kisses!

I've got that feeling that someone is looking at me, which is not a good feeling when you are standing outside the tarpaulin house of a serial killer whilst texting your boyfriend. Is he my boyfriend? Well, I can't internally debate that right now, more importantly, who is looking at me?

I can't really see much but hang on, I'm pretty sure I saw a face at the upstairs window. It moved as soon as I looked up but I'm sure it was there. It looked like it could have been a child, it didn't seem very old, or tall for that matter. But why did it disappear? Something is definitely not right there.

Maybe I should go and knock on the door?

And say what you loony?

'Hi, I just want to check you don't have anyone locked away upstairs.'

Did I just say that out loud? My God, maybe I am mad after all.

Seriously, Gemma, stop looking in people's houses and get on with your own life.

Maybe I was imagining it. It's one thing to deliver a baby

on your walk, but surely the law of averages says you don't find someone else, being held hostage, only two days later. That has to be too much even for my fertile imagination.

It was either nothing or some child messing about. That's it. End of story, Gemma, now get on with your walk, you're nearly at Teapot lady's house. That usually brings something to distract you.

'Morning dear, game played with a young child? Eight.'

'Peekaboo.'

'Thank you.'

Oh, the irony. I swear she's a witch.

DAY SEVENTEEN. WALK SEVENTEEN.

Today is a red-letter day!

After another lovely evening with Dan, where we spent most of the time doubled up with laughter once again, we are going to meet up and he's joining me for my walk.

Consequently, I have spent much longer getting ready this morning. Including the addition of makeup, which quite frankly usually never comes out before evening, if at all, so now I am rushing to get out on time and meet him at the top of the road. I feel rather honoured that he is forgoing his morning run to have a sedate walk with me. Although actually, whenever he sees me out walking, it is far from sedate. I'm usually semi-running, as I try to appear more normal, and attempt to remove myself from whatever traumatic event in which I have become embroiled. But I usually end up looking on the upper end of manic. Luckily he seems to like that look as he keeps coming back for more. However, he may be disappointed when he realises I can't keep up that pace of walking over any distance. I'll have to find lots of interesting things to point out so we can slow right down whilst we have long discussions and I catch my breath.

Oh God, there he is and I must say he looks rather nice. He's not wearing his running gear, which is a relief, but I'm very pleased I made the effort and put on some makeup.

'Hi, you're on time!'

'Actually, Gemma, I've been here 5 minutes as you seem to be running a bit late but that's fine because you look fantastic!'

'Really? Do you need glasses?'

'Stop it and take a compliment when it's offered. In fact, come here and let me greet you properly.'

Oh my word, he's coming in for a kiss. Which way for the head tilt? We don't want to knock noses.

Looks like it's to the right for me. Here goes…

Oh my, that was rather glorious.

Please don't blush, not now, Gemma.

Well, OK, just a small blush then. I suppose that can look fetching, as long as it doesn't turn into the full blotchy chest and neck thing.

'There, our first kiss and I must say Gemma, it was wonderful.'

'Thank you, it was wasn't it.'

Here comes the blush, I'll try and distract him.

'Let's walk shall we, Gemma, show me your usual route.'

What a gentleman, he's moving things on rather graciously. Oh, I could kiss him. Again. But I won't, not yet.

'Come on then, this way for the Gemma guided tour. I hope you can stand the excitement.'

'I'm rather hoping for a quiet stroll. I don't think I could cope with delivering any babies or some other trauma.'

'Well, hopefully, it will be quiet. As far as I know, there

are no babies itching to be born on this particular circuit this morning.'

'Good, lead on then, and I want a full Gemma style description of everywhere we go and the things that you normally see.'

'Really, are you sure? My take on life can be a little, umm, unusual sometimes.'

'I know, that's why I'm here. It's so nice to meet someone with such a refreshing outlook. I can honestly say I have never met anyone quite like you.'

'Excellent, I think. Right, onwards and upwards then. My walk starts with the hill. I devised it this way to really get the muscles working and kick start the exercise.'

'Really?'

'No, but it sounded good didn't it!'

'Ha. See, I'm loving it already!'

'The first attraction we come to is lovingly referred to as the DIY building site. Usually, the dad is lurking around in the background somewhere with a glare that can get his two sons working at double speed in a second. The boys are much more chatty, especially the youngest one. However, as they are at the roofing stage, talking has turned more to shouting in order to be heard.'

'Good start, have you seen this extension going up from the beginning?'

'Yes, it seemed to take ages to get going but now they are getting on with it at quite a pace.'

'That's usually the way, but it's the internal fixtures and fittings that seem to take an eternity for me.'

'Of course, I was forgetting you have a professional interest in this sort of thing.'

'Yes and I'm pleased to say that the work they have done so far looks in pretty good shape.'

'That's a relief I was worried you may spot some glaring error and shut down the whole project. Look, right up at the top, that's the chatty son.'

'Hi Gemma, is that Dan with you?'

'Oh, you've told him about me then?'

'Not exactly, he guessed after the misunderstanding we had over the Jeffrey/Luke episode. Unfortunately, he over-heard the whole thing and has been ribbing me about it ever since.'

'Great, I'm the talk of the town, that's nice to know.'

'Hi, yes, it is Dan, not that it's any of your business.'

'You know you like chatting, Gemma, and I'm very pleased to meet you, Dan.'

'Thanks, likewise. Looks like you are doing a great job on the extension.'

'Dan's an architect so he knows about these things. Unlike me, which is a something you frequently like to point out.'

'Just because you didn't realise we needed to put a roof on the thing! Thanks for the vote of confidence, Dan. It's been a long project and I'll be very glad when it's finished.'

'I bet. They're hard work aren't they.'

'Yes, enjoy your walk you two, you make a lovely couple.'

'Get back to work cheeky and I'll see you tomorrow.'

'Bye, I look forward to it.'

'They seem nice and amazingly normal for two of your acquaintances.'

'Yes, they are, but I do need to break you in gently to the world of Gemma.'

'Really, the mind boggles.'

'Good, I like to keep you on your toes. Now, the next stop is the teapot lady's house. However, it only gets really inter-esting with her on the return journey.'

'Really, why, what happens?'

'I'm not going to tell you, that would spoil it!'

'Oh go on, the suspense is killing me.'

'No, you'll just have to be patient, but I *can* tell you that this is her house. Look there she is, just drinking her tea.'

'Hence the teapot house then.'

'Yup. You guessed it!'

'Should we wave?'

'No point, she doesn't really *do* normal social behaviour.'

'The mind boggles! Drinks tea and doesn't follow social protocol, I like the sound of her already.'

'Oh she's a character alright but forget her for now as we are rapidly approaching tarpaulin house.'

'Please don't tell me this is another house you have a bad feeling about. I wanted mine to be the only one that evoked that sort of emotion from you.'

'Well, yours was kidnapping, this one is more serial killer.'

'What! I was joking! I didn't really think you'd jumped to such wild conclusions for a second time.'

'Oh, it's not since the events at your place, more in conjunction with. I pretty much felt like this about both houses at the same time. It's just that yours has been crossed off the list now.'

'How many houses are on the list? Is there a major incident happening at a number of properties around here? Just imagine if the press got to hear about this, cost of insurance in this neighbourhood is going to rocket!'

'Thank you but there's no need to make fun of me if you don't mind. I admit I made an error of judgement over your house but that doesn't mean I'm wrong this time.'

'I suppose, 'error of judgement' is one way of putting it! But I would have thought that having been caught out once with a particularly overactive imagination that you might have been a little more cautious this time.'

'I am, I haven't been back after dark to snoop around if that's what you mean.'

'That's a relief, not everyone is likely to be as understanding as I was to find someone peering through their window.'

'I must admit you did take it very well.'

'That's because I'd been racking my brains to think of a way to get talking with you and couldn't believe my luck when you literally landed in my rose bush.'

This is so good to hear, he must have wanted to get together with me even before the mishap in his garden.

'Good job I came looking then isn't it.'

'Well, yes, but that doesn't mean something terrible is going on here. Which house is it anyway? Oh hang on, did you say tarpaulin house?'

'Yes.'

'Call me Sherlock if you like but I'm guessing that it must be that house over there. The one with tarpaulin up at the window.'

'Excellent! You're a quick learner.'

'I think it's more likely your less than imaginative naming of these properties that give it away. But that's not a bad thing as it leaves all your imaginative powers free to invent these amazing stories.'

'That's nice of you to say but actually I don't think it's a story. In fact, I'm pretty sure something is happening in there.'

'But why? Just because there's tarpaulin up at the window; surely that just means they are decorating.'

'That's what I thought at first but then I once saw an

incredibly expensive car in the driveway and also a face peeping out from the upstairs window.'

'Oh well, that's conclusive evidence of a crime scene if ever I heard it. Could it possibly be that the owner is successful in his work and he has the decorators in?'

'Of course it could be but I'm pretty sure that's not the case.'

'Really, why?'

'I can't put my finger on it. It's just a hunch.'

'Oh, Gemma you really do make me laugh, in a good way! You're so funny!'

'I'm not actually trying to be funny you know.'

'I know, that's what makes it even more hilarious!'

'OK, well now you have had a good laugh at my expense, once again, shall we move on, and as we walk I shall tell you why I think that sometimes you should believe the unbelievable.'

'I'm all ears, but before we go, can I just say that I think I saw a man with a chainsaw silhouetted behind the tarpaulin.'

'No, really? We have to do something!'

'Gemma, I'm joking. Honestly, I didn't see a thing. Come on, let's get going and you can tell me your tale.'

'OK, this story goes back to when I was a child but it has stuck with me all this time. My brother, Jonny, often told it to me if he wanted to scare me witless.'

'Obviously it worked as you still refer back to it all these years later.'

'No, you're wrong, it did frighten me at the time, and in that sense, Jonny got exactly the reaction he wanted, but now I think the story proves that sometimes you have to think outside the box a little and not always take things at face value.'

'OK, now I'm intrigued, tell your story before we get distracted by another horrifying event on the Gemma guided tour.'

'I will and I want it to be known in advance that I don't care if you believe it or not, the fact that *I* do is what's important.'

'Fine, I promise not to laugh and you might even surprise me.'

'Right, there was once a woman who lived in a semi-detached house on a rather pleasant housing estate.'

'I'm gripped already.'

'You said you wouldn't laugh!'

'I'm not! Do you see me laughing?'

'No, and I shall continue but I will ignore the way your shoulders are already shaking as you try to suppress the mirth.'

'That's perhaps a good thing, go on, I want to know about the normal lady in the normal house.'

'Well, she kept going to the doctors and complaining that her neighbour was trying to kill her.'

'Kill her?'

'Yes, kill her. She said that every evening after dark there were drilling sounds and that the neighbour was making holes in her wall so that she could gas her.'

'That's ridiculous.'

'That's also what the doctor said, along with, 'Pull yourself together, you're just imagining it.' But the problem was that the lady kept on returning to the doctor with the same complaint.'

'Bet he was fed up with it.'

'Doesn't matter if he was or he wasn't, the fact is that he didn't believe her and over time reached the conclusion that she must be mad.'

'How very Victorian.'

'Obviously he didn't just declare this but had her psychiatrically assessed and even admitted to hospital for a short time.'

'Poor woman, it sounds like she needed help anyway if you ask me.'

'Well, I didn't ask you did I?'

'Er, no, sorry please continue.'

'Eventually the woman was released from the hospital and returned home. They had told her she had been under a lot of strain since the death of her husband and that after the treatment she could return home and rebuild her life.'

'Sounds about right, so what's the mystery here then?'

'The mystery is, that on the very night that she returned home there was an explosion at her house. The fire brigade quickly attended and once it was safe to enter they found the woman dead in her armchair.'

'Oh no, that's dreadful.'

'The next part is the really awful bit because an investigation was carried out as to why there had been an explosion. Eventually, they found numerous holes drilled in the wall adjoining the two properties and evidence of a small hose that had been used to pipe gas through to her lounge.'

'Oh God, that's horrific.'

'Yes, isn't it. The poor woman had been right all along but no one would believe her. So she not only ended up dead but for the last few months of her life she was subjected to a hospital admission and being constantly ignored.'

'I must admit that's really sad. But what has that got to do with tarpaulin house?'

'Nothing, apart from the fact that *I* think something is going on there and so far *you* haven't believed me.'

'Fair point and I promise to consider all the facts very carefully.'

'Good, that's all I ask!'

'Well, having considered all the facts very carefully I'm afraid I still think that the tarpaulin house is innocent. I just haven't seen any evidence to prove otherwise.'

'OK, that's fine, neither have I really, well, nothing concrete, but at least you are aware of the place now, and so far you haven't had me committed, so that seems fairly positive.'

'It is and I promise not to whisk you off to the doctor's just yet.'

'Well, that's a relief. Look, I know it sounds odd, I'm not a complete idiot you know, but it's just a feeling.'

'I know, Gemma, but your feelings have been a little off target at times. Honestly, stop worrying about the place and let's get on with enjoying ourselves.'

'OK, you have a point. I shall try to ignore it, after all, there isn't a lot I can do anyway is there?'

'That's not exactly ignoring it is it! That's more putting it on the back burner to see what happens.'

'Yes, true, but that's what I'm going to do. I don't need to stalk the place or anything but I shall keep a casual eye on it when I'm out on my walks.'

'Fair enough, now look, we are nearly back at teapot lady's house, what have I got to look forward to here?'

'Right on cue, here she comes.'

'Threatening, eight letters?'

'Menacing.'

'Oh good. Who's he?'

'A friend of mine.'

'Hello, oh, she's gone.'

'Yes, she doesn't do normal behaviour remember.'

'She's weird. Do you mean to say she comes out, every time you pass to ask you the solution to a troublesome crossword clue?'

'Yes, pretty much. When I go past the first time, sometimes I see her sitting at the table, sometimes I don't. But on my return journey, she always appears. Thankfully, I have managed to get everyone so far. I'm not actually sure what would happen if I didn't know the answer.'

'So you're a bit of a crossword genius on the quiet then?'

'I like to think so! The other thing is that they always seem to be related to something I have seen that morning.'

'Surely that's just a coincidence, you can make anything fit a mood if you really try.'

'I suppose so, but 'menacing'? Don't you find that a bit odd after we'd been viewing the tarpaulin house?'

'No, I don't, because there's *nothing* menacing about that house in the slightest!'

'OK, OK, I get the message. I'm only winding you up and I must say, it's rather easy to do.'

'Thank you, it's nice to know I have such qualities. But we are nearly back at your place now and I would love to continue this conversation but unfortunately, I have a meeting to go too.'

'A meeting? Oh, OK. That sounds important.'

'Important? In a way, I guess it is. A few estate agents are coming around to value Mum's house.'

'Oh, I'm sorry, that's not going to be easy for you.'

'No, I must admit I'm not looking forward to it but at least Elizabeth is still here so she can help.'

'Oh, your sister is still in residence then, she hasn't been called back to London for some important case.'

'No, she's here for a few more days as far as I know.'

'I was going to offer to come and help you but it's probably better to do it with her.'

'That's really kind of you and I would have taken you up on the offer had she been away. But, to make up for it, why don't we go out for a meal tonight?'

'Oh, that would be lovely! I haven't been out to eat for ages.'

'Well, I shall pick you up at 7.30 then.'

'Great, see you later, and thanks for joining me for my walk.'

'No problem, it was an absolute pleasure, and by the way, I think teapot lady is hilarious!'

'Me too!'

Oh, he's coming in for another kiss, head tilt right remember.

Good grief. That was even better than last time. I'm lost for words.

'Finally I seem to have managed to render Gemma speechless! Excellent. On that note, I shall briskly walk off and see you later.'

'Bye, look forward to it.'

Wow. What a lovely morning walk and what an amazing kiss. I really can't wait for tonight.

I'd better start getting ready right now.

DAY EIGHTEEN. WALK EIGHTEEN.

Good job I wrapped up warm this morning, it's cold and wet but at least this jacket has a hood. It isn't the done thing to go for a brisk walk with an umbrella. In fact, I find it impossible to walk quickly with one. I think it's something to do with arm movement. If you are holding an umbrella you can't get just the right amount of arm swing for maximum benefit.

Anyway, my hood is up and managing to keep some of the driving rain from seeping down the back of my neck, but nothing, not even ice-cold rain, is going to dampen my mood today.

We had such a good time out last night. Just when I think it can't get any better Dan proves me wrong by making our evening very special.

We did go out for a meal, nothing fancy, just a pizza at the local Italian, but the atmosphere was great and we talked and laughed for hours.

I honestly couldn't tell you if the pizza was good or not as it really didn't seem to matter.

We managed to get through a couple of bottles of wine,

which is quite an achievement for me. Usually, it only takes a glass or two before I start feeling a bit squiffy. Maybe it was because we took our time and the wine was consumed over a good few hours and a hearty pizza. Not to mention the tiramisu, which was exceedingly moreish. So much so that we actually had two each!

I can't believe we did that. Normally if I go out for a meal with someone I would decline a dessert, as I wouldn't want him to think I was a glutton. But with Dan, we were both so relaxed, obviously aided by the wine, that we giggled as we called the waiter over and practically roared with laughter at his face when we ordered two more.

We did sober up a bit as Dan walked me home. But the kiss he gave me on the doorstep was enough to make my legs turn to jelly again as if we'd had three bottles, not two.

I nearly asked him in, you know, 'for coffee', but, I wimped out when I remembered I haven't yet solved the bikini line dilemma. Just what is the fashion these days? I can't ask him, I suppose I will have to do some research to find out. That should come up with some interesting results.

I must admit though, I do have a bit of a thick head this morning and my waistline really can't tolerate two desserts on a regular basis. But what the heck, we had fun.

To counteract the calories I think I shall go at double speed today and try not to be distracted by anything. Unless some emergency crops up, of course, I mean, I'm not going to carry on walking if someone collapses in front of me or gets run over by a car. But as far as reading anything, or too much, into things I see, well, I'm just going to carry on and burn off some pizza and pudding.

It is nice to have someone to think about and reflect on. If I look back only a few weeks my life was so different. I felt isolated and alone; I rarely left the house and barely took any pride in my own appearance. Now I'm togged up with the latest walking clothes and eating out with a, dare I say, boyfriend? No, not yet, but well on the way to being one I think. No matter what happens I will always be grateful that Dan came along when he did and made me smile again.

'Hey up Gemma, what's with the beam?'

'Oh hi, I'm not beaming, just smiling thank you very much and it's none of your business.'

'I know, but you always tell me in the end. Let me guess, is it lover boy Dan?'

'Excuse me, don't let your Dad hear you talking like that! And no, it isn't about Dan, well, actually it is, but not just him, life in general.'

'See, told you. I think you're in love, you're showing all the symptoms.'

'Get lost and back to your building. Since when did you become an agony Uncle?'

'I'm not! I'm only saying what I see right in front of me, well actually it's several feet below but who's counting.'

'You're a cheeky one, get back to your roofing before I start shaking the scaffolding to dislodge you.'

'Charming! I was only making an observation but if you don't like hearing the truth then that's fine. I'll just carry on with my tiles and leave you to it.'

'Thanks, about time. Hey, stop it. Don't throw cement at me, young man!'

'I won't any more as Dad is just pulling into the road, see you tomorrow Gemma.'

'Yes, see you.'

'It suits you though, this love thing.'

I'm going to pretend I didn't hear that. He does make me laugh. He just says what he wants and doesn't seem bothered about the consequences. Oh to be young and carefree.

Jeez, Gemma, you make it sound like you're over the hill, you're only 22! Get a grip, woman.

There's teapot house and as predicted Mrs Teapot is studying the paper. I wonder what mystery awaits me on my return today?

I shall have to wait and see, oh, that's nice, not-pregnant woman is waving at me from her driveway. I know I said I wouldn't get distracted today but I can't ignore her, we went through so much together.

'Hi Gemma, how are you?'

'I'm fine but more importantly, how are you and little Gemma?'

'We're doing really well thanks. She's such a darling and hardly any bother.'

'Really? I thought they were meant to be ruling your life at this stage. Babies that is.'

'Ha, they do, believe me, I haven't had a minute to myself since I last saw you! But having said that, I wouldn't want it any other way.'

I would. I don't think I could stand that, someone constantly demanding things of me, day and night, especially the night part. I'm not the most responsive of people in the wee small hours. I can barely cope with myself, never mind a tiny person.

'I'm sure you love it, that's what being a mum is all about.'

'You're very perceptive for one so young and childless.'

'I've just got a good imagination apparently.'

'Well you keep using it whilst you can. Once you have a baby, in fact before you have it, something happens to your mind almost as much as the changes to your body. I don't think I have had a clear thought since being about 7 months pregnant.'

'It must be nature's way of helping you deal with it.'

'See, as I said, you're perceptive. That's exactly what my husband used to say when I moaned about my foggy brain.'

'How has he taken to being a Dad?'

'He loves it! He's planning all the big adventures they are going to have over the years. I'm just so happy how things have turned out.'

'That's great and lovely to hear. I must say it's really nice to have something uplifting to listen to instead of the doom and gloom on the news every day.'

'Luckily I rarely have time to watch the news at the moment. But can you hear that? Madam appears to have woken from her nap. I can hear her stirring in the monitor, look, it's tiny and fits into my pocket so I can at least reach the end of the driveway without worrying.'

'That's good, a bit of peace of mind goes a long way. You go off and see to Gemma and I'll see you again soon.'

'OK, nice to see you, Gemma, take care.'

'I will, and you too.'

How sweet. It's lovely to see her so happy after seeing her in such agony. I still have nightmares about the amount of stretching the female body has to do. If I hadn't seen it with my own eyes I doubt I would have believed it. It's more like the special effects department have gone into overdrive on some major film rather than reality, and a horror film at that. Horror and gore, at a cinema near you.

Snort. Oops, I thought I'd got over that habit but obviously, I haven't. Snorting really isn't attractive. I must get to grips with this and stamp it out completely.

Here's tarpaulin house but I'm not going to even look.

Who are you kidding Gemma, of course you are!

Just a little peep, though, nothing major, I did promise myself, and Dan, that I would try and behave in a reasonably normal fashion.

Well, actually there doesn't seem to be anything to worry about anyway. There's no car in the driveway and I can't see any evidence of someone peering out from the upstairs window.

That's a little disappointing. I really wanted to have something mind blowing to tell Dan tomorrow. We're having a day out and driving to the coast. I can't wait, it's been ages since I went anywhere like that and to spend the whole day together is going to be so lovely. I'll have to count a walk on the beach as my daily session as there won't be time to do this route before we go in the morning. Well, I suppose I could make time if I got up really early but that is never going to happen!

I'd sooner wake up at my leisure and spend the extra time beautifying myself before he arrives.

I suppose I'll just have to admit to him that nothing out of the ordinary happened today and he was right, I just have an overactive mind.

As if!

Just because nothing is going on right at this moment doesn't mean a thing. Even serial killers have a day off from time to time.

STOP IT GEMMA.

There isn't a serial killer and if there is, he doesn't live here.

Sometimes I think I am driving myself mad. All I need to do is have everyday thoughts like normal people do.

But what's normal? And wouldn't that be boring?

I'm going to just be me. That's who I am and people, i.e. Dan, can either take me or leave me. But please let it be take, I don't think I want to even consider leave, even at this early stage of proceedings.

The good thing is that all this pondering has got me right back to teapot house and here she comes, brandishing her pen at me.

'Secluded? Eight letters.'

'Isolated.'

'Ta.'

She's off. One day I'm either going to not know the answer or I shall pretend that I don't, just to see what she does. But not today, as I want to get home and not spend the rest of the day picking up the pieces if she goes even more mental than she already is just because she can't finish the crossword.

DAY NINETEEN. WALK NINETEEN.

I am so looking forward to today that I can barely contain my excitement. I've changed my outfit several times already and my bedroom floor looks like the changing rooms of a cheap clothing store on the first day of the sales. Actually, most of the stuff *is* from a cheap clothing store and it's probably why I have rejected it all for a much nicer blouse and a pair of jeans.

I was considering wearing a slinky skirt and skinny top, but it's hardly the weather for it and I'd probably spend most of my time holding the skirt down to prevent my greying knickers from being on display. I really must invest in some more underwear. It's ridiculous.

I think I'll still wear my running shoes though as we are off to the beach for the day and walking is definitely on the agenda. So, just another dab of lipstick and I'm all set to go.

Perfectly timed as here's Dan now.

'Hi, great to see you, Gemma.'

Ooh, nice manly hug, just what I needed.

'Hi, great to see you too, I'm really looking forward to a day out, shall we get going?'

'Of course, your chariot awaits so walk this way.'

'I'll grab my coat, it looks like it could possibly rain later, not that I care.'

'Good, because the forecast isn't great but a walk on the beach will blow the cobwebs away. Let's go. Buckle up.'

'Hang on, did I lock the door?'

'Yes, I watched you do it.'

'I think I'll just check, I don't want to be worrying about it.'

'Go on then Mrs OCD.'

'Am I, do you think I'm a bit OCD?'

'Gemma, I was joking, now check the door and then let's get on our way.'

'OK, done, it was locked but I'm ready to go now.'

'Excellent! It shouldn't take us too long as I doubt there are many other fools heading to the sea when it's as blustery as this.'

'That's exactly why we should go, it will be quiet and the sea will look so dramatic. Perfect Wuthering Heights weather.'

'Except that was on the Yorkshire moors.'

'I know but I'm just setting the scene a little.'

'And a story of revenge.'

'Yes, OK, maybe it wasn't the right example. Anyway, whatever the story I think we shall have a lovely day out.'

'Like your blouse.'

'Thanks, I like your shirt.'

'Good, we're both happy then.'

'Are we nearly there yet?'

'How old are you Gemma, four? No, it'll be a while before we get there. Plenty of time to relax and chat.'

'OK, So, how did you get on with the estate agents?'

'It was good thanks, they all said pretty much the same,

that they didn't think there would be any problem selling Mum's house.'

'Oh, so it's going on the market soon then?'

'Yes, in the next few weeks. Elizabeth wants to get rid of it quickly as she is having work done on her own place and the money would be handy.'

'I thought she was a lawyer and they're always loaded aren't they?'

'She is a lawyer and she is, as you put it, loaded. The house she has is fantastic and she's just making it even better with a loft conversion.'

'So, what happens then? You know, when the house is sold.'

'What do you mean?'

'You know what I mean. Us.'

'I know, I'm only teasing you. I've been thinking a lot about that actually. I can't believe I meet someone I really get on with and they live 300 miles away from London.'

'Who's that then?'

'Gemma, you're fishing now, you of course.'

'I know, I just wanted to hear you say it.'

'As far as I'm concerned it doesn't matter where you live, it's not like you are in another time zone or anything, somehow we can make it work.'

'Are you serious? You want to keep seeing me, even when you go back to London?'

'Of course I do! I can't tell you when I last felt so at ease with someone. I don't want to lose you now.'

Blimey. I wasn't expecting that, not yet anyway, but he feels exactly the same way as I do. I don't think I can keep the grin off my face!

'Stop grinning like a Cheshire cat Gemma.'

'Sorry, I can't help it. I'm really pleased you feel like that because I've been worrying that I might scare you off with my crazy thoughts.'

'It's your crazy thoughts that I like the most, I find it very entertaining.'

'I know, I've seen you laughing at me often enough.'

'Shall we have the radio on?'

'Yes, I'll do it, you drive.'

I'm not in love, so don't forget it, it's just a silly phase I'm going through...

'OK, maybe not.'

'Gemma, you do realise that events around you are not dictated by the lyrics of a song don't you?'

'Of course, I'm not a moron you know, but that song always makes me cry and I spent hours on my mascara today so I'd rather not risk it.'

'Fair enough. So, what do you want to do when we get there?'

'I was thinking a nice walk on the beach, supper as the sun goes down, that sort of thing.'

'Sounds good. I feel rather honoured you have forgone your daily walk to join me. I get the impression it's something of a ritual.'

'It is really, I didn't like it at first but after a few days, I started realising that there is always so much to see. If you keep your eyes open and take the time to look around there are always interesting things going on.'

'I suppose if there isn't you can always make it up.'

'Don't need to funny guy. Who needs to make stories up when you have people like Teapot lady to deal with, not to mention delivering a baby.'

'Put like that I see your point. Somehow you seem to attract unusual circumstances.'

'No, I don't, I just keep an eye on what's going on around

me. I bet things like that are happening all over the place it's just that most people don't look out for it.'

'Most people don't end up stranded in a rose bush though do they?'

'No, I guess not, but what a good job I did!'

'Yes, sure thing. I can't wait to see how the tarpaulin house develops.'

'Um, me too. I hope nothing awful is going on in there and I've been ignoring it. Just imagine how I would feel if I discover the bodies of several victims and could have prevented it if I had only spoken up.'

'Gemma, you don't need to worry about that because nothing is going on in there, and who'd believe you if all you have to go off is a hunch?'

'No one, that's why I'm still keeping an eye on it from a distance.'

'Are you?'

'Yes, why not. If nothing's happening there then that shouldn't be a problem should it?'

'No, I suppose not but don't let your imagination run riot, will you? Not everyone would be as understanding as I was to find you flattening their garden.'

'This is true. OK, what if I promise not to go around there investigating unless I have told you first. How's that?'

'Perfect. Now we can forget the damned place and enjoy the moment because if you look over there you can see the sea!'

'Fantastic. Come on, hurry up, park the car so we can get out.'

'OK, calm down. I love your enthusiasm, Gemma. It's as if you are seeing everything for the first time.'

'When we were young my Mum used to say that I was

like a puppy, everything was fascinating and I needed plenty of exercise.'

'She's not wrong. Come on, here's a space, I'll park up and off we go.'

What an absolutely delightful day. We've walked miles, mostly against the wind, which frankly felt like we were walking in a wind tunnel, and which has left me with a healthy glow. We never stopped talking, and whilst we didn't exactly eat a fish and chip supper as we watched the sun set, the reality was that we had to make a dash for it as the rain started, and finish our meal in the car. The windows got very steamy, not from our antics but from the chips. Shame really, antics may have followed but the coastguard came along and asked us to move the car away as the weather was deteriorating and the tide was due to come in soon. Just my luck!

Still, it's OK because now we are warming up as we speed along on our way home, with the radio playing.

'*So remember we were driving, driving in your car, speed so fast I felt like I was drunk. City lights lay out before us and your arm felt nice wrapped 'round my shoulder...*'

Who said that events around you are not dictated by the lyrics of a song?

DAY TWENTY. WALK TWENTY.

I'm pretty damn grumpy today and I really don't know why.

We had such a lovely time yesterday that I should be singing and dancing on the rooftops rather than wanting to kill someone or something. It started as soon as I opened my eyes, I just thought to myself, now what?

Am I just trying to sabotage my own happiness? I mean everything is going in the right direction. I feel better than I have in months. It isn't just because of Dan, I just feel stronger in myself, and more in control.

My eyes have really been opened to what the world has to offer, so why am I so fed up?

I've even managed to spill coffee down my front, which is very annoying as I was about to go out. But, the difference to a few weeks ago is that I *have* bothered to go upstairs and change rather than just cover the stain with a scarf. I guess in the limited world of Gemma that has to count as progress.

I'm hoping that my walk will help clear my head and get me thinking positively again.

Dan doesn't want a misery guts hanging around him and I don't want to be that person.

So that's it, you've told yourself off, so now get on with the day.

Where did I leave my trainers?

Oh yes, under the radiator, drying out after the drenching we got yesterday. It was worth it though. It's funny how everything seems fun when you're in company. It really didn't matter that the weather was atrocious; we just had a laugh.

Right, that's it, shoes on, slightly squelchy, but nevertheless, away I go.

After I've double-checked I locked the front door. I think that may be the next Gemma tic that I need to gain control over. I really don't want to be Mrs OCD as Dan kindly put it.

'Hello Tortie, how are you, my feline friend?'

Oops. I didn't see her owner there in the background. Somehow I need to turn this pretend scratch to the cat's stomach through a pane of glass into a greeting. Well, a sort of semi-demented wave.

Seemed to work, the owner appears to be smiling at me even if it is in a rather bemused way.

This hill really seems to have shrunk. It doesn't bother me at all any more which is really encouraging. I can set off from the house at a brisk pace and maintain it all the way to the top. Unless of course something catches my eye and makes me slow down to take a look. But overall I think you can safely say my fitness has improved. I'm not up to full on jogging yet and I'm not even sure I want to do that. As far as I can make out it plays havoc with your knees in years to come. But I guess the benefits might outweigh the knee issues. I'll have to give it some thought.

'Hey Gemma, why are you looking so moody?'

'I'm not, well I was, but I'm fine now. Why, was I glaring angrily in your direction?'

'No, but you did look like steam was almost coming out your ears.'

'Thanks, that's a look I've been cultivating for years and it seems I have finally pulled it off.'

'Nice try but actually I think your normal smiley face is the look to go for.'

'Gee, thanks. Stop it or you'll make me blush.'

'You. Blush. I doubt it unless I was to ask you how it went yesterday with Dan, that usually puts some colour in your cheeks.'

'You are getting too cheeky for your own good my boy. But for your information, I had a lovely day out with Dan.'

'Are you seeing him again tonight?'

'As a matter of fact, no, I'm not. He's busy.'

'Oh, busy. Busy doing what?'

'None of your business!'

'I'm only looking out for you, Gemma.'

'No you're not, you're only being nosey. But, for your information, Dan has gone to London for a day or so.'

'So that's why you're miserable.'

'I'm not miserable, I'm quite capable of surviving a few days without Dan whilst maintaining a sense of humour, thanks very much.'

'We'll see how you are tomorrow Gemma, I'm not so sure, I think Dan has taken over your mind.'

'When I want your opinion I shall ask. See, look, I'm all smiley and happy and not a sign of Dan anywhere in the vicinity.'

'OK, you win. See you tomorrow, Gemma. I guess it's a chance to catch up on some beauty sleep whilst he's away.'

'Are you saying I need it Mr?'

'No, of course not, you're lovely just the way you are.'

'You charmer you. Now get back to work and I'll see you tomorrow.'

'See you.'

Cheeky sod. He does make me laugh though. I hope his dad isn't as strict with him as it appears from the outside. I suppose you never really know what is going on behind closed doors. He could be gentle as a kitten when the whole family are safely in the house and the world locked out for another day.

Which brings me to the house of tarpaulin. Yep, it's still there at the window. Whoever they have in to do this decorating really doesn't seem to be making any progress. That's a point, if they had someone in then surely there should be a van or at least evidence of some workmen coming and going? I've never seen anything except the posh car. The more I think about it the more strange it appears.

Perhaps I will have a little look around. I did promise, Dan, I wouldn't go near the place without talking to him, but he'll be stuck somewhere on the M6 around now, and I don't think he'd appreciate my weird theories just at the moment.

Surely a little peep can't do any harm and it might just put my mind at rest and let me forget about the whole silly idea.

There we go, Gemma, you've managed to talk yourself into having a look but how do you propose you go about it?

Umm, tricky, there's no one about on the road, no cars in the driveway and no sign of movement from inside. I think I'll just walk up and see if I can see in through any of the windows.

It all appears very well kept. The lawn is very neatly mowed and there are no weeds anywhere to be seen. So whoever lives here either likes gardening or employs someone to do it for him, or in fact her.

You don't have to be a genius to work that one out Gemma, you'll have to do better than that if you want to find out what is going on here.

So far so good, I'm at the house and as yet I haven't been accosted by anyone or ravaged by a rabid dog.

The outside of the house is also very well maintained, the paintwork is pristine and the doorstep is cleaner than my kitchen floor. So, still nothing to write home about. Maybe I shall just go around the perimeter and see what's around the back.

Gorgeous lounge, I love the settee, it must have cost a fortune. I haven't seen that anywhere, I bet it has been custom made or something and the ornaments are very tasteful. There aren't many of them but the ones they have are very nice.

Jesus, Gemma, you can't just stand here staring into some-one's house uninvited, admiring their furniture. Keep going and stop getting distracted by pretty things. You're like a magpie.

OK, focus. This is the end of the building so I'd better peep around the corner rather than just casually walk into their back garden.

There doesn't seem to be anyone around but I feel a bit exposed out here. Maybe I'll crawl, that will make me less obvious.

Ouch, these pebbles are hurting my knees though.

Blimey, that's the biggest conservatory I have ever seen.

Shit, there's someone in there. I'd better keep completely still as I don't think they know I'm here as they have their back to me. They seem to be engrossed in conversation with someone but I can't see who's there.

Maybe I'll reverse up a bit.

Oh my God, he's hitting them!

Whoever is in there is getting a right pasting. I need to help them.

No I don't, I need to get out of here. I'll be no help to them if he catches me crawling around his garden.

Why did I ever come around the back, or even up the driveway, I should have trusted my instincts and gone straight to the police?

Ouch, that stone really hurt my knee but it looks like the man is too busy slapping whoever is there to notice me reversing out on all fours. At last, at least I'm around the corner now and can stand up and make a run for it.

Thank goodness, nearly there, nearly back to safety and the road.

Has anyone seen me? I don't think so, but wait; there is definitely someone at the window upstairs.

Oh, my God, they have seen me. I'm not sure if they saw me come from the back of the house or just from the front door area.

What should I do?

Why didn't I have some sort of back up plan in case anything went wrong?

Because you're an idiot, Gemma; and once again you have put yourself in danger.

Oh look, they are waving at me. Are they waving as in a greeting or are they actually trying to attract my attention?

I don't know any more. But they look very young, a child even.

I'll just wave back, keep walking and hope for the best.

I can feel my heart pounding so hard in my chest it feels like it's going to explode. Wouldn't that be gruesome?

Yes, it would, Gemma, but not something you need to think

about right now, what you need to do is make it the last few feet
back onto good old council owned pavement.

Here at last. Who'd have thought you could be so
pleased to see dandelions creeping out between the paving
stones and a few pieces of dropped litter.

That was a bit too close for comfort. I can't see anyone at
the window now. Where they really there or did my panic
cause me to see things?

I don't know but I need to get home and think about
all this.

Do I have enough evidence to call the police?

I think Dan would say I haven't. After all, the only thing I
have actually seen is what appears to be a man hitting
someone else. I don't even know if the other person was
male or female.

Well there I was thinking that having a snoop about
would put my mind at rest, but actually, I feel more
confused than I did before.

I can't get home quickly enough, all I want to do is put
the kettle on, relax a bit and assimilate this information.

Oh shit, I'd forgotten about Teapot house, here
she comes.

'Trespasser, eight letters?'

'Intruder.'

I don't believe her. I really don't believe her.

DAY TWENTY-ONE. WALK TWENTY-ONE.

It's no good; I can't sleep.

All I can think about is that person getting a pasting from the unknown, faceless man. Who does he think he is?

I suppose it could be his wife and they've had a terrible argument, but even then he shouldn't resort to punching her. Or it could be a wayward son who has driven him to distraction, and he has finally snapped and hit him. But that's not right either; surely nothing is so bad that you have to resort to violence. However, if it's either of those instances then I guess it would be classed as a domestic, and therefore none of my business. However wrong I think that it is I suppose the victim has to be ready to talk to someone outside the family circle and gradually sort things out. I'm sure there are helplines and charities for these things.

But then I guess, if you are the victim, then it takes a huge amount of courage to actually try and remove yourself from the situation and sort it all out.

I suppose it could have been the first time this has happened, and they are patching things up at this very moment, and he's horrified by what he has done. She will be distraught but gradually decide to use his self-loathing for her own personal gain, by making him pay for his behaviour for months to come.

But what if it isn't family?

It could be a completely different scenario. A colleague from work, another intruder, although I guess he didn't know about me, so technically it would be the first intruder.

Or maybe it was his next victim, and he was softening them up a bit and trying to intimidate and scare them as much as possible before taking them to the kill room. Umm, back to the old serial killer theory.

But what if I'm right and it is his next victim? Every second I waste not intervening in some way could be vital to their very lives. Me dithering about here could ultimately result in an innocent person dying.

I'm going to get up and make some coffee. There's no chance of me sleeping and I need a clear, active mind to decide what to do.

God, I'm freezing now I've left the comforting cocoon of my heavyweight, fifteen tog duvet. That was such a good investment. At the start of my decline, and the beginning of my love for spending hours in bed, day and night, I invested in the warmest duvet around. I think I was suffering from the lack of dog keeping me warm, as the saying goes if it's too cold then just throw another dog on. I suppose it could have been the lack of Luke, and his hairy torso lying next to me, but that's not something I like to remind myself about. No, it's definitely the demise of dear Jeffrey; he was the best hot water bottle around.

Anyway, why am I contemplating duvets when I have much more pressing things to think about?

Where's my dressing gown? I'm sure it's in here somewhere. Where else would it be?

Sod it. I'll just get dressed. In fact, I shall wear my undercover agent outfit. Dark clothing, beanie and running shoes, just in case I decide to go and have another look at tarpaulin house.

But first, I shall have a coffee.

Jeez, why is everything so loud in the night?

The sound of the water running into the kettle, the flicking of the switch, the gradual build-up of steam, all of them seem magnified.

I barely notice these things during the day. I must admit though, I do like the silence of the night. There's something special about being up and about when everyone else is asleep. The world feels fresher somehow, as if it hasn't been worn out by sustaining the inhabitants for another day, and is bracing itself for the next onslaught.

Sometimes, Gemma, your thoughts are so weird.

What was that song, I used to sing it all the time? Oh, I know, *'Sometimes I get so weird, I even freak myself out, I laugh myself to sleep, it's my lullaby.'*

'Anything but Ordinary', that was it. I used to think it was as if Avril had got inside my brain and dragged the lyrics out.

Jeez, this coffee's hot, now I've burnt my lip. Thing is, should I go and investigate or should I be true to my promise to Dan and wait for his return?

What would Avril say?

I know, *'To walk within the lines, would make my life so boring, I want to know that I have been to the extreme...'*

There we go, Avril has spoken, I can't sit back and wait until Dan's home I need to grab life now and go to the extreme, which in this case means a night-time walk, to an unknown house, to observe the goings-on.

OK, I'm not really living my life through the lyrics of a

song, but I know there is no chance of sleep tonight if I don't go and have just a tiny peek at the house. Just to see if everything is all right.

My phone is fully charged, as most unusually for me, I plugged it in last night before I went to bed, with the hopeless idea that I might sleep until morning.

As if, still, it has done me a favour as I don't want to be caught out again with the flat battery scenario.

So, off we go, did I lock the door?

No, I simply refuse to go back and double-check. Of course I did, I always do, and quite frankly if anyone did break in, the place is such a mess they'd probably think I had already been done over and tidy up a bit for me before they left.

Does this actually count as my walk? I guess so, technically it's after midnight, in fact, it's 3 am, so either I get my walk done *much* earlier than normal, which would freak the DIY builders out if they don't see me as usual, or I get to have another walk later if I'm still alive.

Don't be ridiculous, Gemma, of course you'll be alive, this is probably some wild goose chase and you'll be laughing about it with Dan when he gets back in a few days. Or, he might be angry, he did say he didn't want you going anywhere near there on your own.

Oh, he'll get over it. It's not as if he owns me, I have a right to do as I please. So there, blowing a raspberry right at you, Dan.

Poor Dan, he's only trying to look after me. But I don't want to be some pathetic damsel in distress; I want to be able to deal with life myself. So, here I am, being all grown up and making the decision to carry on to the tarpaulin house even though it's bloody freezing.

It's strange how everywhere looks slightly different at

night. I didn't realise there were quite so many trees around this part of the walk. Mind you, these houses are particularly impressive, each one different and set back from the road. I'd love to live in a house with a long, winding driveway, but unless I pull my finger out and get some work that is highly unlikely. Although there is Dan, he's got a good job.

Gemma, stop being such an idiot, you just told yourself you wanted to be in control of your life and in the very next breath you're telling yourself that someone else will be able to provide for you.

Anyway, stop this internal debate, as the important stuff is about to happen. Here we are, the next house along is tarpaulin house and I need to concentrate.

I doubt very much if anyone is awake at this ungodly time, only fools like me and possibly a few burglars. Not that I have seen anyone, which I suppose is a small comfort, I don't really want to bump into a modern-day Fagin and his band of thieves, or any other mobsters for that matter.

Right, keep your wits about you, Gemma; you are at the entrance to the driveway.

No lights on but that's not really a surprise, it's the middle of the night. But it does give me extra cover to get to the house without being spotted. Thankfully there isn't much moonlight tonight; it's too cloudy, which really works in my favour.

It looks like all the curtains upstairs are shut, apart from the tarpaulin room, of course, which seems plunged in darkness with no sign of any movement or small people waving frantically at me. So all is good so far; with nothing much to see.

Shit, this gravel makes a right racket when you walk on it. I seem to remember seeing it on some documentary once that it's a good idea to have prickly bushes around your house, and gravel wherever possible, to let you know if anyone is about.

Seems like the owner of this house was watching the same programme. I'm going as slowly and gingerly as I possibly can and it's still crunching. But I've made it as far as the wall without mishap so I think I'll just go around the back, a quick look in the conservatory and them I'm off.

It's a bit odd that they have left a lamp on. Why would you do that if you'd all gone to bed? There are no lights on in any of the other rooms.

Oh, my God. Maybe it's because someone is up and now I'm stuck at the back of the house surrounded by crunching gravel, with no escape route.

Gemma strikes again and puts herself in danger for no reason whatsoever.

Dare I move and get out of here before I see someone or do I stay glued to the spot for the rest of the night?

Just back up very slowly, Gemma, and everything will be fine. Slowly does it.

Why is there still the sound of gravel grating when I'm barely moving?

Someone must be here.

But where? I can't see a thing.

What's that smell, it's sort of sweet but a bit chemically?

'Who's that? You're hurting me and what are you holding over my face?'

'Chloroform. Relax.'

'Shi....

DAY TWENTY-TWO. MORNING.

Ouch, my head hurts. It's throbbing like mad. Plus there's a scab above my eye so I must have hit it on something. Actually, where the hell am I?

Oh God, it's all coming back to me.

I was at the back of the tarpaulin house when I heard someone come up behind me. They smothered me with something, I don't know what it was but it was a cloth with a chemical smell.

Hang on, someone said, chloroform.

I'm sure they did. Or am I imagining it?

Oh, I don't know what's happening, I really don't.

It looks like the sun is coming up so it must be nearly morning but my phone's not in my pocket so I can't check.

Where the hell has it gone?

OK, Gemma, relax. Relax.

I'm pretty sure someone said that too.

Why would they want me unconscious and why would they tell me to relax?

This is most odd.

I have a horrible feeling that instead of proving to the

world that I can make logical and grown-up decisions that I have got myself captured by a serial killer.

Now there's a phrase I never thought I'd use. Snort.

Stop it, Gemma, it's not funny, this is in fact terribly serious.

What am I going to do?

OK, stop panicking and think.

Looking at the facts so far I strongly suspect that I have been captured. As to who has done it and why, well, I have no idea. I mean even if they did find me trespassing it isn't exactly normal behaviour to knock a person out and dump them in a room.

Actually, I'm really cold and it feels quite damp down here. I don't think I'm in the tarpaulin room as that was upstairs with a big window.

It's really gloomy here and that's allowing for the watery sun that seems to be rather half-heartedly trying to get up.

If I stand up and feel my way around it might give me a few clues.

Ugh, the walls feel damp and clammy, there's certainly no sign of the expensive wallpaper and plush furniture of the house. Maybe this is an outbuilding?

No, I don't recall seeing any outbuildings on either of the two occasions I have ventured here in the past. So, in that case, I'm guessing it's a cellar. The house is certainly old enough to have one and it feels cold and damp in here, which fits in.

Maybe if I can find something to stand on I will be able to see through the little window up there.

OK, this looks promising; it's a small crate. It's very light and feels like one of those crates milkmen used to use to carry their bottles around.

In fact, I think that's exactly what it is.

Well done, Gemma.

OK, if I put it down here below the window I might just be able to reach it.

Umm, just about and if I stand on tiptoes I can make out the lawn in front of me but quite frankly that could be any lawn. Grass is grass after all.

I need to see something that identifies the house. I have no idea how long I was out. I could have been quickly thrown in their cellar or even transported miles away, a different country even. Oh my God, this is getting worse and worse. What if I can't understand a word they say? Even if I escape I might not be able to communicate with anyone and explain I need help.

Hang on, Gemma; the symptoms of distress are pretty universal.

If I manage to get myself out of here and find some trust-worthy people I'm sure I will be able to make them understand.

Actually though, if I stand as far to the right as I can on this crate and stretch right up I can just about make out the edge of a conservatory. Could it be *the* conservatory?

I'm sort of guessing but my gut feeling is that it *is* the one I was snooping around last night.

Well, that makes me feel slightly better. It might still be the home of a serial killer but at least it's in the UK and, if so, *when* I escape, I'll know how to get home and call the police.

Jeez, my calves are aching from stretching up, I'll rest them a bit and see what else is in this dismal room.

A big fat nothing is the answer to that. There is simply nothing else in here. How can anyone have a cellar and not cram it full of bicycles, scooters, gardening tools, stuff like that? Surely no one has a cellar this clean? Well actually, Gemma, they do, because you are standing right in the middle of one at the moment. So get used to the idea that not everyone is as untidy as you are.

So, it seems that the only exits out of this place are the door and the window. I'm guessing the door is locked but actually I might just check it. They could be the most incompetent hostage takers in the world and have forgotten to lock the door.

Sadly, they appear to be highly competent as the door is well and truly locked.

Therefore, barring any secret doors that I have yet to discover, the only other way out is the window. Quite frankly I'm not sure I could even squeeze through there even if I did manage to haul myself up to it. It's tiny, but I suppose it could be worth a try. What other options do I have?

OK, let's pull the crate as near as possible and see if I can get a better grip of the window frame.

Jeez, it's really dirty and grimy; I'm getting filthy here.

Don't suppose that actually matters, does it, Gemma, if they are going to kill you anyway then they surely won't be too bothered about how well manicured your hands are.

If I sort of jump and pull at the same time I can at least get a better view of the window. Unfortunately, this is not very reassuring, as it seems that there's some rather ornate grate over it, they really wanted to secure this place.

However, a small glimmer of hope is that the grate might actually help me. If I can just manage to get high enough up to reach around the bars, I should get a much better grip.

Bloody hell, why did I never learn how to climb? You see these people on TV scaling walls and cliffs as if they are taking a stroll in the park. All I need is a couple of extra inches to reach the damn bars and I can't seem to manage it.

OK, take stock, Gemma, that isn't a lost cause, maybe you

just need to rest a minute and then try again. It's not worth using all your energy up until you really understand the situation you are in.

Having said that, I don't want to understand it I just want to go home.

Oh don't start crying, you stupid woman, it really won't help and you may as well use the time a bit more constructively.

Oh shit, it sounds like someone is coming.

What do I do?

Play dead, or unconscious in this case, it might buy you a bit more time.

Ugh, that means lying on this horrible floor.

Oh, just do it, you stupid cow, right, lie perfectly still and pretend you are asleep on a beautiful beach in the Caribbean somewhere. There is nothing to worry about, the sun is shining, the birds are singing, you have a delightful cocktail next to you waiting to be consumed.

That's all very well but the reality is that someone is turning the key and about to come in.

Sleep. Sleep. Sleep. Pretend like you have never pretended before.

'She's still out.'

'Good, the longer the better as far as I'm concerned.'

'I'll leave her a bottle of water in case she wakes soon, we'll have to deal with her later.'

'Stupid bitch, she should have kept her nose out of it. The boss will be back later, we'll see what he wants to do.'

'Leave her to rot for now. She's going nowhere.'

'Come on, we've more important things to do than babysit her.'

Oh my God, it worked. I should be up for an Oscar for that

superb bit of acting. But it does seem that my situation is rather dire.

Who were they?

I don't think I've ever seen or heard them before. I don't know where they are from but it certainly isn't the UK. They both had heavy accents, but more importantly, they didn't seem at all pleased to see me.

Right, Gemma, I think you are perfectly entitled to have a good old cry now.

That's it. Let it all out.

DAY TWENTY-TWO. AFTERNOON.

I've been here for hours and I have got absolutely nowhere. I have managed to grab hold of the bars a few times, and they do seem to move a little when I pull on them, but I just can't get myself high enough up to try and squeeze through.

This is so frustrating. I tried not to drink any of the water, as I wanted to pretend I'd remained asleep if they came back. But then I realised that they would know the effects of the chloroform would have worn off hours ago.

Plus I was so thirsty and felt it was better to hydrate myself so I could think clearly. Not that it has enabled me to come up with a plan, but it did pass a few minutes and at least I'm not thirsty anymore.

But that was hours ago and now, the natural sequence of events means that I am desperate to go to the toilet.

Do I knock on the door and politely ask to be taken to the ladies room?

That really isn't going to happen. I haven't even dared banging on the door or shouting out of the window as yet. Every so often I see pairs of feet go past the window, it's as if they are patrolling the area.

Well, whatever it is that they are up to, they certainly don't want people knowing about it, so it's highly unlikely they will let me out for a wee.

There's nothing for it, I'm going to have to go in the corner of the cellar. Just try and pretend I am out on some wonderful walk, in the middle of a beautiful forest and I have to squat down behind a tree. See, nothing could be easier. The birds are singing and the river is flowing right next to me. There we go.

It's amazing what you can do when you are absolutely desperate.

Oh, that does feel better.

At least if they come back now I will be able to concentrate on what they are saying rather than my urgent need for the toilet.

But now my mind isn't preoccupied with my bladder I feel incredibly hungry. It must be hours since I ate anything. I've certainly missed breakfast and, judging by the sun, I've missed lunch too. It's probably late afternoon I should imagine.

Oh just think, afternoon tea with scones and jam and a smidgen of cream. Wouldn't that be wonderful! What I would give to see Teapot lady right now and invite myself in to do her crossword in the comfort of her lounge.

Will I ever see her again?

Will I ever see anyone again?

I can't stand it any longer. Sod the consequences I'm going to start yelling.

'HELP. HELP ME, SOMEONE.'

No response.

I'll stand on my old friend the crate and try directing my yell out towards the road. Surely someone will be around.

'HELP. PLEASE HELP. I'M TRAPPED. IN FACT I'M A HOSTAGE.'

'Will you shut up or you'll be sorry.'

'No, I won't, please don't go, who are you? Just let me out and I won't say a thing to anyone. I just want to go home.'

'Well that isn't going to happen is it, you should have thought of that before you came here.'

'Can you at least bend down, so I can see whom it is I'm talking to? All I can see from here are a pair of boots.'

'Tough, I've work to do. Now keep quiet or we'll have to shut you up properly.'

'Oh. OK. I guess I could, and probably should, I'm sorry to increase your workload but I really need to get out of here.'

Here goes.

'HELP ME. I'M IN THE CELLAR. THEY ARE GOING TO HURT ME. GET THE POLICE NOW.'

'It's no use screaming, there's nobody about, but you wouldn't listen would you. I'm coming down.'

Oh no. Why did I do that? Now I'm for it.

For goodness sake, Gemma, think, quickly, what can you do?

Well, I could try and make a break for it when he opens the door. Not the most imaginative of plans but it's all I have in the time allowed.

I can hear him coming. Blimey, he's rather heavy footed and there seem to be quite a lot of stairs to get down here.

Shit, the key's in the lock.

Get ready, Gemma, just run as the door opens.

'You're not very good at this, are you? Did you really think I would open the door and just let you walk out of here? Stop being a pain and sit down.'

How did he manage to hold me back at the same time as

getting into the room? Because he's a vast, lumbering beast, that's how. There's no way I could get past him, he's huge.

'As you won't keep quiet I'll have to tape your mouth shut. It's your own fault, I was happy to leave you just locked up but you wouldn't play nicely would you. So here, keep still and I'd better tie your hands behind your back for good measure.'

Play. Who's bloody playing you giant oaf? Ouch, that really hurts and I can barely breathe. Jesus, he means business.

Me and my big mouth.

'If I were you I'd sit in the corner, really quiet, and hope we all forget about you.'

All. Who are *all* these people? How many of them are there?

At least he has gone and I know for sure that he locked the door. The sound of that key turning the lock had been seared into my brain.

Now what?

Not only am I locked in a cellar but I've also been bound and gagged.

So far you are not doing very well are you, Gemma?

Oh, where's Dan when I need him? I should have listened to him. Why did I go behind his back and come to this awful house, especially when he's away?

He won't even realise I'm missing. I guess he would expect to talk on the phone but he'll just think my battery is flat or something. It's not as if that hasn't happened before. He's actually quite amused at how disorganised I am. But surely he'll start getting worried eventually. I'm not actually sure when he was due to come back from London. He said a couple of days.

A COUPLE OF DAYS! I can't stand a couple more

minutes of this, never mind a couple of days. And will he even think to come here to look for me?

I doubt it. Why should he? He just thinks it's one of my crazy ideas and who could blame him really?

What about the others? The DIY builders for example; surely they will miss me. Well, yes, they will but they are hardly likely to immediately think I've been kidnapped, are they?

Most normal people don't think like you, Gemma. They will probably assume you have a cold or have gone out with friends or simply can't be bothered to take your walk.

Not, Gemma hasn't been around today she must be in danger, being held hostage somewhere and most likely in the hands of a serial killer.

No. It isn't going to happen. I need to sort this out myself.

Not that I have been hugely successful so far. All I have managed to do is get myself tied up to add to my misery.

Misery. Now there's another great film, mind you, it's probably best not to think about 'the' leg scene, it's all a little too close for comfort. This is really not the time to be reminiscing about that, in fact, I feel quite sick at the thought of it.

My wrists really hurt too. The more I wriggle the tighter it gets. This is horrendous. What can I do?

I could try again to get up to the window. But that's hardly likely now, is it? I couldn't reach with my hands-free, never mind with them tied behind my back.

God, you are so pathetic, Gemma.

I wonder if there are any secret doors in this room? That would be perfect, you know, the sort of film where the heroine stumbles across a lever, hidden behind a bookcase or something, and the whole thing swivels around to reveal a secret staircase. Inevitably it leads to freedom and she is reunited with her tearful family.

OK, so that obviously isn't one of the most exciting plots ever but surely there must be something here.

Nope. I'm painstakingly going around the whole room, kicking and head-butting every brick within reach, trying to find some solution to this dilemma, but nothing gives. Literally, nothing gives. These walls were made to last and seem extremely well cemented in place.

So much for that theory.

I think I'll have to be more proactive than hoping that some distant, long gone builder foresaw a hostage situation centuries later and provided an escape route, just in case.

Maybe I can dig my own tunnel. That has definitely been done before. I mean look at Steve McQueen. If only I had a baseball glove and ball, I could sit sullenly in the corner and pretend I'm in 'the cooler'. Except I couldn't throw the ball as my hands are bound behind my bloody back.

Apart from that, I don't have to pretend. I am in the cooler. It's cold, damp, solitary and I am captive. Which brings me right back to square one.

So get on your knees and start digging.

It's not easy to even get in position like this and scratching at the floor is only tightening the binding even further.

The floor is so solid; my hands aren't making even a tiny dent in it as I claw away. However, I have broken several nails by the feel of things, which is unfortunate but hardly my main concern at the moment.

Maybe if I snap a bit off the crate and use it as a tiny spade, God this is tough, I'll try stamping on it.

Ouch, I've got a piece, but also managed to cut my leg in the process.

Shit, Gemma, you're such a clumsy oaf.

I've not even got anything to clean it up a bit. I suppose I'll just have to use the edge of my t-shirt, although this does require me to be something of a contortionist.

But I've managed to wipe the cut a bit; it doesn't seem to be too bad really, although now my t-shirt is even more of a mess. Shame really as it's my favourite one and there's no way you can get dried blood off a white shirt.

Whatever. It hardly matters now, does it? If I ever get out of here I can treat myself to a whole wardrobe full of t-shirts if I want. If I don't get out, well, I'm not going to think about that. The prospect of seeing out my days in this place is just too grim to consider.

Oh, God. Someone's coming again. I can hear him. I think it's the same man judging by the footfall.

You'd think they'd put some oil in that lock, it makes such a racket.

'Here. Eat this.'

'Mmmm mmmm mm.'

'Keep still, I'll pull the tape off.'

'Ouch, that really hurt! You could have done it gently.'

'Stop moaning and eat.'

'OK, thanks. I was rather hungry. What is it?'

'Who cares? You're lucky to get anything. Here's some more water too. I'll leave the tape off while you eat but one sound from you and it'll be back on. Turn around, I'll release your hands, but same goes, any trouble and it will be back on.'

'OK, I'll be quiet as a mouse. Honestly.'

'Quiet as a mouse? You English are weird. I'll be back soon.'

So, a cheese sandwich, I was hoping for something a little more exciting, especially if this is going to be my last meal. Even prisoners on death row get to choose what they want to eat before their execution. There isn't even any margarine or mayonnaise on it.

This is scandalous.

Snort.

Gemma, you really are a one. Here you are, captive with nothing but a dried out cheese sandwich to eat, and you're more concerned about the lack of mayonnaise than the fact that it really might be your last meal.

Oh well, may as well eat it. A girl has to keep her strength up.

I refuse to admit that this is the end. Something will happen. An opportunity will arise and I can make my escape or beg for forgiveness or something.

At least that has taken the edge off my hunger. I could certainly do with a nice mug of hot coffee and a chocolate bar but I guess that's not an option.

Shouting is my best chance. It might just be that a few people are walking home from work and may hear me. It's worth a try.

'HEY, HELP ME. PLEASE, SOMEONE, HELP ME. I'M OVER HERE, IN THE CELLAR.'

Nothing.

Nothing that is except Igor is on his way back.

Here he is.

'I did warn you. Why did you shout again?'

'Why do you think, you idiot? Because I want to get out of here, please, just let me go.'

'Nope. And for your pains, the tape goes back on and the hands are re-tied. Maybe eventually you'll get the message.'

'Umm mmm mmm.'

'Shut up, no one can hear your pathetic mumbling.'

Off he goes.

I'm back in solitary and in exactly the same predicament.

Brilliant job, Gemma.

I may as well lie down for a bit.

There's no one about, I'm locked in, my hands are tied and I can't shout.

This is a hopeless situation.

DAY TWENTY-TWO. NIGHT.

I must have fallen asleep, it's pitch black out there and I'm freezing. Ouch, my whole body aches and my wrists are so sore.

I really should have kept quiet; at least I'd be marginally more comfortable now.

I'll have to pace about to try and warm up and get the blood circulating again.

One. Two. Three. Four. Five. Length.

One. Two. Three. Width.

Well, that didn't take long.

I suppose it's better than nothing though and I've always found I think clearer when I'm on the move. I've proved that with my walks. It's amazing how much I've sorted out in my mind by simply walking every day.

Not that this miserable distance is anything to shout about, and not that shouting is an option.

Oh, Gemma, you really did it this time.

I can hear a car.

Quick, get on the crate and try and peep out to see what's happening.

I can barely see anything and it's making my legs ache again.

It looks like the posh car I saw here before. Damn, I can't see who is getting out but two doors have slammed shut so I'm guessing there are at least two of them, maybe more.

Judging by the noise the gravel is making I would say two, umm, possibly three. They're talking but it's so quiet I can't make anything out and it sounds like they have gone in the house now. That was probably the front door closing.

How frustrating, so near to seeing the man with the car and yet so very far.

It's probably a good thing actually. I really don't want to see, hear, or feel what he has in store for me.

But here's a thought. Don't serial killers work alone?

Surely there isn't a serial killer society where they all get together and chat about their latest conquest? Or a forum they can join to meet up with like-minded murderers and plot a joint venture? No, I've always thought they were more isolated, psychopathic misfits. But what exactly does an isolated, psychopathic misfit look like?

Fact is, that they probably look pretty normal. It isn't as if they will have 'murderer' tattooed on their foreheads, is it?

But the thing is, if the big cheese is a serial killer then why are all these other goons hanging around?

Something in my theory isn't adding up.

Could it be that I have got the whole thing wrong?

Well yes, I could have.

But that doesn't explain the fact that I am in a cellar, bound and gagged. Whilst the top man may not be a serial killer he certainly isn't the gentle, sociable sort.

In some ways, I do feel a little better about it all.

I mean if he isn't a serial killer then my chances of survival must have gone up slightly.

I don't think I'd like to work out the odds though, but that would certainly make an interesting, and rather unlikely, phone call to Ladbrokes.

'Oh hello, I'd like to know the odds on a young woman surviving if she's bound and gagged in the cellar of a serial killer, compared to the cellar of just a simple sociopath?'

'OK dear, let me just take a few details.'

If only.

Just imagine how easy all this would be if I only had my phone. I could simply call the police; tell them exactly where I am, and sit back waiting to hear the sirens getting nearer and nearer.

Or would I call Dan?

No, I wouldn't want to put him in danger, and anyway, it would take him hours to get here from London. No, it would have to be the police.

I'd probably tell them to send an armed response unit, as who knows what weapons these guys have. I'm pretty sure they must be armed to the teeth. I mean men like this don't just walk about with a lace-trimmed handkerchief in their pocket do they?

I would feel dreadful if any policemen were hurt whilst trying to save me. But would the police even believe me? Surely it's not every day they get a call from a distant, disembodied voice? Snort. Maybe disembodied isn't a phrase I should use whilst I'm still unsure if my head will remain on my shoulders for any length of time. But anyway, they get a call from me, unable to talk because of the tape.

Oh.

There goes that dream. If I can't talk, how am I going to tell them where I am?

Surely they can track the phone or something.

Gemma. Stop it.

You don't have a phone. Some lunatic has taken it, so all of this is pointless.

Sigh. At least it passed a few minutes. Just for a few precious moments I felt that there was something I could do.

Sometimes escaping into imagination can be really useful.

Although I think I have proved, beyond all doubt, that sometimes my imagination can lead me into serious trouble.

I CAN'T STAND FEELING SO HELPLESS. SOMEONE GET ME OUT OF HERE.

Screaming inside your head really doesn't have the same effect, or release the tension, half as much as yelling out loud would.

Now I'm getting pins and needles again. I suppose I should heave myself up and do a few turns of the prison.

Prison. That's exactly what this is, a prison. I really don't think I would cope very well being in prison for any length of time. I've only been here a while and I feel like I'm already starting to lose any sense of reality. At least if you are in prison, presumably you've done something wrong, although some might argue against that, but I don't think they'd live in conditions like this, and certainly not unsure if they were going to be around to see another day.

Oh God, the tears are coming again. I think I'm entitled to another cry, just a small blubber, I don't want to choke to death because of the tape, wouldn't that be ironic?

Get a grip, Gemma, and heave yourself up off the grimy floor. Make yourself move around, you don't want to seize up.

Ouch, it really hurts my wrists when I move, just when I think this binding can't get any tighter it does.

At least I'm on my feet now. I'll do a couple of circuits,

that shouldn't take more than a few seconds. See, back to the beginning.

I'll get on my crate and see if I can at least draw a few breaths of fresh air. If I stretch up as much as possible I can see the grass again. It looks so green and inviting. How I'd love to be running barefoot across the lawn right now.

The night air smells so refreshing, it's cold but it feels like it has woken me up a bit and cleared my head.

I wish my calves could tolerate standing at full stretch for a little longer but sadly they can't.

Shit, now I've lost my balance and it's so hard to stabilise myself with no hands. So here I am face down in the dirt.

Lovely.

I must look delightful.

Double shit, Igor's coming. Well, it sounds like him but I suppose it could be any of those lunkheads.

Maybe he'll at least help me up from the floor.

'Come on, get up.'

'Ummmm. Ummm.'

'OK, I'll take this off your mouth, just for a minute.'

'Ouch, thanks. That's so much better. Can't you leave it off?'

'No. Now get up.'

'I can't, my wrists are too sore.'

'Don't be pathetic. You don't know what pain is yet.'

Charming. That really isn't the response I was hoping for.

'Oh alright then, here, I'll pull you up.'

Excellent, the man does have a conscience after all. Or maybe I was just taking too long.

Whatever, it spared my wrists another twist of the binding.

'Come on, I'm taking you upstairs.'

'Why, who's there? Can I go now? Are they going to hurt me?'

'Shut up, so many questions and you're not really in the position to ask them are you?'

'Oh, I don't know, it's good to keep yourself informed.'

'Don't you ever stop? Look, I'm taking you up to the main house so take my advice and shut up. If you carry on like this with the boss I can't see him liking it. You've already caused us enough trouble.'

'Oh. The boss. Right. I'm not sure I'm ready for this.'

'You don't have a choice, do you? Now, drink this.'

'Why, what is it?'

'Don't worry, it's only water, but I don't want him thinking we've mistreated you.'

'I suspect the binding and tape marks may give you away, but thanks, I was pretty thirsty. Can't you leave the tape off now? Promise I won't say anything.'

'No, it goes back on. From my experience you aren't able to keep quiet and yelling at the boss will make your life much, much worse.'

'Please, I won't talk.'

'No, here, it's going back on. If he wants me to remove it when we're up there, well I will.'

'Ummm ummm mmm.'

'Stop struggling and walk. It's time.'

Oh. My, God.

He really is taking me up to the house. Suddenly I don't want to leave the cellar. It isn't that bad after all. Especially when I'm heading towards my doom.

No, Gemma, think positively. Something good might come of this. Maybe he'll be reasonable and set you free.

Yes, right. They don't seem to be a particularly reasonable bunch to me.

Negotiating all these steps isn't easy with my hands behind my back. Good job Igor is holding tightly onto me although I strongly suspect that's to stop me running off rather than to steady me.

Oh, how lovely. The moon is shining and it looks so beautiful, I wish I could stand here and watch it all night.

Ha. Like that's going to happen, Igor is already pushing me forward towards the house.

At least it's a nice place. I can see the lounge; it looks like that's where he's taking me. That was the room with the very nice settee I seem to remember. Maybe I should compliment him on his taste in soft furnishings to lighten things up a bit.

Well, I can't because I can't say a thing can I?

OK, here we go. Time to meet *the* boss.

Just a few more feet, Igor wants me to stand still; it looks like we have to knock before we go in. It's a bit like being sent to the headmaster at school. Although slightly more traumatic, but I guess that depends on who your headmaster is.

At least I haven't lost my sense of humour, yet.

'Come in.'

Shit.

'So, here's the woman causing so much trouble. What exactly are we going to do with you?'

What does he want me to do? I can't speak; I'll try looking imploringly at him.

'Good, you're scared, that always makes compliance easier.'

What does he mean? I'm trying to look belligerent. I must say I'm a bit disappointed; he's only small. I imagined him to be huge like the others.

Who else do we have here? I think I can sneak a little look around.

Well, three men. The other two look like Igor's siblings. They're huge. This situation is not really looking any better.

'Someone get Simon.'

Looks like we are being joined by another goon, Simon doesn't sound like a particularly foreign name, maybe I can work on the fact that we have nationality in common and try to get him on my side.

'Simon, evening, come in, I have a little problem here and I need your help.'

'Yes, I heard about it. Don't worry, your 'little problem' should be easy to deal with.'

WHAT. I DON'T BELIEVE IT. THIS CAN'T BE HAPPENING.

That's not Simon; it's Dan.

DAY TWENTY-THREE.

I can't stop crying, which has made my nose run, and now the tears and snot are mingling into one disgusting mess and trickling off my chin.

My face is sore from this damn tape and my wrists have started bleeding by the feel of things.

But none of this is as bad as last night.

The shock of seeing Dan almost made me faint. Luckily, Igor was still holding onto me otherwise I'd have ended up on the floor. At least he had the decency to steady me without making a big deal of it. I suppose he's used to that, it must be a pretty common occurrence in his line of work.

I tried to speak, but of course, I couldn't, and Dan just looked blankly at me as if he had never seen me before. There was no recognition on his face whatsoever.

How could he erase all those memories and treat me like that? It doesn't make any sense.

None of this makes any sense.

Then they talked about me as if I wasn't there. I must say I wish I hadn't been in the room as the way the conversation was going it didn't seem very positive.

The boss man certainly isn't happy to have me staying at his house.

Ha! That makes it sound like I'm here as a guest, of my own free will, not a hostage being held in his cellar.

Some of the time they talked openly in front of me, but mainly they took themselves off to stand next to the fire and talked in hushed tones, so I couldn't make out what was being said.

At those points, Igor and I just looked at each other. I was hoping he was beginning to feel something for me; a little pity wouldn't go amiss, but sadly there has been no sign of that.

I must have stood there for 15 minutes, just Igor and I staring blankly at each other.

Then the boss came back over and stood right in front of me. Dan joined him and stared at me with such cold eyes I couldn't believe it. I tried speaking but that came out as mere grunts, which was impossible for anyone to decipher.

I also tried to use my eyes to get some sort of recognition from Dan. After going through my entire repertoire of pleading, sad, imploring, hateful and confused looks, none of which got any sort of response from Dan, I went cross-eyed in the hopes of eliciting something from him.

Nothing. Well, not quite nothing, I swear there was the smallest smirk, for a split second, but it was so minimal I may have just been imagining it.

Dan then gestured to the boss that he wanted to talk some more and they walked off.

As there wasn't a lot else I could do I stared vacantly into the middle distance. Well not exactly the middle distance, I decided they wouldn't break my spirit and spent the time studying the various framed prints on the walls.

I must say the artwork on display was all truly fantastic,

but, put together in such a way as to remind me of the unhinged nature of my host.

I mean, who puts, 'The Arnolfini Marriage' by Jan van Eyck next to Munch's, 'The Scream'? Although the wonderful colours in Klimt's 'The Kiss' did warm me slightly, but next to Rubens 'Massacre of the Innocents', seriously?

This wasn't reassuring in the slightest.

Murder and trauma seemed far too readily reflected in his choice of art.

By the time I had identified Caravaggio's 'Beheading of Saint John the Baptist' I had decided that I couldn't take anymore and focused back on Dan.

He, however, was still completely ignoring me and talking to the boss like long lost buddies.

I couldn't hear anything but there was the occasional nodding of the head from Dan and once he shook it very vigorously. I would love to know what that was all about but, at the same time, I'm pretty terrified of actually finding out.

All the time I couldn't get the thought out of my head that this was Dan.

What on earth was he doing and why do they think he's called Simon?

Maybe I'm the one who has it all wrong. Maybe he is called Simon and he has been lying to me all along. I mean I was wrong about the serial killer...I think, so I could have got it all wrong about Dan.

After all, my previous choice of male companion wasn't too successful. But although Luke was a complete bastard he wasn't mixed up in hostage taking and God knows what else.

These thoughts kept swirling around my mind all the

while I was waiting for the boss to finish his discussion and I'm still thinking about it now.

Eventually, they seemed to tire of the apparent skulduggery that was going on between them and they came to face me once again.

Igor took a polite step backwards, presumably to give them some space, but, as he had still been supporting me, I lost my balance and slipped very ungraciously to the floor.

Dan just stared at me and didn't move.

The boss looked irritated and turned to Dan and said, 'Are you sure, look at her?'

My heart was in my mouth. What was Dan sure about that the boss wasn't?

Dan replied, 'Yes, it's too risky, put her back in the cellar.'

PUT ME BACK IN THE CELLAR.

That's what he said, calm as anything, as if he was suggesting taking me out to the cinema to watch the latest blockbuster or a restaurant for a delightful meal and a bottle of the finest house wine.

And that was it.

No further discussion and certainly no explanation to me.

The boss nodded at Igor, he stepped forward and pulled me up from the floor before frogmarching me out of the lounge and back outside.

Just as we were leaving the room Dan shouted, 'And leave the tape on, she'll only scream the place down if we take it off.'

I couldn't believe it. Dan, who only a few hours' earlier I had been imagining would rescue me from this nightmare, was now taking control of it and demanding I remain bound and gagged.

Igor didn't pause to let me enjoy the cool night air or a

glimpse of the stunning moon, but walked me unceremoniously down the steps and slung me through the cellar door, before stepping back and securely locking it.

As I slumped back on the damp, cold floor I started crying and basically managed to keep it going until dawn.

Even as the watery sun tried to brighten the day a little I was still crying, and felt frightened and certainly betrayed.

But that was hours ago and now I'm starving.

Nobody has been to see me or even offered me a drink. I'm cold, hungry and tired.

But the more I think about it at least I'm alive.

Before I went up to the big house I was certain that would be it, end of Gemma.

Now I'm not so sure.

I mean, if they wanted me out of the way surely they would have done it by now?

I still have no idea what these people are up to or how they think keeping me in a cellar will help?

Maybe it's better not to know. Maybe they are only keeping me here for the time being and have other plans for me?

But what, whatever they are up too is surely illegal otherwise why all the secrecy? Which brings me right back around to why are they keeping me alive?

I can't stand it any longer; I need something to drink at the very least.

Maybe if I keep kicking the door Igor will take pity on me and come and see what I want.

Now I have a sore foot to go with all my other problems but at least someone is coming.

'Stand back or I won't come in.'

'Umm, mmmmm.'

Should I tell Igor that I know Simon, but as Dan, and that he is, or rather, very much *was*, my boyfriend?

No. I don't think I will, I don't understand what is going on or who I can trust, I think I'll keep quiet and hopefully get the chance to talk to Dan/Simon soon.

Right after I've poked him in the eyes; and kicked him in the testicles.

'Here, let me take this off so you can eat.'

'Bloody hell, I told you to do it gently last time, that was even worse.'

'Stop complaining or I'll put it back on and you'll only be able to smell this lovely pasta I have brought you.'

'Pasta, you brought me pasta?'

'Yes, we all had a take away this evening and Simon said to order something for you, in fact, he suggested pasta but also a tiramisu.'

'Really, that's my favourite?'

'Your lucky day then isn't it. Now eat up, here's some water to go with it, I'll be back in 5 minutes. The tape goes back on whether you've finished or not.'

'OK, OK, go and let me eat. This smells fantastic. Oh, blimey, it's the best meal I have *ever* eaten.'

Oh, he's gone. Still, at least I can enjoy it in peace without his gormless face staring at me.

Umm, creamy pasta, how delightful, but as soon as I've shovelled that down I'm diving straight into the tiramisu.

Why would Dan suggest they order me a dessert and especially Tiramisu? He knows it's my favourite.

Is he trying to tell me something? Yes, probably that this is your last meal so you may as well have something I know you like.

What a bastard.

But, whatever happens next I may as well enjoy this. How could I not? It's fantastic.

Why does it seem so weird that a bunch of criminals have ordered in a takeaway?

It seems so odd. Surely they should be keeping a low profile, not slinking off to the shops and buying loads of meals.

Oh, I can't be bothered to think about it anymore. I'm not getting any answers but I am starting to feel a little more human now I have eaten. Mum always said I got grumpy when I was hungry and I think she's right. But there isn't much use getting grumpy when there's no one around to listen to you.

I've been putting all my energy into staying alive and not freezing to death.

Oh shit. Surely that wasn't 5 minutes, I still have half my tiramisu left and I can hear bloody Igor coming.

Oh, wait, someone is talking to him. It sounds like Dan, or whoever he is.

'Give this to the girl. We can't have her dying on us just yet.'

'Yes, anything else? Like a book or something to keep her busy?'

'She's not on holiday, are you going soft on me?'

'No, no Sir. I, I'll just give her the blanket.'

'Do that, then get back out here, the shipment will be arriving soon.'

'OK.'

What shipment? And why can't I have a book Dan you miserable sod? Igor's only trying to help; just you wait, I'll, I'll, well, I don't know what I'll do but you can rest assured it will be unpleasant. I can't believe you, Dan.

What a complete shit.

Here comes Igor.

'Thanks for trying.'

'You heard? You were not meant to hear.'

'Well I did and I thought you were trying to be very kind. It's a shame Da...this Simon bloke isn't as nice as you.'

'Take my advice, don't let him know you heard him. He's a very dangerous man and you don't want to upset him.'

'Then why did he speak right outside this room? He might be dangerous but he's not very bright is he?'

'Shhh, he may hear you; I don't know where he went. Look, I must put the tape back on. We are very busy now.'

'Please don't, my mouth is so sore.'

'I must. But hopefully, it won't be for long.'

'Oh yes, the shipment. I guess that's what you are all waiting for?'

'You must forget you heard that, seriously, they will kill you if they know you heard. Now, sorry, but keep still, I'll try not to make it too tight.'

I guess he's trying to be nice but there's a limit to what he can do given the circumstances.

If I ever get out of here I will put a good word in for him to the judge, unlike Dan, who I'll suggest they chuck into prison and throw away the bloody key.

DAY TWENTY-FOUR. DAY.

Well, I didn't get much sleep last night and it wasn't due to the lack of a bed, although that was obviously a contributing factor.

I mean, I haven't slept straight onto the floor since, well, ever actually. Even when I was growing up and friends came to stay, a camping mattress or at least a pile of old blankets and duvets would appear to make our guests comfortable. Thinking about it though, not much sleep happened on those occasions either but it wasn't because we were uncomfortable, more because we were so excited. Eventually, we would start telling each other ghost stories until we were too scared to sleep, but would finally drop off, in complete exhaustion, just before dawn. Consequently, we were grumpy all the next day but that's part of growing up, isn't it?

They could do with a nice inflatable double mattress down here. Actually, it wouldn't fit in this miserable place, unless it was a single one. Which is a bit like me, once again.

Anyway, the fact remains that I barely had any sleep.

I did nod off for a while after the lovely pasta and the delicious tiramisu, I was so pleased to be feeling full rather than that horrible, grumbling, emptiness, that I just drifted off, right there on the floor of the cellar.

But my beauty sleep had hardly kicked in before I was woken up by the sound of a lorry arriving. The gravel around the house certainly works as a way to alert home-owners of an intruder. Although in this case, I suspected the intruder was expected.

I jumped up onto my crate to try and get a look at what was going on.

It turned out it wasn't a lorry but a large van. It was the sort of thing you see driving around towns all the time, often with a name on the side. My dad has often said to me, usually after some disaster with a conman builder, 'Don't employ a workman if his name's on the side of his van. If he's any good then he'll be kept busy by word of mouth.'

That could well be true, and if ever I am free from this place and need any work doing I shall retest Dad's theory, but in this case, there was no name on the van, and I strongly suspect the owner was far from reliable. Unless you're of a criminal bent, in which case he could well be very accommodating.

I could hear voices as the boss and his henchmen spoke with the driver, although I was too far away to make out what they were saying. There seemed to be a lot of gesturing and smiling going on though, and a certain amount of back-slapping.

It seemed to me that the boss was very pleased to see the man and his van.

It was still dark and the moon was high, so I could see pretty well considering it was the middle of the night.

Eventually, the driver unlocked the sliding door on the side of the van and everyone took a step back.

After a few seconds, I found out why. There was an

horrific smell coming from the van. It was like a drain had been blocked for weeks and the decaying food and other unmentionable matter had been seeping through the ground.

Igor and one of the other big guys peered into the van whilst covering their mouths and noses with towels.

'Move it,' was all I heard and then gradually lots of pairs of feet started appearing.

It was so frustrating as I couldn't see the bodies that were attached to them but they appeared to be of all sizes.

I tried to keep count but it was difficult as some of them seemed to be having trouble standing. But at a guess, there were probably six or seven males, the same of female-sized feet and then maybe three or four much smaller ones that could well have been children.

What on earth were all these people doing stuffed in a van?

The smell was appalling and seemed to get stronger with every person who spilled out.

Igor then reappeared with a hosepipe and I heard him instruct the unfortunate people to strip off. Whilst I still couldn't see much it sounded like he was hosing them down.

Another man came out of the house carrying a large bag which he flung on the floor and asked the people to find clothes that fit them.

Each one was then given a bottle of water and the lines of ankles and feet were led away.

From what I knew about the layout of the house they seemed to be going around to the side, where there was another entrance.

After they had all gone Igor hosed out the van and gradually the awful smell receded.

I got down from my crate at this point, as there wasn't really very much to see.

That was all some hours ago, as the sun has since risen and is now high in the sky.

I haven't heard anything from the people since then, and have no idea where they are or what they are doing.

Once again I'm hungry, but after seeing this miserable sight, under cover of darkness, I doubt I could eat anything.

I've spent all this time thinking about them all, and wondering what they are doing here.

It certainly looked like they didn't have much choice in the matter.

I am now very anxious to know where they are. Could they be in the tarpaulin room? After all, that's in the main part of the house and I would imagine the side door would give them access to the upstairs. I keep thinking back over my various walks and the odd occasions when I felt sure that I had seen someone at the window.

I'd even mentioned it to Dan but he'd briskly brushed off my concerns. Looking back at it now I can understand why. He certainly didn't want me nosing about when he was involved in whatever criminality is going on here.

I strongly suspect that these people have been brought in from abroad. God knows where, it's hard to tell from ankles and feet. But the shuffling gaits and stiff movements make me think that they have been confined in that van for some considerable length of time.

Could it be that that Dan, Igor, the boss and all the others are involved in some sort of people trafficking?

What exactly does that mean? I vaguely remember watching a programme about it during my, 'can't move from the settee phase', and it was very moving and extremely shocking. But surely this sort of thing doesn't go on around here?

It's the sleepy suburb of a nondescript town for god's sake. Nothing ever happens here.

But then I suppose that makes it the perfect location. Who in their right mind would suspect this smart, expensive home of being involved in people trafficking?

Obviously, I'm *not* in my right mind, as I knew something odd was going on here.

I don't know if that's a good thing or a bad thing but I do know that my hunch has got me into serious trouble.

These men really don't care about people. I mean *really* don't care. If they can treat them like cattle, crammed into the back of that van, then they are capable of anything.

You've really blown it this time, Gemma.

The more I think about it the more I realise that I am probably right. The serial killer theory has been blown away by the facts in front of my eyes.

OK, I admit, I'm relieved I don't think I'm dealing with a mass murderer anymore, but is this any better?

Surely they will realise I've seen too much and they can't possibly let me go now.

There has been very little movement outside all day but I have heard mobile phones ringing constantly, they are always answered within two rings, but it seems to have been relentless.

What are they doing? Who is making and receiving all these calls?

My guess is that the first phase of their plan has been completed, they have the people here but they need to move them on as quickly as possible.

But where, where do you send a group of people and why would you?

Money must be involved and you can be sure these poor unfortunates don't see any of it.

Oh Dan, what have you got yourself into?

I refuse to feel sorry for him, he has proved to be a monster, way worse than anything I could have imagined, but he may also be the only way I can get out of this mess.

Somehow I need to break through his ice-cold exterior and remind him of the fun we have had over the last few weeks.

But that seems hopeless. I've only seen him a couple of times and the boss has always been around. He's hardly going to spring me in front of the big cheese, is he?

My guess is that if he were going to do that it would have happened by now. The longer I'm here the more I see, and presumably, that makes the outcome for me increasingly dodgy.

I either need to contrive some reason to be alone with Dan, or I have to win over Igor, he has seemed a little more caring in the last few hours. Maybe he does have a conscience after all.

Shit, I can hear voices again. I'll get back on my bloody crate and see what's going on.

This takes so much effort, my poor wrists have gone past feeling sore and now my whole arms are just numb. But heaving myself up from the floor and trying to balance on this crate always set it off again.

Still, there's nothing much else to do, Gemma, so quit complaining and hoick your silly arse up and try to work out what's happening now.

I know those ankles, that's Dan and it looks like he might be talking to the boss. This is probably not good. If they are out and about then something must be happening.

Now Igor's standing in front of the grill so I can't see anything but his nylon socks.

Nylon socks? Who wears nylon socks these days? I really need to tell Igor that he needs to get cotton socks before his feet start rotting.

Focus, Gemma, Igor's socks really aren't the issue here.

Oh, here comes Dan, walking this way. Should I try and attract his attention?

No, the boss is over there, Igor's in the way, and Dan knows I'm down here anyway.

I'll just listen and see if I can glean anything of interest.

Please, just a little nearer guys; I can't hear you.

Ha! It's almost like I said that out loud, they are very accommodating and have stationed themselves right by the grate to my prison.

'Is everything ready?'

'Yes Simon, everyone has been contacted.'

'Good. I don't want to wait too long, we've never taken on as many as this in one go, and once they recover from the journey they may be inclined to start making a racket. We really don't want that. Keep going in to let them know they have to keep their mouths shut. Make it quite obvious. You understand?'

'Yes Simon, I think they have already got that message loud and clear.'

'Good, well, we are aiming for tonight. There are just a few more things to put in place, so keep alert. Alright?'

'Yes, of course, there's plenty of time to rest after this deal is done.'

'That's right, but there will be many more where this came from if all goes to plan tonight. Oh, make sure she's fed, will you? I keep forgetting about her down there.'

'I will, but what are we going to do with her? She knows too much.'

'Don't worry, we have plans for her, she won't be bothering you for much longer. As soon as we've dealt with this lot, we'll sort her out.'

'OK, shame, she's a pretty girl.'

'Is she? Hadn't noticed. And don't you go getting attached, it's no good in this trade.'

'I know, I won't. Thank you.'

'See you later, I've more calls to make.'

'Yes, OK.'

How dare he? Hadn't noticed if I was pretty? I could wring his bloody neck. Forgetting about me? If I could only pinch myself I'd wake up from this nightmare. Surely it is a nightmare, it must be. It can't be reality, can it?

DAY TWENTY-FOUR. EVENING.

Today just seems to have gone on and on.

Igor came down a few times to throw some food and water at me but apart from that, it has been quiet. I tried talking to him but he seemed very preoccupied and wouldn't be drawn into conversation. Anyway, I was desperate to eat the dried out sandwich he gave me and wash it down with some tepid, bottled water. He didn't even leave me alone this time but just stood there, staring at the walls whilst I ate. When I had finished he bound me again with the dreaded tape...

It looks like it's early evening now but I don't expect anything to happen here until the middle of the night. They certainly won't want any local residents seeing anything strange going on, so will have to wait until the streets are quiet.

I've spent all day trying to work out how I can get out of this place, but as I'm still sitting here, I think it's true to say I have been highly unsuccessful at reaching a satisfactory conclusion.

Actually, strange as it may seem, I'm bored. Really bored.

Who would have thought that, when faced with possibly your last few days on the planet, boredom could be an issue?

There are so many places I would love to visit, people I'd like to talk to and things I want to do. But for some reason, I seem unable to even think about any of that. Maybe it's self-preservation. If I was to start pulling up images of mum and dad and thinking about what I would say to them, if it were going to be the last conversation I was going to have, I might just go mad. Or perhaps I should say even madder.

But now I've had that thought I've gone into free-fall. I won't ever see the DIY builders completed project, or see little Gemma grow up, or have any children of my own for that matter. To be honest, it stinks. This whole situation really stinks.

Snort.

How very British, here I am faced with death, and what do I find myself thinking? That the situation stinks.

Gemma, surely you could come up with something a little more fiery than that!

Oh, what does it matter really? Whatever I'm thinking is stuck in this room with me. I could go as crazy as I liked and nobody would care.

But I need to stop feeling sorry for myself and try and stay calm.

That's it; stay calm.

Well, that's easier said than done.

If only I had a crossword or something. That would pass the time. Oh God. Crossword lady. Will I ever see you again?

Who's going to help you now?

Me. I will.

Somehow I am going to get out of here and back to my old life. Except it will be different. It's impossible to go through this without it having an effect on you. I'm certainly going to make the most of every single day, no, every single hour, once I'm free.

I know; I'll keep my brain active with crossword clues. Well, I've got to keep my hand in.

How about Calm, eight letters?

Oh yes, easy one, Gemma, that has to be 'composed'.

I am now calm, composed, sedate, at ease, serene, need I go on? OK, I know they aren't all eight letters but they are synonyms. That's the point; I could have said any number of letters. The rules in this Gemma crossword are rather loose, mainly because I have no crossword, pen, paper or anything but a crate to stand on. So this is more a mental exercise or workout. Oh God, now I've started, I can't stop.

What about prisoner?

Hostage. Suspect. Detainee. Jailbird.

Jailbird, never again will I look at a bird in a cage without feeling deep sympathy for it. In fact, I'd go as far to say that I would make every attempt to release the poor thing. It should be soaring free, way up high, not perched on a plastic ledge looking at the world through bars.

In fact, I feel like that about all animals now. I never really gave it a thought before but why should they suffer in captivity for our pleasure? Maybe I'll turn into some sort of animal freedom vigilante. It's not compulsory to wear over-sized clothes, have straggly hair and never shave your legs, is it? Whatever, I'd have to give it a bit more thought I think. You can't exactly rescue a polar bear from a zoo and set it free on the streets of Greater Manchester. It's not really going to be familiar terrain, is it?

Actually, this is all proving a bit more problematic than I realised. In fact, whatever happens to these poor people could be just as confusing as it would be for the polar bear. One minute they are at home with their families, and the next they are stuffed into a lorry and find themselves in a different country, unable to communicate, and with no means of getting home.

Not so different after all. What is the fate of these poor people? Where are they going? Do they have a choice?

I doubt it by the look of them they are scared and isolated.

However I manage to escape from here I'm just going to have to take them with me. I couldn't live with myself if I finally got away, had a lovely bath, something gorgeous to eat, tucked myself up in bed and then remembered all these unfortunate people still stuck in the house.

No, I'll have to free them somehow.

So now I'm also responsible for all fifteen, sixteen, seventeen or however many there are of these poor folks. Umm, not really making life simple, but then I never have. Why start now?

As to how this is going to happen I have simply no idea. I think I'll get back to my crossword practice and hope inspiration strikes once I've fired up a few more neurones.

How about something more positive, happy for example? Well, cheerful, joyous, one of the seven dwarfs.

Now I'm just getting silly.

Acting. Now there's another thing I wish I had done but never got around to it. Actually, it wasn't that I didn't find the time but that I felt I wouldn't be good enough. Why? Why would I talk myself out of something without even giving it a go?

You've been such a fool, Gemma.

So many wasted opportunities, at the very least I should join a drama group or something, maybe get on an agency as an extra and just see what happens. There's the small problem of my camera phobia and complete inability to have even a photo taken without gurning, but that's a minor problem. I'm sure there must be a way to get around that and retrain my face *not* to contort the minute someone points a camera at me.

See, I'm already realising that I am capable of so much more. Why on earth did it take being held hostage to face the fact that I simply need to have more confidence and give things a go?

Oh shit, someone's coming.

Just as I was about to enter the fantasy world of Gemma, and imagine I was Scarlett to Clark Gable's Rhett, when I'm sent crashing back to reality by the approach of Igor.

'Shall I let her out for a while, it really smells down there?'

'Absolutely not. It's far too risky now, and to be honest I'm starting to question your emotional involvement with this woman.'

'No, Simon, honestly, I don't care what happens to her but I thought a bit of fresh air might make it a little more bearable.'

'She's not going to need to bear anything for much longer. Leave her there but take her another drink. I suppose that can't do any harm.'

'OK, I'll do that. Don't misunderstand me. I really don't care about her.'

'Don't worry, luckily for you I can see that you are good at your job in so many ways that I can overlook your moment of sympathy. Give her a drink and then get back to work. There are only a few more hours to wait now.'

'Yes, Simon. I'll do that. Thank you.'

'Just get on with it.'

Bloody hell. I didn't think I could hate Dan anymore than I did five minutes ago but it turns out I can. What a slithering, slimy, shit-bag. Why won't he let Igor take me above ground for just a few minutes? It would be such a relief to get out of here and I might even be able to find a way to escape.

Well, that answers your own question, doesn't it?

Dan really doesn't want me escaping, end of story. But looking on the bright side he did say there are only a few more hours to wait. I'm sure I can stand that. After *days* of this place, a few more hours is nothing.

It's a good job Igor didn't let me out. If I came face to face with Dan again I think I would have to kick him very sharply in the testicles, and that would just be for starters.

Clunk. Clunk. Clunk. Here comes Igor. I wonder what his name really is? Igor actually suits him but I doubt he would be too happy about the name I have given him. As he seems to be the only person even remotely concerned about my welfare then I guess I just won't tell him.

Oh, here he is, turning the creaking key in the oversized lock. I suppose that at least adds to the drama. A slick, streamlined Yale wouldn't be quite so emotive.

'Hi, not long now. Here, let me take the tape off, but don't shout as the boss is getting restless, I wouldn't be able to stop him if he came after you.'

'Ummmmm, ouch. Thank you. It feels better already just being able to stretch my jaw. Don't worry, I don't mean by screaming, only to release some of this tension.'

'Here, have some water. I shall be busy for a while so you will be left alone. But don't think you will be able to get away; there are a lot of men around now. You have no chance. Take my advice and sit tight.'

'Right, so you suggest I sit back, relax and wait for whatever fate has in store for me?'

'Yes.'

'I can't.'

'You have no choice.'

'*You* do. You could choose to untie my hands right now and forget to lock the door as you went. Who could blame you? After all, you said you were very busy. It would only be a *tiny* lapse in concentration for a single moment. Just imagine, your problem, me, would just resolve in a matter of minutes.'

'No. My problem would become much greater, as the boss would kill me as soon as I'd been out and found you. So it isn't going to happen.'

'Right. I suppose there's no point in me begging?'

'None.'

'Pleading?'

'No.'

'Crying?'

'Just shut up, the tape is going back on. There is nothing more I can do for you. I have to go.'

Charming. He stuck the tape back on and left in such a hurry. Maybe I was actually getting to him and he wanted to help? More likely is that he has work to do and doesn't want Dan/Simon on his back about going soft on me.

Whatever, I'm still here, exactly as I have been for ages now. The only good thing is that it does appear that things are starting to hot up.

There's more activity, albeit very quietly, and the moon is high in the sky.

It must be very late now.

DAY TWENTY-FIVE. BEFORE DAWN.

What was that?

I can't believe I fell asleep again. God, I'm so stiff and sore after sleeping on this bloody floor. I must look a complete fright and I'm pretty sure I smell awful.

It's getting so difficult to heave myself up; I doubt my arms will ever be the same again. Not that it will matter. Things are looking far from rosy as far as I can tell. By the time the sun comes up, it could all be over for me. That is if it's true about tonight being the night.

Whatever it is that these morons are dealing with is about to come to a head, which means they then need to decide what to do with me. Who am I kidding? They already know what they have to do; it's just a case of carrying it out.

Oh, stop whimpering, Gemma, and take a look outside. It sounds like there are a few cars pulling into the drive.

No, they're vans, several of them. What on earth is going on? There must be at least two, if not three, men getting out of each van, and they look like a pretty mean bunch. Jeez, I thought Igor looked like a thug; well he's positively a choirboy in comparison. This lot ooze evil. I can actually feel cold sweat trickling down my back. I always thought that was just a saying, that it was something that happened in times of extreme stress, but only in films. Well, I can vouch for the fact that it isn't Hollywood make-believe, I definitely feel the beads rolling down my back *right* now. Actually, it's more of a torrent, like a waterfall, than beads of sweat, but I think I should focus my attention on more relevant things, such as what is happening outside.

God, there are so many of them.

It's getting worse. They are most definitely armed. Now, I'm no armourer, in fact, I doubt I'd know one end from the other really, but the guns these men are carrying look very powerful. They also look like they are ready to use them at the slightest provocation. There is no way I'm going to shout out now, any surprise noise would get this jittery bunch firing randomly at anything.

Maybe that would work. I could create chaos by causing some sort of distraction and hope that they all just shot each other.

As plans go I think that is possibly the worst one I have come up with yet. I would imagine they are a little more disciplined than to fire randomly at each other until no man is left standing.

I wonder if they know I'm down here? Somehow I doubt it. Only the original bunch of loons will be aware of my presence. The big boss man won't want any of this lot being more hyped up than they already are.

Actually, I think I'm doing rather well at analysing them. Maybe there is a future for me as a detective or something? There's a lot to be said for first-hand knowledge.

One big problem with that theory is that I am unlikely to

make it out of here alive, so a career as a police officer seems unlikely.

Oh, stop being so defeatist, Gemma; it's not over until the fat lady sings.

Sadly, I have seen no evidence of a fat lady. I suppose I could be thought of as a little chunky compared to the poor souls shut up in the house, but not actually fat. Plus, I can't sing.

Here I go again, random thoughts that seem to go off at a tangent. I've always done that, even as a small child. If something was happening that I wasn't keen on I just entered my mind and made up a more pleasant situation.

But I can't do that now, I really need to concentrate, there may be one last chance to get out of here. I don't want to miss it just because I've been pretending I'm lying on a beach, cool breeze drifting over me, my toes playing in the sand as I sip a cocktail.

No. Stop it. Watch and keep quiet. That's the best plan I have, the only plan I have.

Well, it looks like that's all the vans; they seemed to arrive pretty much at the same time. I guess there are about five of them. So that makes at least ten more goons, quite possibly more. From here it looks like they are all getting ready to receive the goods. By 'goods', I'm sure they mean the poor people inside. Igor looks like he is going in, probably to get them.

It's eerily quiet, no one is talking except in hushed whispers, and they are all standing guard next to their vans with their guns at the ready.

This is scary. I'm actually rather pleased I have ten feet thick brick walls to protect me.

Oh for God's sake, Dan's standing right in front of the grate. I could recognise those feet anywhere.

'OK, I'm in front of the cellar.'

What's he on about.

I know he is, he's blocking my view, and just when it was all getting exciting.

Bloody hell Dan; as if I wasn't mad enough at you already. If this is going to be my last few hours on earth you could at least move out of the way so I get a good view.

What was that?

I'm sure I heard something in the road outside.

Maybe it's another van. But the rest of them didn't seem to notice anything.

Oh here comes the boss and it looks like he's going to speak to them all.

You might be in my way Dan but I can just about see his feet, I know those brogues belong to the miserable man.

'Everyone, listen. We don't have long and we must be as quiet as possible.'

Not that quiet, I can hardly hear you and you're only a few feet away. Speak up, man.

'Our guests will be brought out any minute. You will be handed your people and you must get them in the van as quickly and as quietly as possible. I doubt they will make any noise as we've gagged them but once you have left these premises, and are a reasonable distance away, it's up to you what you do with them.'

Charming. He's talking about the poor people as if they were slabs of meat.

'You're individual bosses will have given you a package to hand over to me. One of each team should step forward now and hand the package to Simon here.'

Your lucky day Dan, it looks like you get to take charge of all the boss's money, drugs, whatever it is.

Here they come, one by one, silent, creeping feet walking past me.

Dan stop it, you're putting all the packages in my way. I can hardly see anything.

Shit. I can only see out of one tiny corner now.

Looks like the packages have all been received and Mr Boss is gently kicking each one.

'Right. The first part of our deal is complete so now I will carry out my side of the bargain.'

Is that Igor loitering in the background? I think it is and it looks like he has the poor people with him.

This is it. This is the end.

What the fuck is that flying over the wall?

Oh, my God, there's smoke everywhere.

'PUT YOUR GUNS DOWN AND STEP AWAY.'

Who said that?

What's going on?

I can't see anything.

Oh no. They are all running around by the sound of it, which is nothing like putting your gun down and stepping away.

CRACK. CRACK. CRACK.

Oh my God, it's so loud. There's gunfire everywhere.

The acrid smell is choking.

Arghhhhh. I've been hit. I'm covered in blood.

It doesn't hurt like I thought it would.

Gemma, you silly sod, it isn't your blood.

It must be Dan's, I can't see his feet anymore but it looks like he's lying on the floor.

Oh no. As much as I hate you, Dan, I can't believe you're dead.

I can't stand this noise. It's like a shootout at the O.K Corral.

I'm going to get hit by a ricocheting bullet if I'm not careful.

Drop down Gemma, curl up on the floor and keep out of sight.

Sirens. I can hear sirens.

There are definitely sirens and blue flashing lights. Oh, thank God. Someone is coming to help us.

That sounds like a helicopter.

Oh, I can't stay down here I need to see what's going on.

One last time, Gemma, find the strength from somewhere and get on your crate.

It is! It is a helicopter. They're throwing a massive beam of light down on us all.

This is fantastic. Well, apart from all the dead people who seem to be all over the place.

Thankfully it looks like Igor and the poor hostages are still in the house. Hopefully, he had the sense to keep them all out of the way.

Never have I been as pleased to see a beam of light as now.

It feels like I'm on a film set and the heroes are arriving, I should be standing out there with my hair being whipped around by the downdraft from the helicopter.

Actually, no, there are still too many shots being fired.

Armed police are over the wall now. Maybe, just maybe they are getting on top of this situation.

Dan's still there but I think he may have moved slightly.

I'm sure he was face down before and now he's on his back.

Oh no, the boss has seen me. Never has eye contact felt more dangerous than right now.

He's coming over and he has his gun out.

So this is it.

This is how my story ends.

Shot in a cellar. No way to protect myself, and certainly not looking at my best.

Here it comes.

I'm sorry mum, sorry dad. I love you so much.

CRACK.

Why am I still here?

He was aiming right at my head.

Dan. Was that you?

Did you just shoot your boss?

I can't be sure but I think he did. I saw his hand go up and I know he had a gun because I saw him using it just before he got shot.

What on earth is going on?

I feel like a cat but I have definitely lost at least two of my lives in the last few minutes.

God, there are police everywhere now and the shooting is slowing. In fact, I think it's safe to say it has stopped.

The helicopter is still hovering and it looks like a massacre out there.

What on earth are the neighbours thinking?

Snort.

Trust you, Gemma. In a time of extreme and life-threatening tension, you wonder what the neighbours make of it.

My legs.

My legs are going. I can't hold myself up anymore.

Why am I crying?

I don't seem to be able to stop crying.

Oh, Igor's there. He's come out of the house and run to Dan. It looks like he's pressing on some wound in Dan's chest. But what's he saying?

He's pointing.

Pointing at me.

He's betraying me. After all I thought about possibly

breaking through his armour, at the last moment he's betraying me.

I'm done.

I can't stand up any longer.

I'm just going to lie here in the mud, sobbing to myself. I don't care that I smell. I don't care that I'm covered in mud, blood and goodness knows what else.

I'm just going to cry.

They're opening the door.

'Gemma. It's OK. It's the police.'

I can hardly breathe; this tape is killing me.

'Keep still, let's take this off and undo your arms.'

Thank God.

'You can stop crying now, you're safe. It's over.'

'I can't. I just can't stop.'

'That's OK, you're OK.'

'Can I have a hug? I know we've only just met and I'm covered in snot but please, can I have a hug?'

'Yes, course you can, come here.'

Never has human contact felt more reassuring than at this moment.

'Thank you. Thank you.'

'No problem, you've been very brave.'

'Can I go home?'

'No, love. Not yet. We have ambulances on the way. You need to go to hospital and get checked over.'

'No, please, just let me go home. Oh God, how could I have forgotten? You must save the people. The people are inside. They're frightened and I don't know what was going to happen to them but you must help them. I'm not going anywhere, not even hospital until you do.'

'It's OK Gemma, they are all safe now. A team of officers

are looking after them right now. Come on. Let's take you up.'

'Oh. OK. They're alright?'

'Yes, they're fine. Come on, I'll help you.'

'I'm not sure I can walk. My legs feel like they belong to someone else.'

'Well you don't have to, look the paramedics are here. We'll get you on a stretcher and carry you out. You'll be fine in no time.'

'Thank you. Thank you all so much. I'm not dead?'

'No, you're not dead. You're talking way too much to be dead.'

'Ha. That's always been my problem.'

'Here we are, love, we'll wrap you in this blanket and get you sorted shall we.'

'It's so soft. Thank you. Thank you.'

'You don't need to keep saying thank you, we're just pleased you're going to be fine.'

'Thank you. I can't seem to keep my eyes open.'

'Shut them and rest. Your body and mind have been through quite a trauma. Go to sleep and we'll look after you now.'

'Thank you.'

DAY TWENTY-SIX.

'Come on dear, sit up, we need you to start eating now. I've brought you some toast and a nice cup of tea.'

'Oh. Thanks. Umm, I don't suppose I could have a nice cup of coffee instead could I?'

'Course you can, after what you've been through; I think you should have whatever you fancy. I'll be right back.'

This feels so surreal.

Here I am, lying in a hospital bed. I've been pummelled and prodded from every angle but apparently, I'm surprisingly fine. All I have are a few bruises around my wrists, some grotesque looking sores around my mouth from the dreaded tape, some abrasions on my knuckles from trying to tunnel out and severe dehydration. At some point in the night, the staff removed the drip that was flooding my veins with much-needed liquid as I kept complaining about how uncomfortable I was.

That's a laugh! This is complete luxury compared to the cellar but I seemed to slip into whining mode. Eventually, they took the drip out but made me promise to drink all the water in the jug before morning.

I kept my side of the bargain as I didn't want to get them in trouble and actually, I've felt incredibly thirsty ever since I arrived here.

The rest of yesterday all seems a blur now.

Apart from being checked by a number of doctors and the nurses taking my blood pressure every five minutes, nothing much happened.

Mainly because I was asleep; I have never felt so tired in all my life. It was as if I had run a marathon *after* climbing Everest. Every muscle, tendon, and every nerve in my body, seemed to ache.

But now it's morning again and I must say I feel a little more human. Almost 24 hours of sleep was apparently what I needed, plus the fluids dripping slowly into my arm.

All I know is that the police need to talk to me again but the doctors wouldn't let them wake me yesterday. Consequently, there was a young officer placed at the foot of my bed, standing guard.

I kept waking up with a start and it was very disconcerting to find a body looming over me in the semi-dark, eventually, the night staff asked him to wait at the end of the corridor as they thought I might go loopy if I had yet another fright.

After that, I slept like a baby.

Not that they sleep much from what I hear, but that's how the saying goes.

So here I am, in bed, dragging my very weary bones into a sitting position, as I can see the nurse returning with a steaming cup of coffee.

'Here you are, drink this and eat that toast before it gets cold. I'll be back soon to help you with a wash.'

'OK, I will, promise.'

Hopefully, that was my most sincere smile but the

chances of me eating that toast are minimal. I just don't feel hungry. I'm sure the urge to eat will return shortly, probably at the same time as I leave here and can go and buy lots of chocolate. Yes, that's what I need, chocolate. It's the answer to most of life's problems.

Oh my, this coffee is sublime. Never has a cup of weak, instant coffee tasted so good. Blimey, I'm having a caffeine rush similar to a cocaine hit. Not that I actually know what that would feel like but this must be a much cheaper option. I can feel the coffee as it starts filtering through my brain and reactivating every synapse.

Glorious.

Just glorious, what was it I told myself when in the cellar? Oh yes, that I was going to enjoy every minute of every day. Well, so far so good. That drink really hit the spot. Shame they only have thimbles for cups. What I really need is a bucket-sized mug to really top my levels up properly. Mind you, that may not be a good idea given how my mind is already racing.

I need to know what happened back there. How are the other people? How many were killed? What was it all about? Why was Dan there? Is he dead?

It all seems such a blur now. Did Dan shoot his boss? Was he aiming at someone else? Is he dead or alive? I thought he was dead but then I'm pretty sure I saw him moving. Oh, I don't know. It was all happening so quickly and there was so much noise. I really don't know what to think anymore.

'Well you haven't done very well with the toast but at least you've drunk your coffee. I can always get you something to eat later if you start feeling peckish.'

'Thank you, you're very kind. Umm, do you think you could tell me what happened, you know before I came in here? I just don't know what to make of it all and it's driving me mad.'

'I'm sorry dear, I'm afraid we can't talk to you about it yet, not that we know very much really, but you have to speak to the police first. The doctor will be around shortly and if she thinks you're up to it, then the police will have a chat with you. You can ask them all about it.'

'Oh, God. I don't want to speak to the police, I feel like a criminal. I really do, I shouldn't have been there. They'll probably arrest me and lock me up.'

'Well, that's certainly not the impression I have of the situation! Relax, I'm sure they'll fill you in with all you need to know and you'll feel much better about it all.'

'Thanks, I don't know about that, I seem to have caused quite a commotion. I just hope the police are as understanding as you are.'

'Look, here's the doctor now, let me have a word with her and see if she'll take a look at you now, put you first on her list, we don't want you getting all agitated now do we?'

'No. We don't. Thank you. Everyone is being so kind, it makes me want to cry again.'

'Well go ahead, dear. Crying is good. Let it all out. I'll get the doctor.'

What a wimp, Gemma, here you are sobbing again. At least the staff have kindly left a box of tissues by the bed.

Unfortunately, I have nearly used them all up, just in the last hour. Well, she did say crying was good so maybe that isn't such a bad thing.

Oh, here she comes. That looks like one of the doctors who saw me last night. Do these people never go home?

'Hello Gemma, do you remember me, Dr Jones, I spoke to you yesterday.'

'Yes, I remember. Well, a bit of it. To be honest it all seems a little fuzzy.'

'Fuzzy is fine. Honestly, it's just your mind protecting you as it tries to make sense of all you have been through. Physically you are in much better shape than you were when you arrived, the bloods we took this morning are nearly back to normal, but we want to keep you a little longer, just to be sure. Is that OK?'

'Of course. I was hoping to go home but quite frankly I don't care where I am as long as it isn't a cellar. I just want to feel safe.'

'Well you are safe here, there are lots of staff around and even a policeman outside the door.'

'I know; I believe they want to talk to me.'

'They do, do you feel up to it?'

'I guess so, if I have to.'

'I'm afraid you do, but I'm sure there's nothing to worry about. They only want to know what you saw or heard whilst you were there. I'll let the policeman know you're ready and they'll send the detective down for a chat. OK?'

'Yes, OK. Thanks again. By the way, do you ever go home?'

'Ha. Not often, or it seems that way. But don't worry about me, you've enough to deal with!'

Oh, God. I feel like I'm waiting for the executioner. Well, maybe that's a little dramatic. Especially as only yesterday I thought I really *was* waiting to be executed, but I'm not looking forward to this.

I'll lie back and rest my head on these soft pillows and hope it all goes away.

'Gemma. Gemma. It's Inspector Clarkson. Can we have a chat?'

'Um. Oh. Who. Inspector Clouseau?' Snort.

'Clarkson. Inspector Clarkson, Gemma.'

'Oh, sorry, I was half asleep. I do apologise.'

Not a great start, Gemma, you fool.

'Don't worry, it's rather amusing actually. I was a big fan.'

'Me too! I used to love watching those with my brother and we'd…'

'Sorry to interrupt, Gemma, but can we get on with our little talk? There are some things I need to ask you.'

'Yes, of course. Sorry, again.'

Gemma, stop randomly gabbling away to everyone, these people are busy and don't have time for it.

'Right, well, how much do you actually remember?'

'Everything I think. It all seems to be gradually coming back to me. It was terrible. I've never seen so much blood or even a dead body for that matter. Well, I have now; lots of them. Thankfully not mine though. Although I wouldn't be looking at it would I if it were mine.'

'No. No, you wouldn't. That's true.'

'Sorry. I'm doing it again. I'm afraid I'm rather agitated still and I tend to go on a bit when I'm scared.'

'Yes, yes, I can see that. But don't worry, you're not in any trouble, we just need to know a few details. We already know why you were there.'

'You do? How come? I thought nobody knew I was there apart from the thugs.'

'Well, look, we had an agent in there. Undercover. So we knew you were captive the entire time. But we couldn't risk the case falling apart as we didn't want you or the other hostages getting harmed.'

'You knew. You knew I was there?'

'Yes.'

I think my head is going to explode. The police knew I

was there all along. But it must have been days. Days and days of trauma.

'Look, I can see this has all been a real shock to you. It would be a shock for anyone. All I can say at the moment is that we knew you were there. We knew you were basically OK but very uncomfortable, and we had to make a decision. Ultimately we decided we had to maintain the cover to protect the cargo they were bringing in.'

'The cargo?'

'Yes.'

'By cargo, you mean those people?'

'Yes.'

'Oh.'

This surely is being filmed and is some elaborate hoax. The whole thing is so weird. I really can't get my head around it.

'Look, Gemma, the police have been working on this case for nearly two years. Everything was in place to finally bring them all to justice and stop the trafficking of all these people, hundreds of them over time. Unfortunately, you managed to get caught up in it.'

'Caught up in it? I was a hostage!'

'I know, but I can assure you that we have been keeping a very close eye on you, from a distance.'

Oh no. I hope that doesn't mean they saw me weeing in the corner.

'How close? Could you see me?'

'No. We couldn't see you but there were two agents in there.'

'Two agents?'

'Yes.'

'Who? This is bizarre. Two agents. Why didn't they tell me? I was terrified.'

'I know and I'm sorry. We didn't want it to turn out like this but you left us no option.'

'Me. *I* left you no option?'

'No, once you were caught by them we had to make a decision. Dan felt you could cope with it. He wasn't happy, but you were already captive by the time he found out. There wasn't much he could do to get you out until the whole case wound up. Not without the risk of you getting hurt.'

Dan. So it was my Dan, the real Dan.

'But Dan's an architect. How does an architect end up getting involved in something like this?'

'He's not an architect. He was undercover.'

No. No. So many lies; I can't stand this. I don't know who or what to believe.

'Look, Gemma, I know this is an awful lot for you to take in but the important thing to remember is that you are now safe, you're getting better, and that by staying in the cellar and keeping reasonably quiet, you allowed us to trap these men and uncover the whole ring.'

'But Dan. Is he, is he dead?'

'No. No, he's not dead but he is in theatre. They are operating on him right now. They had to stabilise him overnight and now they are repairing the damage to his chest.'

'Oh God. Will he live?'

'Yes, yes he will. They say he will make a full recovery. I spoke to him last night and he was very keen to talk to you. He said he had a lot of explaining to do.'

'Too right he does! But why didn't he? Why didn't he come and see me?'

'He couldn't. He wasn't well enough and you were flat out, I think they gave you some sedation in the end, to make you rest. Apparently, you wouldn't stop talking.'

'Oh. Really? That sounds like it could possibly be true.'

'Yes, I noticed.'

He looks weary. Inspector Clouseau, I mean Clarkson, so tired. Shit, I have caused such a lot of trouble. All because I wouldn't listen to Dan and stay away from the house.

'Can I go to him now? Have we finished?'

'We've finished, yes, you will have to come down to the station in a few days time, when you are fully recovered, and make a full statement. We will be able to go through it all with you then. I'm sure you will have a few more questions by that stage too.'

'Yes, so am I. There's so much to take in, but Dan. Can I see him?'

'No. Not now. But I'll tell the doctor that as soon as Dan's fit enough you can have a chat with him. Now, you get some rest young lady. You've had a bit of a time of it.'

'Yes, something of an understatement, but yes, I have. Oh, by the way, you should get some rest too, you don't look like you've had much sleep recently.'

'I haven't. This has quite possibly been the most unusual case I have worked on. We don't generally make it common practice to allow members of the public to participate in a case unwittingly.'

'No, I don't suppose you do. Oh, one other thing, who's the second agent. You said there were two undercover? Was it Igor?'

'Igor, no, don't know who that is, no, this was Stevens. He was the one who saw you the most. He brought you food and things and feels awful about tying you up.'

'It is Igor. I knew it. I just knew I was breaking him down! Actually, I feel a whole lot better. Maybe I'm not as bad at reading people as I thought. Thank you. Now, I suggest you go home and write your report up, or whatever you need to do, and then get some rest.'

'Yes, Miss. I think I shall do exactly that. You've been quite a worry to us young lady but thankfully it turned out better than we had hoped.'

'Well, that's good. Please, don't forget to tell the doctor that I can see Dan as soon as he is well enough.'

'I won't. Now you take care, Gemma, and I'll see you soon.'

'Bye.'

Well. What do you make of that, Gemma?

It seems you have been unwittingly solving crimes. Who'd have thought it?

'Nurse. Nurse. Do you think I could have another cup of coffee?'

'Yes, sure, I'll bring you one. Oh, and by the way, a message from the other ward, Dan has had his operation. Hopefully, you'll be able to see him, but not until tomorrow.'

'Thank goodness. That's a huge relief. Please, tell me as soon as I can go there.'

'I will, don't you worry. Now I'll get you that coffee.'

Here they come. Here come the tears. Again.

I can see the headlines now, 'NHS finally broken by huge tissue bill.'

DAY TWENTY-SEVEN.

Well, that's me done. After a full day of care from the long-suffering staff, I can't remember how many times I hassled them about Dan, and a very good night's sleep, I do actually feel much better.

Apparently, I can go home later today and I'm absolutely delighted about it. I think.

There's a small bit of me that's rather concerned about being on my own, but I suppose that's normal. The doctors have all said it will take time to really get over, 'the situation' as they like to call it, but that's not surprising really. I guess I shall just have to take life by the scruff of the neck and get on with it.

Mum and Dad did ask me to go back to stay with them for a while, but I feel I need to face the fear right now and stop it from taking hold. If I don't go back to my little house and try to settle down now, then I may never return. I think they understood, but I can also understand why they would want to keep me close to them. It has all been a huge shock for them too. Actually, at the moment, it's worse for them as they have journalists camping outside their house. The hospital won't let them anywhere near me, so the papers have gone for the next best option and are stalking my parents. They'll hate that. Not being able to leave the house without running the gauntlet of cameras and microphones being stuffed in their faces. They are very private people and won't welcome the intrusion. Just another thing they have me to thank for. I really have made their lives difficult this time.

It's not as if they actually have any details of what happened, well not really. We did discuss it when they visited but I couldn't bring myself to tell them exactly what it was like. Maybe I will in time, or maybe they'll find out from the papers once the story all comes out, but either way, I feel sad that they are going through this.

But I can't dwell on that at the moment, I know they will be fine and I have to think about myself, and Dan.

The doctor said I can visit after lunch, and before I go home. His surgery went well and he is now awake and talking.

Consequently, this has been the longest morning in living memory. There are only so many times you can talk to the lady in the next bed about her grandchildren. They do sound very nice but the poor dear obviously can't remember that she told me the same story six times already this morning. I have resorted to closing the curtains and pretending that I am having a snooze. Every so often I do a little snore, just to prevent her from peering in and telling me about her daughter Glenda's children, who live in America, yet again.

It's probably quite selfish of me really. She's only lonely, and quite probably scared in her own way, but I do feel I have to be a little bit selfish right now. Perhaps, once I'm better myself, I'll call in to see her. She doesn't seem to have many visitors, any in fact. Poor thing.

Now I feel really guilty.

I'll pull the curtain back and humour her for a few minutes.

Oh. She's asleep. Well, at least the thought was there. If she wakes up before I finally get released I'll give her my full attention.

So the morning drags on.

Thankfully I could get up to go and have a bath today. That certainly beats a bed bath. When the nurse said she'd come and help me with a wash I'd no idea she meant literally. How humiliating!

So escaping to the bathroom was a complete delight. I did have to find a cloth and some cleaner and give the whole bath a scrub before I got in myself, but that's just my OCD tendencies showing. How am I to know who was in there before me?

But after giving it a good clean I ran a very hot bath, eased myself in and lay back to soak. It was very relaxing and I felt so much better. You wouldn't believe the colour of the water when I got out. It looked like I'd just come off a football pitch, having done several slide tackles, in the middle of winter.

But then I had been sleeping on a cellar floor for a few days so it isn't so surprising.

I actually got out of the bath and then had a shower, just for good measure, and my hair now feels soft and bouncy instead of being stuck to my head with grease and mud.

I usually wash my hair most days, so not washing it was probably one of the biggest traumas of the lot. Well, not really, I didn't actually think of it at the time as I was concentrating on trying to stay alive, but as soon as I got out of there I must admit I did become rather preoccupied with my hair. The night staff refused to let me up for a shower on the first night, as they said I wasn't well enough. I think it was shortly after that they brought out the sedation, probably to shut me up as they had much more important things to deal with than chatting with me about the benefits of various shampoos.

The only downside of the whole bath/hair wash routine was that there was a mirror in the bathroom. I caught a glimpse of myself and really wish I hadn't.

I'd no idea I looked so dreadful, the hospital staff are certainly good at not allowing their faces to reflect what they must surely be thinking.

The sores around my mouth are now all crusty, which is not a good look, and I don't think I have ever been as pale.

Anyway, I'm not going to dwell on that, it will all resolve over time and is a small price to pay for actually still being alive.

Here come the porters with the lunch trolley. They are always so chirpy; I don't know how they do it. They spend all day wheeling people about and trying to keep patients smiling, yet they must have concerns of their own. It's the same with the cleaners. The number of times they have mopped around my bed whilst keeping up a running commentary of jovial issues is amazing. Not one of them has asked me about what happened, although I strongly suspect that's because they have been told not to. I have caught a few of them looking at me closely, but then who wouldn't when I had greasy, muddy hair plastered to my face and sores around my mouth.

They must all have a basic idea of what I've been through, if only from the papers.

Oh, come on. Serve the meal up so I can pretend to eat it and go and see Dan. This morning is interminable.

Oops. Did I say that out loud?

Get a grip, Gemma; they are going as fast as they can.

Here it comes, delightful, sausage, mash and questionable gravy. How nice. Well, I'll cut it all up a bit, and move it around the plate a lot, and see if I can get away with not eating anything.

Actually, the potato isn't too bad, I'll force some of that down; just so they let me out of here.

At least they have finally realised that I rarely drink tea and much prefer coffee. I don't have to ask anymore, they just bring me a mug. After I had a detailed conversation about the size of the cups, the nice lady who makes the drinks now uses a staff mug, just to shut me up I suspect. Not that the staff ever seem to have time to go on a coffee break. I swear the same people seem to be here all day long.

It does appear that I have convinced them that I am now eating as they have removed my plate and say I can start getting ready to go.

I can't wait.

I shall get dressed and go to see Dan on my way out. At least the hospital can reuse my bed that way. I'm sure it will be filled pretty much as soon as my feet step over the boundary of the ward.

Thankfully Mum thought to bring me in a change of clothes. I must have left them at her house last time I was over. They certainly wouldn't have been my choice of outfit to go and see what Dan has to say for himself. Will he be able to take me seriously in an oversized tracksuit? Did I ever actually fit this thing? I guess the regular walking has helped my figure more than I thought. Well, that and the near starvation of the last few days.

Oh, stop being so shallow, Gemma. Dan won't care what you are wearing; he has had enough troubles of his own.

At least the operation went well, according to the staff

who I quizzed on a half-hourly basis throughout the night and most of this morning.

But now I'm ready and I have started feeling anxious. What do I say to him?

'You OK, Gemma?'

'Oh, hi, umm, no. Not really. Now I can actually go home I'm not sure I want to. Maybe I've become institutionalised.'

'You're fine, Gemma, once you get home you can relax and try to forget about all this. I would leave by the back door though, there are a lot of journalists about.'

'Oh shit. I can't face them. I don't want to talk to anyone. Well, apart from Dan. Can I go to see him now?'

'Yes, that's what I was coming to tell you. Go and see him. Have a chat and sort it all out. You'll feel better for it. Then, when it's time to leave ask one of the porters to show you the back way out.'

'OK, I will and thank you for all you've done. You all managed to make a horrific situation seem much better, I couldn't have done it without you.'

'Yes you could, and you will, over the coming weeks. Don't expect it all to go away overnight, Gemma; it will take time. Don't be too hard on yourself.'

'I won't, thanks again. Right, I'm off.'

'Bye dear, at least I can have my mug back now.'

'Yes, you can. It was much appreciated!'

There she goes, back to work whilst I try and decide what I'm going to say to Dan. I don't know whether to be angry or happy or cross or furious or sad or relieved.

Whatever; get yourself over there Gemma, and play it by ear.

'Bye love, you take care.'

'Oh, bye, I hope you get to America soon to see your grandchildren.'

'Don't need to, they're coming over for a visit next week, our Glenda just called the hospital to tell me.'

'That's fantastic, you have a great time when they get here and take care.'

That's so lovely. I hope Glenda realised just how happy she has made her mum. Maybe I should try to get in touch, just to let her know. Oh, stop interfering, Gemma; you have enough troubles of your own. Stop avoiding the situation and walk the short distance across the corridor to Dan's ward.

Ok. I'm doing it.

I've done it.

I just need to go in and ask where Dan is. But now I'm here I'm terrified.

I can't. I'll just go home.

'Gemma, what you doing standing there? You've been asking about this Dan chap all morning, here, I'll take you in.'

'Umm, no, it's...'

'Look, that's his bed, right over there. He's seen you, now off you go.'

'Oh. Thanks. Suppose I will then. Umm, bye.'

'Bye, you keep yourself out of trouble young lady.'

'Oh, I will. I've definitely decided the thrill-seeking life is not for me.'

'That's good, see you then.'

'Yes, bye.'

Oh God, he's looking at me.

Now he's waving me over. There really is no escape. I have to go and speak to him now.

'Gemma, God Gemma, I'm so pleased to see you. Come over here and let me hug you.'

'Dan. I thought. I didn't, I don't know, oh what the heck, here give me a hug.'

This feels so nice. But aren't I meant to be angry?

'Gemma, I'm so sorry, you must be furious at me.'

'Well, actually yes, I was. But now I don't quite know how I feel.'

'That's not surprising is it, given the situation?'

'Situation. Everyone keeps talking about the 'situation'. I could have been killed, Dan. But that's not all. It's the lies. I don't know what's true and what's not. Who are you? What do you do? How much of your life is simply a lie?'

'Gemma. Gemma, please, calm down. Most of it's true. Honestly, I felt so bad lying to you but I had no choice. I wasn't meant to fall in love whilst out undercover.'

'What did you say?'

'That most of it was true.'

'No, not that bit. The important bit.'

'That I fell in love?'

'Yes. That bit. Really? Do you mean it?'

'Of course I mean it. How could I *not* fall in love with you? I knew for sure the moment you went cross-eyed in front of me when I was talking with the main man.'

'I know when you mean. I don't walk around cross-eyed very often, in fact in the last few years I can honestly say that was the first time I've done it.'

'Well, it nearly made me laugh, which would have completely blown my cover, but I just wanted to hug you and tell you everything would be alright.'

'Let me get this straight. All that was needed for me to get a man to fall in love with me was to go cross-eyed? Jeez, if I'd have known that I'd have been walking around like that years ago.'

'Seriously Gemma, I hated doing that to you, but when I

found out they'd caught you, there really wasn't another option.'

'You could have told me your form of architecture wasn't exactly conventional.'

'I couldn't. Too much was at stake. Obviously, I'm not an architect, I'm a detective.'

'I managed to work that one out. Admittedly with a little help from one of your detective friends. Inspector Clouseau.'

'Clarkson. Yes, he told me you'd been talking.'

'Yes, that's it, Clarkson. Anyway, what I need to know is how much of your life is a lie? Your house, your Mum, your sister Elizabeth? There are so many parts to this. I'm confused.'

'I'm sure you are, and I really am sorry. The problem was that we have been working on this case for so long and knew that another shipment of people was on the way. We couldn't risk you or them.'

'Basically, that is my mum's old house and I am selling it. It just proved useful as a base, to make my story ring true but I will be selling it now. Obviously, I'm not an architect but I couldn't risk you asking too many questions. You are after all, um, inquisitive.'

'True. I get that. Go on.'

'Well, the only other thing is Elizabeth, she isn't my sister; she's a colleague. They sent her up to see what was going on when they realised I had gone and fallen for a local girl. It really wasn't in the plan.'

'Oh. Well. I like to shake things up a bit.'

'You're telling me! I got into a lot of trouble over that, but actually, when you inadvertently got involved, it actually turned out to be an excellent distraction.'

'Distraction?'

'Yes, the traffickers became so engrossed in what to do with you that it bought me a lot of time.'

'I'm delighted I proved to be a very good decoy.'

'I knew you could cope.'

'How? How did you know that? I barely function in the real world. I can't even remember to charge my phone at night. How does that equate with coping in a hostage situation?'

'I think it was the time I found you upside down in my rose bush. The way you bounced back from that was very, well, imaginative.'

'Oh, right. Yes, how could I forget that episode? Well, I'm delighted you thought me such a capable person because, frankly, it isn't the way I would have described myself.'

'Ultimately the decision was taken out of my hands anyway, Gemma. The Home Office had the final say and they went with the, 'keep you hostage' approach.'

'Home Office. You mean the Home Office have been discussing me?'

'Yes. They had too, it was all becoming so complicated.'

'That's what Clouseau said. Complicated.'

'Clarkson.'

'Yes, him. So are you saying I have done my bit for Queen and country?'

'Absolutely. You're a heroine. You're in all the papers and most likely the story will hit the T.V. once you get out of here.'

'Oh, God. I just want to go home and get some peace.'

'You can. Everything will calm down, you'll see.'

'Tomorrow's fish and chip paper I suppose.'

'Exactly. Anyway, am I forgiven, Gemma?'

'I suppose so. How can I stay angry with you after all

this? It seems you were only trying to protect me, granted, it was in a rather unusual fashion but, hey, what a story!'

'It certainly beats a, 'We met online' kind of scenario.'

Snort.

'That's for sure. Anyway, when can you get out of here? I think we should start again. Put all this behind us and get to know each other. No lies.'

'I was hoping you'd say that. I'll be out in a few days, and on sick leave for a while, so, plenty of time to renew our acquaintance.'

'Excellent. I shall look forward to it. In the meantime, I need to get home and sort all this out in my mind.'

'Of course you do. But before you go, can I say one thing?'

'OK, what?'

'Those sores around your mouth are damned attractive.'

'Don't push your luck, my friend, you've Igor to thank for that.'

'Igor?'

'Yes, Igor. Your mate, the one who kept feeding me, what was it? Oh, yes, Stevens I think he was called.'

'Ha. He'll find that hilarious! You called him Igor?'

'Not to his face, remember I thought he wanted to kill me. I'm not completely stupid.'

'Far from it Gemma. You're fantastic. Come here, can I have a kiss?'

'Only if you don't laugh at my sores again.'

'I won't.'

'Dan, are you, oh, it seems you have made it up with Gemma. I'll, well, I'll leave you to it.'

'Umm, oh, thanks, Igor.'

'What?'

'Never mind. I'll speak to you later.'

DAY TWENTY-EIGHT.

I feel like a new woman after a gorgeous sleep in my luxurious bed. Those hospital mattresses are the pits. All plastic so you get hot and sweaty within minutes and every time you move the sheets nearly slip off the bed. Not to mention the noise. How is anyone meant to sleep in a hospital? All the staff kept saying; 'Get some rest, Gemma,' yet they woke me up every five minutes to take my temperature or blood pressure or simply stand staring at me as they stood at the foot of the bed. It was most unnerving.

Also, Clapham Junction has nothing on the activity in a general ward overnight. I swear a trolley trundled past every few minutes with a writhing, groaning patient waiting to be transferred from the trolley to a marginally more comfortable bed. I sound ungrateful now, but I'm not. I'm full of praise for the staff and the difficult work they do, but, a night in my own bed, in my own room, of my own house has never felt so good.

In fact, I think I shall just stay here all day. Lying, cocooned in my duvet with my head sinking into this pillow is all I need, apart from the toilet.

Oh God, why is it that just as I realise how comfortable and dozy I am that I also realise I need the toilet.

I suppose I'll have to move, once you have had that thought there is no way it is going to go away. There is an up side though. The floor is nice and soft with my springy carpet instead of the cold, Lino of the hospital. Even worse than that, was the dirty, damp floor of the cellar. No. I can't think about that part yet. It's making me feel queasy just to remember the cellar floor. I'll go back to enjoying the comfort of my own bathroom instead. At least I don't feel the need to scrub the toilet before I use it.

OK, leap back into bed, Gemma, and get comfortable again. There's no need to get up, you have nothing to do but rest and recuperate.

Even the police have said they will leave me alone today so that I can relax.

Jeez. Now I can't get comfortable. How can a bed that felt so inviting a few minutes ago now feel lumpy and too hot?

I give in. I'll get up and make some coffee. Yes, that's what I'll do. Maybe even a slice of toast. Oh yes, I think my appetite is returning, toast and marmalade, that's exactly what I need.

I'm not putting that awful tracksuit on again there must be some clean clothes in the drawer. It's not as if I've been wearing them recently. But did I do any laundry in the last few months, that's the question?

Yes, I must have been feeling better. Here are some jeans that fit quite well, and a reasonable t-shirt. This old jumper will also do, as it's one of my favourites. It's so soft and baggy I can almost disappear into it.

Socks. I need socks. Well, they don't exactly match but who cares? There's only me here, it isn't as if I need to dress up to impress Dan. Apart from the fact that he's still in hospital it seems that all I need to do to reel him in is to go cross-eyed. Sometimes I simply don't understand men.

Right. Downstairs and kettle on, I shall find my largest mug and make the strongest coffee I have had in days. It seems the biggest mug I have has a picture of Rudolph on it, but as far as I am aware, there isn't a law about using seasonal cups out of sync with reality, besides, it's one of my favourites. So, Rudolph, it is and just to soothe the rebel in me I shall use a Santa plate for the toast.

Oh. There's a fatal flaw in my plan. This milk stinks. Ugh. Really stinks. I guess it has been sitting in the fridge for quite some time. Don't I have any more? Surely there must be some? Maybe I put it in the freezer, for emergencies.

Of course, you didn't, Gemma. The chances of you even considering that as pre-hostage Gemma are minuscule.

Perhaps I will have to venture out and go to the shops after all. Let some light in Gemma and see what sort of day we have.

Oh my God!

Quick, shut the curtains. Shit. Oh, god, they saw me and now they are ringing the bell.

There must be hundreds of people out there. Journalists, cameras, people just gawping.

There is no way I'm going out and there is no way I'm answering the door either. Why can't they leave me alone?

Because I'm today's news. Maybe I shall camp out here until they get bored and move on.

So, black coffee it is then.

That was my phone, sounded like a text coming in. Now, where is it?

Blimey, Gemma, that's a first, you actually put it on the counter in the kitchen to charge. Maybe this, 'situation', has done you some good after all.

Yup, it's a message, from Dan.

'Nice jumper'.

What does he mean? OK, 'What are you talking about?'

'I like the colour of your jumper, it matches the scabs on your face.'

'You're freaking me out Dan, what are you on about?'

'Turn your TV on.'

TV, has he gone mad? Right, here we are, BBC or SKY? Bloody Hell. It doesn't matter which one. I'm on both. Jesus. I only opened the curtain for a second and they all managed to capture me on film. This is awful. I look like some dishevelled mad woman. No wonder they have stopped ringing the bell, they probably think I'll come out and chase them down the street I look so demented.

Or it could be those two policemen that seem to have arrived and are now stationed at the end of my drive.

Dan again.

'Sit tight, they'll go soon and we arranged some security for you.'

'Gee, thanks; a prisoner in my own house now, frying pan and fire?'

'Nah, none of this lot are trying to kill you. Just relax and enjoy the show. Xx'

Two kisses. That's good. Actually, it's quite nice to sit and watch the front of your house on TV. I can pretend I have the best CCTV around, courtesy of all the major news networks.

Let's hear what they have to say:

'It seems that Gemma is now resident back at her home but still suffering from the trauma of her ordeal. We hope to speak to her personally in time but the police have advised us that this may be some hours away.'

'Meanwhile, we can report that several arrests have been made following the dramatic events and a number of major names associated with modern slavery are now being questioned at police stations around the county.'

'It appears that human trafficking is far more prevalent than was first thought. We have known for some time about the plight of some who have been forced into domestic servitude, brothels and prostitution, their passports removed and no wages paid, but there appear to be many more cases being discovered, thanks to this incident. This highlights aspects of human trafficking where the individuals are hidden in plain sight. Nail bars, takeaways, hotels, car washes, basically, anywhere demanding cash only payment, should start alarm bells ringing. We, as a country need to get on top of the exploitation of adults and children within our society...'

Turn it off, Gemma.

I can't watch it. They are talking about the poor people I saw getting out of the van and taken into the house. It sounds like many have gone before them too. No wonder I've made the news.

It seems that I have inadvertently got myself involved in a rather large case.

I actually feel quite proud of the small part I have played in breaking the system. I'm not so sure that is how the Home Office will feel about it. I don't suppose they really wanted a member of the public caught up in the whole gruesome scenario, but as Dan said, once I was captured they didn't really have much choice.

Snort.

Who'd have thought that little old Gemma would make the news headlines!

The whole thing was awful. I have never been so scared

in all my life, but, now that I'm home and the feelings are slowly fading, I can see that I managed to help those poor people in a strange sort of way.

Apart from anything else, the fact they are talking about modern slavery on the news is fantastic. The more people who are aware of the tell-tale signs the better as far as I'm concerned.

In fact, I'm going out there. I want to tell them just that. How important it is that we all look out for this dreadful way of life that some people are forced into.

'Dan, I'm going out.'

Right, where are my shoes?

'Don't. You need to be briefed first.'

'It's a free country, I can talk to whoever I want.'

'Oh God, Gemma. Don't you ever listen?'

'No.'

That looks a bit harsh, I'll send a belated kiss.

'xxx'

There, three for good measure.

Take a deep breath, Gemma; they are only people. There is nothing to be scared about. At least you are facing cameras this time rather than guns. It has to be easier.

Here goes.

'Hello.'

'Gemma, Sky news, can you...'

'BBC here, we want...'

'Daily Herald, do you...'

'Stop, everyone, stop. I'm not answering your questions today but I will say a few words. But that's it. Once I have finished you can all go home and leave me in peace. As you know it has been a difficult few days, and firstly I want to thank the police and hospital staff for their excellent work.'

'If any good can come from this horrific experience then I shall follow that up in the days and weeks to come, but for now, the very fact that we are talking about human trafficking on national television is a huge step forward. The plight of the frightened people, I witnessed with my own eyes, was horrendous and there will be many, many more people dealing with similar situations. This topic needs to be discussed openly within society so that we can all be alert to its dehumanising nature. More has to be done to prevent the physical and mental abuse taking place in our country. This affects adults and children alike. In due course, I will hold interviews with the relevant people to publicise a greater awareness, but for now, I need to recover. So thank you all and please feel free to go home now.'

'Gemma, just one thing,'

'No, sorry, I won't take questions today.'

'Wait, it's the police, we have something for you, sent by a well-wisher.'

'Really, what?'

'Umm, bread and milk. Do you want it?'

'Why didn't you say earlier, course I do. I wouldn't have come out at all but I was trying to get rid of this lot so I could go to the shop. Thanks. That's great. See you.'

My heart's pounding. I bet my face is as red as a beetroot. I can't believe I just said that.

Shit. Bet it's Dan with another message.

'You were doing so well, right up to the bread and milk...'

'Was it you?'

'Course it was. Who else would send a colleague over with some milk?'

'Much appreciated. Do you think I came across OK?'

'Would have taken you more seriously if your socks had matched and you'd remembered some shoes. Apart from that...great x'

No. No. No.

Thought my feet were getting wet.

Will I never learn?

DAY TWENTY-NINE.

Thanks to Dan, and his thoughtful gift of some bread and milk, I was able to remain inside for the entire day yesterday. It was handy really as I could take my time trying to re-establish some degree of normality back into my life. Putting the washing in and running a Hoover around the house are excellent ways of bringing you crashing back to earth with a tiresome thump. So whilst my lovely home is looking much smarter than it has done for many months, my soul is screaming.

I'm so bored.

Who'd have thought that resting and recuperating, as all the hospital staff and come to think of it, the police, have told me to do, could be so tedious?

After the cleaning frenzy yesterday I spent the rest of the day flicking between channels on the TV and watching the horrible image of myself being played over and over again. If I shut my eyes and just listen then I feel a whole lot better about it. Some of the things I said actually sound quite convincing. It's almost as if I knew what I was talking about. But, a soon as I take a peek and see my pale face with huge dark rings under my eyes, not to mention the baggy jumper that looks like it's a historical artefact that was dug up from some ancient burial ground. Oh, and try to forget about the mismatched socks and lack of shoes, well, I mean, who on earth could take me seriously?

Once again I have ignored Dan at my peril. I should have listened to him and stayed away from the windows and certainly not have given an impromptu statement without any advice or debriefing.

Well, there's nothing I can do about that now but I did mean what I said. Once all this has calmed down and I feel better I really will try to highlight the problem of modern slavery, but next time in a more controlled fashion. Maybe I will get proper interviews on TV, where I can explain exactly what happens to these people. I think I will have to discuss this with Dan first and see what he thinks. After all, I expect there will be some sort of court case following all those arrests. Presumably, details of the event can't be made public as this may interfere with court proceedings, or influence the jury, or something technical like that.

No. Much better to wait and talk to Dan, I really don't think he, or all the rest of the police, would be too happy if all the criminals got off just because I had opened my big mouth. I've caused them enough trouble as it is. Even the Home Office got involved for God's sake.

Snort.

Actually, every time I think about that I can't help but laugh. I have this image of a very posh office with a huge desk sitting right in the middle. A bespectacled, suited and very efficient looking man is peering over his glasses as the Chief Constable fills him in about the wayward girl who appears to have been taken hostage by a gang of criminals. He sighs, coughs to clear his throat and declares I should be left there to prevent the case from falling apart. He probably then went home and forgot all about little old me whilst he sipped a gin and tonic in his sumptuous house, stroking a black Labrador sitting patiently at his feet.

OK, so most of that is the result of a very active imagination but the point is that *my* name was discussed at the highest levels. That's hilarious.

The good news is that Dan is making an excellent recovery and will, in fact, be released from hospital later today. The bad news is that I won't be able to see him until at least tomorrow. Apparently, he will be taken straight to some official offices for debriefing, and he will be there for some time. Not only will they discuss the case and the outcome so far, but they will also want to assess him and his mental state following the surgery, and his emotional involvement with me. ME. Once again I am causing Dan a few headaches. I'm actually starting to feel a bit sorry for him.

That's a turnaround, I hated him not that long ago but I keep telling myself I wasn't aware of all the details at that point, and actually, was pretty stressed myself.

The thing is I don't seem to be able to think about it all without sniggering. I'm not sure if this is a delayed reaction and I'm actually losing my mind or whether it's just relief that it is all over. Or at least the trauma part is over.

Whatever, I guess all will become clear over time. I will be speaking to the police at some point but they don't seem to be in any sort of hurry, which is absolutely fine by me.

But right now I feel like a caged animal. I've had enough of being trapped in a cellar, hospital and now a house. I need to get out and resume my life. I've really missed my routine. Who'd have thought I would miss my walking?

It took superhuman strength on my part to lever myself

out of the house and start this walking therapy lark, but boy has it made a difference.

My life has certainly changed. Admittedly, not quite in the way that was initially expected, but that somehow just adds to the whole experience.

But right now I need to stretch my legs and get back out there. I'm sure it will help to clear my head, which will be an added bonus.

So, firstly, let's peep outside and see if the coast is clear.

Hang on, Gemma; before you do that you should at least brush your hair?

Good grief, have I actually learnt something? That's a first.

Mind you, it was wasted on this occasion, as the coast does seem to be clear. There's not a soul in sight. That's a bit disappointing really. It seems the press have moved on to some other story and forgotten about me already.

How dare they!

Yesterday they would have done anything for a few words from me but today they couldn't care less.

I suppose that was my fifteen minutes of fame. Sadly, my fifteen minutes involved me looking like a crazy woman ranting on her doorstep, minus her shoes, in the middle of winter. The only thing that could have made that worse would have been if I had been wearing a pair of novelty slippers.

See, there's always a bright side.

However, just in case there are any journalists hiding in the undergrowth, I will have a quick wash and then get my newest joggers and boots on before I go for my walk. For good measure I think I'll wear this baseball cap, I want to be incognito today.

Oh, my word. It is so good to get out in the fresh air. Umm, huge lungs full of glorious, free air. It feels great to be alive.

Admittedly, I actually feel a bit stiff now I've started walking but that will wear off I'm sure. It's amazing how quickly your body will adjust. Here it is complaining as it hasn't been used for a few days but it will be fine in no time.

Dear little cat, have you missed me? Look, I'm sure she has, she's leaning into the window to say hello. Oh, bless her, 'I've missed you too my tortoiseshell friend.'

Seems like the cap didn't trick you did it?

'I bet you wondered what had happened to me didn't you?' Well, maybe that's going too far but I'm very pleased to see you again. 'Now you go back to sunbathing on the windowsill whilst I continue my walk.'

Blimey, this hill feels steeper than it did, has someone tilted the road whilst I've been away?

Of course not, Gemma; just put your back into it and work up a sweat. You'll feel much better afterwards.

Oh God, here comes a woman walking towards me.

What's the betting she ignores me completely? They usually do, generally you have to drag a hello out of everyone.

'Morning, dear, lovely day isn't it?'

Blimey.

'Umm, morning, yes, glorious isn't it?'

Well, that's a turn up for the books, no begrudging smile or forced hello, just an exchange of pleasantries. That's more like it! People being nice to other people, it really doesn't take much. I feel quite heartened by that.

Actually, there seem to be an awful lot more people out and about. What's going on? There aren't many cars but lots of people walking. How strange.

I wonder if they are all patients of Dr Wright and he's on

some sort of one-man crusade to make the local population healthier and happier?

They don't look depressed but then what is depression supposed to look like?

Stop analysing everything and just enjoy your freedom and your walk.

'Gemma! Thank goodness, we have been so worried about you.'

What the... Oh, it's the DIY builders, didn't realise I'd got as far as that so quickly, I must be more adrenaline-fuelled than I thought.

'Hi! Oh, you've come down from the roof. I must say, you're much taller than I thought you were, but then I've only ever seen you when you've been up a ladder or hanging onto the scaffolding.'

'Gemma, what on earth has been happening to you, you've been all over the news? When we didn't see you we started worrying but thought you were just at home or away with Dan. Then, there you are on the front pages of all the newspapers and talking on your doorstep, with no shoes on incidentally.'

'You saw that then?'

'Everyone did, I've been telling all my friends how I know you. Come here, give me a hug, it's such a relief to see you again.'

Blimey, a hug too. I'm a real celebrity.

'You can let go now, but thank you. Shit, your dad's coming, you had better get back to work.'

'No, it's fine, look, he wants to shake hands with you.'

'Me? Why?'

'Because you saved all those people, you're a hero Gemma.'

'Heroine, but, no, I'm not. Really. I'm not.'

'Yes, you are. My whole family have been talking about it and how honoured they are to be able to say they say hello to you every day.'

'Give over. That's ridiculous!'

'No, it isn't. Here, father, this is Gemma.'

'Very pleased to meet you, Gemma, and to shake your hand. You are a very strong woman who has done a lot of good.'

'No, really, you've got it all wrong, I was in the way mainly.'

'You can protest all you like, but we are very proud of you and would like you and Dan to call round for a meal when you feel ready.'

'That's very kind of you, thank you. We shall do that once Dan has fully recovered.'

'Good, now back to work for us, you take care.'

Cheeky wink there, hope his dad didn't see it.

'Bye, and thank you, I shall look forward to the meal.'

That's nice, who would have thought I could break down the barriers with DIY Dad? That's amazing and has put a real spring in my step.

Life suddenly feels very good.

It's like Clapham Junction here today, now there's a lady with a pram approaching. Can we make it three positive meetings in a row?

Oh my God, of course we can, it's little Gemma!

'Gemma, how are you? What a dreadful time you've been having but what an incredible outcome.'

'Hi, well, yes, I suppose so. To be honest, I wasn't really expecting all this acknowledgement, it's a bit unnerving.'

'Enjoy it! We are, we're telling everyone that our Gemma's namesake is a real hero.'

'Heroine, but no, I'm not. Honestly.'

'Yes you are, as if delivering my gorgeous little Gemma wasn't enough you go and rescue all those people.'

'Umm, it, well, it wasn't really like that.'

'Don't be so modest, look, I can't stop now, we're off to the doctors for Gemma's checkup, but please, do come round to see us soon and you can tell me all about it.'

'Umm, thanks, I will. I swear Gemma has grown already, it's amazing.'

'Oh, she has. Not surprising really the amount she eats. I'm up every two hours day and night feeding the little blighter.'

'Ugh, that's horrific!'

'No, horrific is what you had to deal with, for me, feeding Gemma is a delight. Look, must go but call in soon. Bye.'

'Yes, bye, will do.'

Well, she's taken to motherhood rather well and it suits her, she seems so happy and positive. That's another reason to feel that life is very good today.

This walk is certainly doing me good.

Well, it was.

But that's *the* house. THE HOUSE WITH THE CELLAR.

Why didn't I think about the fact that the very house where I've been held hostage is on my walking route?

Of course it is, you idiot, that's why you got in this mess in the first place.

I'll pull my cap further down to hide my face and just stroll past.

There are plenty of police around, doing whatever it is they do at a crime scene, but also plenty of press. It's too late to detour now; I'll just walk on by as if the whole place has nothing to do with me.

'If you see me walking down the street, and I start to cry, each time we meet, walk on by, walk on by...'

Made it and I don't think anyone realised it was me. That's a relief; I'm not ready to look at that place again just yet. I think I may well have to change my route after today. How stupid not to think of that before.

Maybe I'm not as well adjusted about the whole thing as I thought I was.

Still, we live and learn, hopefully.

Oh great, I've run the gauntlet of the press and tarpaulin house, but coming right up is Teapot House. Will she be expecting me? After all, it has been a few days.

Oh, yes, of course she will, here she comes.

'Sommelier's stockroom, six letters?'

'Oh God, cellar.'

'Excellent. Thank you and good to have you back.'

'You missed me...'

Of course, she's gone.

Witch. She's definitely a witch.

DAY THIRTY

So here I am. Awake and staring at the ceiling as if Michelangelo had painstakingly re-created a fresco from the Sistine Chapel, right here in my bedroom.

Actually, all I can see are a few smudges, probably the remains of a tiresome insect or two, and the damp outline left after a leaking roof incident. None of which is very inspiring and the more I look at it the more annoying it is.

It must be nearly morning. I've been awake for ages. It's still dark so I know I haven't miraculously slept in. Oh, how I wish I could. I miss those days. You know, when you don't seem to have a care in the world and simply sleep until your body and brain decide it's time to surface.

Who are you kidding, Gemma? You've always been worrying about something even as a teenager.

Especially as a teenager come to think about it. I never seemed to have the right mascara or latest clothes or anything that would make me blend in with the masses. Maybe that's because subconsciously I didn't want too. Perhaps I've always wanted to be just a little bit different from everyone else.

It certainly feels like it. Why is that? Why do I feel out of sync with those around me? Why am I so restless? Why am I asking myself so many questions?

Oh for God's sake it's only 4.30 in the morning. Why did I look at the clock?

STOP IT GEMMA. Stop asking yourself questions, when you don't have the answers. It simply makes you sound and feel like more of a loon than you actually are.

What if I am actually mad?

I certainly felt like I was drifting that way before Dr Wright stepped in and suggested these walks.

Now I'm being dramatic. Of course I wasn't mad, just, well, anxious maybe, or stressed, or perhaps a tiny bit unhinged, but not actually mad. I think life just got the better of me, temporarily. I was at a low point but thankfully I was able to drag myself out of it.

But life is always going to have tough times. Nobody gets through it without some sort of trauma. Who'd want to, it would be a pretty dull sort of life if you ask me. I guess it's all about balance.

What people need is a certain amount of excitement in their daily lives just to keep them interested. Occasionally a curveball will be thrown and you have to deal with it, but that's just how it is. People do deal with it and seem to manage quite nicely thank you very much.

I need to stop analysing myself. I'm obviously hopeless at it and, frankly, it's a job that should be left to the professionals.

Maybe I'll get the chance as part of my debriefing from the police. It all sounds very official.

They'll have a field day with me. The girl who thought she was stalking a serial killer but it turned out to be a syndicate of human traffickers.

OK, maybe not so sane after all.

Right. It might only be 4.35 in the morning but I am going to get up and make a drink and some toast. That's the beauty of living alone, you can get up in the middle of the night and no one actually cares.

It doesn't matter that I've stood on the creaking floor-boards instead of avoiding them, as there's no one here to wake. Annoying though, I don't normally misjudge my footing like that, perhaps I'm half asleep after all.

Downstairs looks a bit creepy, I think I'll put all the lights on before I go down and make that drink.

That's better, there are no lurking maniacs; it's just my imagination. I seem to be scared by my own shadow at the moment.

Oh, Gemma, it doesn't take a bloody genius, does it? You've been through a massive trauma, now stop being so hard on yourself and make a drink.

That's better, steaming coffee, toast and marmalade and I'll flick through the news channels and see what is going on in the world.

How disappointing, I'm not on any of them and to be honest, it's all a bit tedious. Same old rolling news, being delivered by amazingly fresh-faced presenters, trying to jolly it all along in their bright and breezy way.

I could do that.

No, really, I *could* do that.

Maybe I have inadvertently stumbled upon my next career move?

I mean, my one experience of dealing with the media may not have been a complete success, but it wasn't *that* bad.

Plus, I had been involved in the trauma I was talking about. These TV people don't actually have to be *in* the incident, they just talk about it. It's not like I want to be a roving war reporter or anything like that. No, I've had my fill of guns and battles thank you very much. Also, I really don't think a flak jacket would suit me. It's bound to make me look fatter than I actually am. They aren't exactly flattering, are they? Not that they are meant to be, it's far better that they can stop a bullet in its tracks rather than make a killer fashion statement.

Snort.

Killer. Maybe the wrong word to use in the circumstances.

But seriously, Gemma, you could talk to camera, surely.

In fact, you did it and what you said, which incidentally was off the cuff rather than autocue, went really well.

It was your appearance that was the problem and that is something that you could work on, especially if it was your job.

Now, I'm not saying anyone can work in front of a camera because they certainly couldn't. I doubt I could before this 'situation'. I was far too self-conscious for anything like that.

But now, yes, I really think I could.

Maybe I'm kidding myself and I'd end up looking like a fraud and an idiot, but there is a chance that the whole experience has altered me for the better. Could it possibly be a fortunate stroke of serendipity?

I shall have to give this some serious thought.

I need a job and it seems like the perfect time to challenge myself and try and improve my lot in life.

It was me who said I would make use of every single minute of my life if I ever got out alive.

Well, here I am alive, if a bit sleepy.

Maybe I'll go back to bed now I've had today's brainwave.

It is only 4.58 am.

Who'd have thought that I could turn my life around in under half an hour?

Right, lights out and sleep until at least 9 am. Please.

No.

It just isn't going to happen.

Damn you head, don't you realise this girl has to get some sleep?

She needs to be fresh and rested when Dan comes around tomorrow, not looking like Edvard Munch's lesser-known painting, 'The Whimper'.

It's no good. I can't stand staring at the ceiling and its corpse-ridden blemishes. I'm going to have to paint it.

Yes, that's what I'll do.

I'm pretty sure I have at least one tin of paint in the cupboard under the stairs. I remember buying it when I intended to freshen up the lounge, but by the time I'd got home the feeling had well and truly left me, so I shoved it in the cupboard and forgot about it.

Lights on again, let's go and have a look.

Yes, fantastic!

Not only do I have the paint but also a reasonably decent looking brush. If only *past* me had realised how happy *future* me would be that I shirked the job last time.

Right, all I need is this old sheet to throw over my bed and I can crack on.

Eggshell blue.

Not exactly what I was thinking but now I've stirred it up a bit it doesn't seem quite as shocking. I suppose I must have thought it a good idea once.

Jeez, it's splashing all over me. Dan will think I've got some sort of pox if he sees me covered in light blue dots.

I know, back to the cupboard, I've just the thing to keep me looking good whilst the ceiling gets an overhaul.

That's it, perfect!

Now, back to it. It's already 5.23 am and the first coat is nowhere near being done.

A little music is needed I think, let's see what the radio has for us at this ungodly time of day.

How appropriate, I love this:

'Blackbird singing in the dead of night, take these broken wings and learn to fly, all your life, you were only waiting for this moment to arise'.

'Blackbird singing in the dead of night, take these sunken eyes and learn to see, all your life, you were only waiting for this moment to be free'.

'Blackbird fly, blackbird fly, into the light of the dark black night'.

'Blackbird fly, blackbird fly, into the light of the dark black night'.

'Blackbird singing in the dead of night, take these broken wings and learn to fly, all your life, you were only waiting for this moment to arise, you were only waiting for this moment to arise, you were only waiting for this moment to arise.'

It has to be an omen. The teapot house woman, the songs, everything seems to signify it's time to change; that there is more to life for me than I thought possible a few weeks ago.

'Still don't know what I was waitin' for

And my time was runnin' wild
A million dead-end streets and
Every time I thought I'd got it made
It seemed the taste was not so sweet
So I turned myself to face me
But I've never caught a glimpse
How the others must see the faker
I'm much too fast to take that test'

'Ch-ch-ch-ch-changes
Turn and face the strange
Ch-ch-changes...'

Oh for goodness sake. That's it. The radio is going off. As much as I love this song it's just too much. My feeble mind really is starting to read too much into practically everything now.

I shall immerse myself in my painting to the exclusion of all else.

Apart from the fact that this is quite boring.

What did you expect Gemma? You're painting a ceiling not creating a masterpiece.

Just put your back into it and you'll be delighted when it's done.

Blimey, I must have got really absorbed in the tedium of the task; the sun is high in the sky. What time is it?

Jeez, it's 10.30 am.

Where did the rest of the night go?

Oh shit, that's the doorbell and I'm balancing on the bed with a paintbrush tied to a broom.

'OK, I'm coming, I'm coming, no need to keep ringing.'

'Gemma, is that you?'

'Of course it is, who do you think would be answering the door in my own house?'

'Well, it's hard to tell when you're wearing a bright yellow sou'wester hat that's covered in a million sky blue dots.'

'Eggshell actually and sorry, I forgot I was wearing a hat.'

'Better than ending up with a blue rinse I guess.'

'Very funny but you don't have to stand on the doorstep, you can come in you know. I was expecting you it's just the time seemed to run away with me a little.'

'Yes, I can see that painting seems to be your therapy. Which is actually rather appropriate.'

'What you talking about Dan?'

'Wait there.'

'What's all the mystery? I've not even asked you how you are yet?'

'Don't worry about that now, there are more important things to deal with.'

'You're not making a bit of sense Dan.'

'Just close your eyes, I'll be right back.'

'Close my eyes? Why?'

'Stop asking questions and for once, please, just do as you are told!'

'OK, OK, they're closed.'

Don't know where he's gone but that sounded like a car door shutting.

He must have gone back to his car for whatever this surprise it.

'No, peeping.'

'I'm not peeping Dan but the suspense is killing me. Hurry up!'

'I'm going as fast as I can, now, stand still.'

'I am still.'

'No your not, you're hopping from foot to foot, which, incidentally, is speckled with blue, much like your hat.'

'Forget all that. What is the surprise?'

'Hold your hands out.'

'Oh good grief, it's wriggling. It's no use, I *have* to look.'

'Go on then.'

'Awwwww, it's, she's, he's, whatever it is, awww, so beautiful. A Dulux dog, now I get it, appropriate. Ha!'

'*Your* Dulux dog actually, or to give *her* the correct name, *she's* an Old English Sheepdog.'

'Mine. You can't be serious. Mine. Really. Mine?'

'Yup. She's all yours. She's 10 weeks old, and well, when a friend told me about her I thought it would be the perfect gift for you.'

'For me. Really?'

'Really, yes, she needs a good home and you need someone to keep you company on your walks. I'm hoping that if all your attention is taken up with this young lady you may just be too busy to get yourself into any other sort of mischief.'

'Mine. Really.'

'Stop saying that, yes, all yours. Why are you crying?'

'Because I'm so happy. She is absolutely adorable and I'm so pleased with her, and I didn't get you anything, and I didn't even make myself look nice for your arrival, and...'

'Gemma, stop. Honestly, seeing you standing there, wearing a blue spotted, yellow sou'wester is just perfect. I'd have been too shocked to speak if you'd been given a complete makeover.'

'I love her. She is so beautiful, just like a little teddy.'

'She is, but not for long, she'll get pretty big.'

'I don't care, I love her and she's just what I need. Thank you so much, Dan. I don't know what to say.'

'How about, 'come in' to start with. The neighbours are beginning to peer through their curtains at the latest floor show from Gemma's house.'

'Oh, yes, come in, please, come in.'

'Now, if you don't mind putting her down for a minute there's something else I need to do.'

'Oh, do I have too, she's so cuddly.'

'She needs to have a look around her new home and, well, hopefully, you'll like the next bit too.'

'The next bit?'

'Yes, come here, it's time we had a lengthy kiss and, quite possibly, lock the door for the rest of the day.'

'Well, why didn't you say? Come on Sherlock, you have a look around the kitchen, your Dad and I have things to do.'

'Sherlock? She's a girl?'

'So, it suits her. She can help me solve the next mystery, we're going to be a great team.'

'No. Please tell me your joking, no more excitement Gemma, I don't think I could stand any more traumas with you.'

'Traumas, no. But excitement; we'll just see about that. Come here.'

'Thought you'd never ask....'

DAY THIRTY-ONE.

What a day, and night, I had yesterday.

Eventually, after much fussing and petting of dear little Sherlock, I got around to asking Dan about his injuries and operation. He didn't really want to talk about it, but eventually, he let on that he was still rather sore where the tube had been in his chest, but that he'd be fine in a few days.

Personally, I think he's being a bit optimistic with the 'few days', I'd be crawling around on all fours to gain maximum sympathy if I were him.

He seemed to want to go the other way and try and pretend he was absolutely fine, and that nothing untoward had taken place.

So eventually I took the hint and stopped trying to pump him for information.

We had a little trip out to the pet shop where he spent a fortune on 'essentials' for Sherlock. Obviously, this included a bed, food, lead, toys, water bowl etc. but I don't think a dog garden fountain can be classed as essential. Plus, Sherlock is way too young to learn how to press a button to release the water. Dan wouldn't be deterred though so we now have a fountain in the middle of the lounge, standing on an old bag, as we thought it too cold for her to be using it outside.

Ideally, I think we need to train her to wee outside before we start introducing even more fluids into the house, but it's all part of the fun of parenting this little individual.

Secretly, I'm delighted that Dan is as besotted with her as I am, and I can't wait for her to finish her injections so we can take her for long, rambling walks together.

But the best part was the night.

After all the pressure and tension we have both been living with it was just sublime to lie in my bed, staring at the pale blue ceiling, and trying not to choke on the overpowering smell of paint.

Eventually, we gave up and dragged the mattress into the spare room, where we finally snuggled down and simply enjoyed holding each other.

Of course, it couldn't last, Sherlock wouldn't keep still and needed to go out, so Dan valiantly volunteered to pace around the garden in the dead of night until she had carried out her bodily functions.

But when he returned, by some miracle he had managed to settle her in the kitchen and we finally got some time alone.

Admittedly it wasn't quite as romantic, or energetic, as it may have been under normal circumstances, but then Dan does still have stitches in his side and bruises covering most of the top half of his body. Not to mention the highly unattractive sores around my mouth, which failed to be protected by the sou'wester so now have a slight dusting of pale blue. But the way I see it, if we both still find each other desirable under these circumstances, then imagine how we are going to be once we have both healed.

We did talk about the future too. This took me by

surprise, as previous boyfriends have had to be practically forced to face the inevitable conversation about where this relationship is going.

But Dan is quite clear that he wants us to be together and somehow we will work out how we can do this.

OK, so he lives and works in the south and I'm based in the north but that's a minor technicality.

I was also very brave and discussed my idea of a career in television.

Admittedly he laughed for a full five minutes until he realised I was being serious but then said he would support me all the way.

So who knows what will happen over the coming months. I can hardly dare think about it all.

But one thing we both decided is that we have to make the most of every day. It's a shame really that it takes a near death experience to make you realise that life is precious.

But it is and we intend to live ours to the full.

He has now gone off to speak to various people at work, and fill in forms or something boring like that.

I wanted him to stay, and he didn't want to go, but the sooner he passes on all the information he was able to get whilst undercover, the sooner he can take a proper break and we can really relax and get to know each other.

Apart from that, I also remembered that I have a doctor's appointment today.

I really can't believe that a whole month has passed since I saw Dr Wright. I feel like a different person to the one that he spoke to only a few weeks ago.

I told Dan I had the appointment and was even considering cancelling it at one point in the wee small hours of the morning, but Dan insisted I should go and see him. Apart from the fact that he has been so good to me over the last few months, and always had time to talk to me when I felt that there was no one else I could turn to, Dan also pointed out that it could be therapeutic. He said, and I suspect this is the result of many management courses over his career, that talking to Dr Wright could give me some sort of closure regarding this whole stage of my life.

I must admit this caused some mirth on my part initially, but we talked for a while and I really do think it will help.

It isn't all about the hostage thing, the shootings or the fact I was living in fear of my life, but the *whole* month.

I started out feeling insecure, distracted and quite frankly, rather a mess. I didn't seem able to hold on to any positive thoughts and was flailing around in the dark as to how my life should move forward. I know it all happened as a result of a number of incidents, Jeffrey's death and breaking up with Luke. Wait, that sounds too wholesome. I was unceremoniously dumped and I only went to the shops, plus there was losing my job, and they are only the big things. There were countless little events that seemed to cement themselves in my mind causing me to fret and worry. When I reflect on it now I really can't believe it. Did I honestly get so angry and cross just because someone walked past me without saying hello?

It just shows that, when at a low ebb, everyday events can take on a whole new meaning. I bet you none of the people who set off those various rants, had any idea of the effect they were having on another person. I will certainly try and look at life in a fresh way from now on, and try to be as pleasant as possible to those around me, whether I know them or not. At the end of the day, we are all just humans trying to forge a pathway through life.

Get me! Gemma contemplates life, the universe and everything. Well, not quite, but it is worth thinking about.

But that's enough reflection for now; I have Sherlock to take in the garden, it's time for her two hourly stroll. Exactly how long does it take to housetrain a dog? I'm exhausted already.

Then I shall have a lovely soak in a nice hot bath before going to the docs.

As the appointment isn't until 6.30 Dan said he'd bring something home with him to eat. Bring something HOME. Those were his exact words and although I have been repeating them over and over in my mind for the last few hours, they still make me tingle with excitement.

Repeating things over and over. Does that mean I'm going all OCD again?

Give over, Gemma, you're happy. Just happy, leave it at that and stop being so stupid. You cannot let yourself sabotage this newly acquired state of being.

Good.

Now I've sorted that out in my mind it's time to go.

Here, Sherlock, have one of the numerous chews we got for you yesterday. Hopefully, it will keep you occupied until I get back and save my furniture from being mauled. I doubt it, but, actually, I don't care either. What a relief!

A few teeth marks in the sofa are well worth it for the pleasure this little girl is giving me.

Plus, I never liked that settee anyway, Luke chose it, so quite frankly Sherlock, give it all you've got.

Right, off I go. I shall walk at a nice brisk pace as I didn't manage to get out today, and I did promise Dr Wright I would walk every day for a month.

Obviously, I didn't manage that whilst I was locked in a cellar but that can surely be put down as 'circumstances beyond my control'.

Nor the time I was in hospital come to think of it. But

hey, the new Gemma isn't going to worry about that minor detail.

'Hi, it's Gemma to see Dr Wright.'

'Oh Hello Gemma, take a seat. The doctor has been so busy today as he's just back from a conference in America. It feels like the entire list of his patients have been trying to see him.'

'Oh, don't worry, I'm in no rush.'

'Actually, you're lucky, it looks like his previous patient didn't need very much, after all, you're in next and you're also his last one of the day, so take your time.'

'Excellent.'

'Gemma, do you want to come in?'

'Yes, thank you, how was America?'

'Busy, very busy, I feel so out of the loop and I was only away a week. But, wow, blimey Gemma, you look well.'

'Thank you, shall I sit?'

'Sorry, yes, please do. It seems that a daily walk has done you good. I hope you've had a peaceful month which has given you time to rest and recuperate?'

'You really are out of the loop aren't you?'

'What do you mean?'

'OK, maybe you should sit down too, this might take a while.'

MAILING LIST

If you have enjoyed my book then please join my mailing list to receive free bonus chapters, information about forthcoming books and publications plus the chance to become an advance reader of new releases!

It is completely free to sign up and you will never be spammed by me as I'm far too busy writing my next book. You can opt out easily at any time.

Please visit my website to join my mailing list:

www.annakeenanhill.com

PLEASE LEAVE A REVIEW!

Gemma has become quite important to me over the time I have been writing about her and if you have enjoyed this book I would be delighted if you left a review.

Reviews help to bring my books to the attention of other readers who may enjoy them.

One Month In My Mind

Thank you!

ACKNOWLEDGEMENTS

Whenever I read a book I always take a few minutes to look at the acknowledgements, probably as I am fundamentally rather nosey, but also because I like to try and read between the lines regarding the relationships of the people mentioned.

It wasn't until I came to write my own acknowledgements page that I realised just how difficult it is. Essentially, everyone I meet, influences me, in one way or another, and it isn't just those I meet during the writing of a book. Some ideas stem from previous years, and even decades, and can lie dormant until the appropriate moment presents itself.

But there are always a few people who require special mention for their role in the whole process. So here they are:

My husband **Robin**, who has patiently read, reread and deliberated endlessly from start to finish. Alongside this, he has encouraged when the task ahead felt too big, reassured when confidence was ebbing and generally been supportive from start to, well, it hasn't finished yet.

My boys, **Oliver** and **Felix**, are an endless source of amusement and support. I am so proud of them, and all they have achieved themselves in such a short time. They have never once doubted me and patiently waited for delayed meals whilst generally living with a distracted mother for some time.

My Mum, **Pip Keenan** and partner, **David Straw**. They have always been there for me, and the rest of the family, whatever the situation, and it's difficult to put into words just how much they mean to me and what a huge part of my life they are.

Lesley Danson and **Rachel Britton**. Lesley produced a wonderful cover, for which I shall always be extremely grateful, and Rachel's skill with design and setting finished it off beautifully. Apart from these essential contributions to the process, they both kept me sane through some tricky times with the aid of coffee, cakes and endless laughs.

Helen McCloud, my sister, alongside my Mum and David, were the first people to read the finished product. Their thoughts and input were invaluable.

Angela and **Len Funk**. They are two of the nicest people you are ever likely to meet and have been a constant positive force in my life.

Obviously my cats, Satchmo & Hobbes for sitting on my computer whilst I worked and my dogs, Coco, Pugwash & Floyd for giving me a cuddle when I needed it.

Finally, if you've made it to the end of the page, thank you for reading and I hope you enjoy this book and all those that follow.

Anna Keenan Hill

SOCIAL MEDIA

There are plenty of places to find me and I'd love to hear from you. If you can't decide which one, then why not try them all!

Anna Keenan Hill - website

Facebook: AnnaKeenanHill

Twitter: AnnaKeenanHill

Instagram: Anna Keenan Hill

FILM REFERENCES & DIRECTORS

Fargo – Joel & Ethan Coen

Sliding Doors – Peter Howitt

Wuthering Heights – William Wyler

Misery – Rob Reiner

The Great Escape – John Sturges

Gone With The Wind – Victor Fleming, George Cukor

SONG REFERENCES & ARTISTS

I'm Not In love – 10cc

Fast Car – Tracy Chapman

Anything But Ordinary – Avril Lavigne

Walk On By – Dionne Warwick

Blackbird – Paul McCartney

Changes – David Bowie

BOOKS BY ANNA KEENAN HILL

This is Anna's first book.

One Month In My Mind

ABOUT THE AUTHOR

Anna was born in Rochester, Kent, but has spent much of her life in the north of England where she lives with her husband Robin and their sons Oliver and Felix, (along with three dogs and two cats!).

She has always enjoyed writing, which has provided an escape from reality for many years.

A full and hectic life has ensured there have been many everyday situations to draw from and get the creative juices flowing. Whether that's from working in a busy A&E department, her background in psychology or managing her guitarist husband, Robin Hill.

You can find Anna on:

www.annakeenanhill.com

www.twitter.com/AnnaKeenanHill

www.facebook.com/AnnaKeenanHill

www.instagram.com/annakeenanhill

38503348R00181

Printed in Great Britain
by Amazon